POISONED

THE BOOK OF MALADIES

D.K. HOLMBERG

ASH PUBLISHING

If you want to be notified when D.K. Holmberg's next novel is released and get free stories and occasional other promotions, please sign up for his mailing list by going here. Your email address will never be shared and you can unsubscribe at any time.

www.dkholmberg.com

STAFF TRAINING

S am leaned over, resting her elbows on her knees, slowly trying to catch her breath. She ached all over from the countless blows that she'd sustained, a mass of bruises blooming all over her abused body. She managed to look up, her dark hair hanging in front of her face, and stared at a woman she had long thought dead.

"You still react too slowly," her mother said.

"Too slowly? I'm practically flying with my canal staff."

Her mother took a step back, tapped the staff on the open lawn, and casually soared twenty feet, landing in a quick roll. She bounded back to her feet and shot Sam a satisfied expression.

"Like I've told you before, I need my augmentations to manage what you're doing."

Elaine shook her head. "You need no such... augmentations. All you need are your natural abilities. You are descended from Kaver blood, and you don't need augmentations to grant you your abilities."

Sam wasn't about to argue with her mother. In the

months since they had been reunited, she'd learned that her mother was fairly rigid with her beliefs. She had no tolerance for Sam's attitude—which often wasn't nearly as compliant as Elaine preferred. Then again, some of that attitude was well-deserved. Sam had thought her mother dead.

This time, it made no sense to argue with Elaine. She'd seen the way Marin could jump the canals, managing to do so with amazing deftness, her skill putting anything Sam could accomplish to shame. Sam had a similar ability when augmented, though with Alec continuing his studies at the university, they had fewer opportunities to work together to practice those augmentations.

"If you would only show me how to do that, then I wouldn't need my augmentations."

Her mother approached slowly, the slender canal staff gripped lightly in hand. It still impressed Sam that she could break her staff down so that it was no longer than her forearm. Each piece slid neatly into the other, hollowed out, and still was sturdy enough for her to balance on. And here Sam had thought her two-piece canal staff something to be excited about. She kept waiting for Elaine—or the princess, though she rarely saw her—to offer her a staff made similarly, but they never did.

"You're learning slowly, Samara."

Sam let out a frustrated sigh. Slowly. Always slowly. It seemed the theme for her. She'd never been tall enough, or strong enough, and now it seemed she wasn't even smart enough.

"Well, maybe it's because Marin made a mess of my

brain," Sam said, slapping her canal staff into the hard-packed earth.

She still couldn't believe that Marin had wiped her mind, convincing her that her mother had died, making her believe that she was alone—and that she had a brother. What sort of augmentation had she used on Sam? If she ever managed to reach Marin, she was determined to find out. The problem was that since learning about her mother, Marin had essentially disappeared. There was no sign of her at her home, her belongings having been packaged up and taken... somewhere.

Her mother's hardened expression seemed to ease, albeit barely. "You can't continue to blame her for what happened."

"Not blame her? Who should I blame? She took me from you. Why aren't you angrier?"

Sam had so few memories of her mother, something she should have thought strange before. Since being reunited, her mother had yet to show much emotion—at least no positive emotions—almost as if she had been happier when Sam had been out of her life.

Had she not wanted Sam?

She tried not to think that way. Doing so only left her with mixed emotions.

"Angrier? You don't think I was angry? I spent years searching for you, Samara. Years when I thought Marin had stolen you from the city and taken you to the Thelns as a bargaining chip, and ultimately had come to terms with the fact that you had possibly already died. There are limits to a Kaver's ability. Finding you was all I wanted, but not something I ever thought I would succeed in doing. Instead of focusing on your own anger—or questioning my lack of it, you should concentrate on our reunion and how relieved I am to have found you once more."

Sam swallowed the lump that formed in her throat. She had wanted to hear words like that—*needed* to hear them. It wasn't that she didn't think her mother was pleased to see her again, but she'd begun to ask herself whether she had wanted to find her for the sake of finding her daughter, or if she had wanted to find her to use her in some way.

"We will find Marin," Elaine said. "We will uncover what she did. And we will help you unlock your true potential."

Sam could only nod. At least Elaine had said *we*. It meant she wasn't abandoning her. She didn't expect that she would, but a part of her had wondered whether they would be more interested in using Sam to track down Thelns than allowing Sam to participate in the search for Marin.

"Tray deserves to know," she said.

Elaine furrowed her brow. "Trayson does deserve to know but knowing in his case places him in a unique position. Once he learns what happened—and how you were used as part of Marin's plan—how will he react? Will he assist you? Or do you think he will side with Marin?"

Sam could only shake her head. What answer was there to the question? Regardless of what Marin had done, the way she had used not only Sam, but Tray, left her with no real answers. How could anyone use her own son in such a manner? It was horrific and painful. Still, in spite of everything, he was her brother. How could he not be when memories of what they had gone through together remained in her mind?

"I don't know how he'll react. Probably the same way I did."

"I doubt that," Elaine said. "You've been angry, which is understandable, but you have allowed yourself to keep a measured response. When he learns the way his mother used him—and you, the person he believes is his sister— do you think he'll remain calm?"

Sam considered her mother for a moment, before realizing Elaine wasn't at all worried about the information Tray would receive—or about his reaction. It was something else. "You're concerned because he's part Theln, aren't you?"

Elaine's gaze went distant for a moment before returning to meet Sam's. "Should I not be worried?"

"If Marin is a Kaver and Tray is part Theln, what will that combination mean for him?"

"I don't know. I suspect that's part of the reason she's kept him here, keeping him close—protected—so the Thelns can't get to him. They would be interested in that combination as well. Gaining that understanding would likely lead to much heartache for the Kavers and Scribes."

"Why not bring him to the palace? With the princess—"

"We don't know what he is capable of. We don't know what he might do. And until we find him, we won't know."

Had they been looking for Tray? Sam thought only she had been. "Capable of? He's my brother."

"No. He is not. He's Marin's son, not your brother."

Sam turned away, gripping her canal staff tightly in

her hand. What could she say that would convince Elaine that Tray would do the right thing? Probably nothing, she decided. Elaine had already made up her mind about Tray. Which meant that the princess had already made up her mind, too. Did that put Trayson in danger? She hoped it didn't, but they hadn't allowed her to get close enough, to learn enough about their plans, to understand exactly how Trayson might factor in. Somehow, she had to believe that he did.

"Now, it's time to continue. Do you think you're ready to focus again?"

Sam slammed her canal staff into the earth, the frustration rising within her different from before. She was ready, and she was determined to figure this out, partly so that she could learn the skills that, as a Kaver, she was born to, but partly so that she could keep Marin from hurting her if she came across her again—and so that *she* could get answers.

Sam spun the staff and stepped back, ready to face Elaine. She tipped her head in a quick nod and barely had time to react when Elaine swung her staff.

2

THERAPY

"I know that you have a friend within the university. You could speak to him."

Sam looked up at the master physicker. She was an older woman, heavy-set with thick jowls, but she had kind eyes and looked at Sam in a way that few physickers had done. She was one of several from the university that the princess had brought in to try to heal Sam. She carried with her a stack of books that she'd set on the table in the small sitting room the princess had agreed they could use. So far, all of their attempts to help restore her memories had failed. They had no idea what Marin had done, or how she had used particular augmentations to block Sam from remembering her family.

Sam had wondered if that was the reason Elaine had been so distant with her. Was she upset that Sam didn't remember her at all? Memories of her mother were faint, little more than snippets of happy times, but Sam wondered if those were even to be believed. Maybe whatever Marin had done had permanently damaged her and had permanently taken away any hope that Sam had of remembering her family.

"He is… new to the university," Sam said.

She looked down at her hands, wishing she had a knife or her canal staff or something to keep her from feeling so helpless. But who did she need protection from? It was a strange sensation to be stuck in this room. She had to believe she was safe, but was she? Did she trust her mother? The princess? They seemed to be acting in her best interest, trying to help her restore memories of a life she hadn't known. But she felt like she didn't belong, that she hadn't earned this. It was a hard transition for her to go from believing herself lowborn to thinking that she might be something more. But isn't that what she'd always wanted? More? It had been hard enough learning that she was a Kaver and that Alec could be her Scribe.

"I see," the physicker said, nodding to herself.

Sam didn't want to tell the woman that Alec might know just as much as many of the master physickers. She had seen several times the way he had demonstrated his knowledge. And had seen him recognize symptoms and diagnose conditions that she doubted even the masters at the university would have done as quickly. Then again, Sam was biased.

She looked around the room. It was nothing more than a sitting room. There were several plush chairs covered in brightly colored fabrics, with the ornately carved armrests that were so typical in the palace. There were paintings along the walls, most with the look of significant skill to the technique. Bastan might be better able to assess how well-made they were, but that would mean revealing to him what she'd been through. Eventually, she knew she would have to. He deserved that much from her since he had helped her more than she had ever realized.

"From what I understand, there's a belief that your potential is locked within you by what was done to you."

Sam nodded. Elaine had alluded to that fact, but she wasn't sure what to make of it. *Could* she have her Kaver abilities restricted in some way? She and Alec had managed to perform augmentations, but it was apparently possible that she was capable of much more, especially after what she saw of Elaine.

"Today, I'm going to try a different strategy."

Sam turned her attention back to the physicker. "Not medicines today?"

The woman shook her head. "Medicines have failed us. Whatever was done to you will not respond to any of the typical medicinal treatments that I know."

That had been the only question Sam had asked Alec. He had known of nothing that would reverse what had happened to her and hadn't any idea of how to restore her memories. If he had, she felt certain that he would have attempted it.

She kept expecting Elaine and the princess to attempt an augmentation to reverse it, but neither of them had made that suggestion. Either they didn't believe they would be successful or they didn't have the necessary knowledge to reverse what Marin had done.

As much as Sam might want Alec to experiment with augmentations, performing one that would affect her memories and possibly change her way of thinking bothered her. She didn't think she could do that, though she might want to.

"If not medicines, what are you going to do?"

The physicker scooted forward in her chair, shifting so that she tottered on the edge. With her weight, she practically crushed the chair. An image of it collapsing beneath her weight flashed through Sam's mind, and she had to suppress a smile. It would do her no good to upset the physicker assigned to work with her, the physicker to whom both Elaine and the princess felt comfortable enough to reveal what had happened to her. Sam needed to regain those memories, but she wondered whether anything would change if she did.

"We're going to talk."

"Talk?"

The physicker nodded. "There is a strategy that I have read about," she said, passing one of the books on the table next to her. "It's not one that I had been familiar with before, but I think it would be applicable with what you've been through."

Sam shrugged. Anything was worth trying at this point. Maybe if the physicker could help her regain her memories, it would unlock something within her that would allow her to use her abilities in the way they expected of her.

"What can you tell me about your past?" the physicker said.

"We've been through this before."

"We have, but not this way."

Sam held her gaze and noted a hard intensity there. What was the woman doing with her today?

"I don't remember much of my past," Sam said.

"Tell me what you *do* remember."

Sam tried to think back, working through what she

remembered, but all of her memories seemed fairly recent. That had never troubled her before, but it should have. She was nearly eighteen, and most of her memories were of the last eight years. Why hadn't that struck her as odd?

Though had she thought about it, she would have thought it was related to losing her mother and thinking that the trauma of that time had kept her from remembering it.

"I remember… Bastan."

"Bastan?"

Sam nodded. "He's a tavern owner. He allowed Trayson and me to stay with him. He gave me safety and asked that I do some odd jobs for him."

That seemed as open an explanation as to Bastan's work as she was willing to give. She wasn't about to bring him to the attention of the palace.

The physicker had pulled out a slim journal and smoothed it open on her lap. She jotted down notes on the page. Sam smiled to herself, thinking of how Alec did the same. He claimed it was the expectation of his father, but in reality, Sam suspected that his documentation of symptoms had helped hone his mind.

"This man, Bastan, is one of your earliest memories?" The physicker leaned forward, tapping the feathered end of her quill pen against her lips. With each tap, her jowls jiggled slightly, forcing Sam to suppress a smile as she watched.

"He's one of the first," Sam said.

She didn't know if he was only one of the first, or if he was her first memory. Bastan had been a part of all of her memories, always seemingly there, watching over her.

Using her. He could be hard, but then again, many in Caster were hard, and Bastan was no harder than any others.

"I remember him taking me in and giving me a room to stay in."

She frowned with the memory. Maybe that *was* the first memory she had. Bastan had been intimidating then, but in spite of his intimidation, she hadn't feared him. Maybe because he had laughed easily. He'd jump to anger almost as easily, but often had reasons for that. He had a difficult position, one that required him to maintain control so that others didn't attempt to usurp him.

It was that way throughout much of Caster. Power was held until it was not. Often, it was best that he be the one to hold it, mostly because he had never abused his power, at least not that Sam had ever seen.

"Why do you think he took you in?"

Sam shrugged. She had asked Bastan that at one point, and he had answered that he felt sorry for her. And then she became useful to him.

"Several reasons, but probably mostly because he thought he could get cheap labor."

"Cheap labor? You would have been a child. From what the princess and Elaine say, you would have been no more than eight or nine."

"I think I was ten," Sam said.

The physicker nodded. "Still young. At that age, you wouldn't even be allowed an apprenticeship yet."

Sam stared at her, thinking that she'd made a joke, and started laughing. The physicker frowned back at her, and Sam realized that it hadn't been a joke.

"How much time have you spent in Caster?" The wide-eyed look of horror answered that more quickly than the physicker could have spoken her response. "That's what I thought. Things are different in Caster."

"Things are much the same throughout the city," the physicker said.

"Are they? In Caster, I don't think we necessarily have the same form of apprenticeships as are found in other sections. Employment regulations aren't nearly so enforced."

"And you didn't have a problem with this?"

Sam laughed and leaned back in her chair. It really was a comfortable chair. She should be thankful that the princess gave her such a nice place to work with the physicker. She could have forced her to go to the university and suffer through this assessment in one of their more sterile environments. Alec had told her all about the types of rooms that were used there. Sam didn't think there would be anything therapeutic about that.

"I didn't have much of a choice, did I?"

"No choice? You could have demanded that he follow the rules set forth by the king."

In her time within the palace, Sam had yet to come across the king. She had met the princess several times, but the king had remained something of a mystery, as did the queen.

"Had I forced him to follow the regulations of the king, I would have been kicked out of the tavern and forced to sleep on the streets."

"Children never have to sleep on the streets. Not in the city."

"The alternative isn't any better. Children may not have to sleep on the streets, but the orphanages aren't kind to children. It's actually been a blessing that I never had to end up in one." Sam thought of the people that she'd known who had spent time in orphanages. Most were traumatized in some way, and at least Sam hadn't had experiences quite like that. Bastan allowing her to stay truly *had* been a blessing, though she did wonder why he had been so willing to allow a ten-year-old girl and her supposed brother to stay with him. She might have been inexpensive labor, but Bastan didn't struggle with finding cheap labor.

Maybe there was more to it than what she had known. When she had free time, she needed to go to Bastan and see what memories he had of those first days when she'd come to him.

"Let's simply agree that we have differing viewpoints," the physicker said.

Sam shrugged. "Fine. Differing viewpoints, it is."

"What other memories do you have?"

"Most of the memories I have are tied to events, rather than people or feelings. I remember slipping near the canal at one point, terrified that I would fall in."

"Terrified? Why would you be terrified of the canal?"

"Have you ever swum in the canals?"

"I have not."

Sam grinned. "Well I have. It is… not pleasant."

"It's only water. Why is it not pleasant?" The physicker asked.

"Water with damn eels swimming in it. You know those eels are thirsty for blood." She shuddered at the thought. Feeling the eels in the water had unnerved her. She'd already had a close call and wasn't willing to risk it again. She remembered all too well how they had swum near her, far too close for her comfort level.

The physicker only shook her head. "The eels are little more than a legend."

"Legend? I felt one swimming alongside me. The damn thing wanted to get my blood."

The physicker frowned. "Honestly, I've heard some people believe there are eels throughout the canals, but they have never been seen. Perhaps what you experienced was something else."

Sam shivered at the thought that there might be something else like the eels in the canal. There were fish, of course. Enough men stood along the canals with their long, bamboo rods hanging in the water that she knew there had to be fish, but what fish was as large as the thing that had swum alongside her?

Nothing but a nightmare.

"When did you fall into the canal?" the physicker asked.

"I was traveling between sections of the city. I slipped—"

"Slipped? As in you slipped off one of the bridges and into the canal?"

Sam met the woman's gaze. "There are other ways of crossing the canals."

"That is forbidden. Crossing by jumping over has been outlawed by the throne."

"When you live in Caster, you don't have the same respect for the throne."

The physicker pursed her lips together, tapping the feather quill against the side of her cheek as she considered Sam for long moments. "And now you reside in the palace. You have led quite the interesting life in your brief years."

"Interesting. Dangerous. I suppose all describe me equally well."

"Yes. Equally well, and likely why the princess has asked me to help understand you."

"I thought the intent was for me to regain my memories."

The physicker nodded. "You are to regain your memories, but to do so, I must understand you first. I think there is much about what you've been through that we need to talk through."

"Will talking through it help me understand what happened to me?"

"It is not uncommon for trauma to suppress memories. It certainly seems as if you have experienced significant trauma."

"I thought the only real trauma I had experienced was losing my mother. I remember that she had been a part of my life, and then knowing that she was not."

"Yes. Your mother. You speak only of her, but you have not yet told me anything about your father."

"What's to say?" Sam asked with a shrug. "I don't have any memories of my father. I was told he died when I was young."

"And you trust the memory of being told this?"

Sam frowned. Should she trust that memory any more than the others? Was that why Elaine seemed annoyed with her most of the time? Was she angry that Sam had not gone in search of her father?

But Sam remembered being told when she was no more than five years old—and believed—that her father had died when she was very young. Marin couldn't have implanted that memory as well, could she?

"I see that you don't know. Perhaps we should meet again in a few days and see if you've been able to recall anything else."

As the physicker stood, Sam could only nod. Why couldn't she remember her father? Why couldn't she remember anything else?

Her frustration was enough to push her to the edge of sanity.

She needed to find Elaine and ask those questions. Maybe her mother would be able to give Sam more background that might help her remember the person she had been and the person she was supposed to be. If she didn't, there was another way she could find those answers, but it involved learning where Marin had gone.

With all the training she'd been undertaking, she hadn't been able to look. Perhaps it was time to change that.

3

MAKING A VISIT

Caster had a dreary look about it, especially compared to where Sam had been spending the majority of her time. The days that she'd been gone had changed her. Sam didn't know whether to be happy about such change or to hate it.

She had grown accustomed to the finer things around her, from the expensive and plush fabrics to the cleanliness of the streets. Was she becoming what she had hated all those years? Was she somehow becoming highborn?

There was a time when she would have scoffed at the idea. Had she longed to escape the life of the lowborn? Yes. But one simply didn't go from lowborn status to highborn status, even though that seemed to be what she had done. How else could she classify herself? She lived and trained in the palace, ate in the palace kitchen, and had access to all sections of the city with paperwork prepared by the princess herself.

Sam was no longer lowborn.

She worried she'd betrayed the person she had been,

and all of the people she had known and cared for growing up. At the same time, she didn't have the same worries that she'd once had. She no longer had to fear finding her next meal or being asked to sneak into various places on Bastan's behalf. She no longer had to steal.

Why, then, did she miss it?

She reached Bastan's tavern and paused at the door. His first tavern had been destroyed by the Thelns, and she had feared they would easily reach other places throughout the city, but the more she learned of the Thelns, and their relationship to the Kavers and Scribes, the more she understood that there were reasons the Thelns weren't allowed into the city. They shouldn't have managed to reach as far as they had.

The door to the tavern banged open, and a man stumbled out, heavily intoxicated for this early in the evening. Sam smiled to herself. She rarely saw men quite so intoxicated near the palace or even the surrounding sections of the city.

She slipped inside and surveyed the tavern. Tables were fairly full for the time of day, and the food being served smelled delicious, making her mouth water. It was simpler fare in Caster, not any of the formality that she had in the palace, and certainly none of the fine wines that were often served. Sam didn't have a taste for wine and preferred ale, something that was considered uncouth in the palace.

She saw a familiar face and nodded to Kevin. He was a youngish man and had always been friendly to her. He dropped off a few mugs at one table before weaving toward her. "Sam? Where have you been? Bastan won't tell us, and it's had the rest of us worried."

She grinned. "You were worried about me?"

Kevin shrugged. "Well, we got used to seeing you every couple of days. Everyone knows you're Bastan's favorite, so when you didn't show, we..."

"You thought the worst?"

A relieved expression swept over his face. He stepped toward her and slipped an arm around her shoulders, giving her a tight squeeze. "I am glad you're well. I'm sure that wherever you went was on some job for Bastan. The great gods know that he probably has more jobs than he could ever accomplish. Even now, he's making a place for more of his art."

"What is it this time? Some sculpture by a famous artist?"

Kevin chuckled. "I don't know where he would put another sculpture. His office is filled with them, and that's nothing compared to his warehouse."

Sam had never seen Bastan's warehouse, but there were rumors that he stored enormous amounts of art, stockpiling it. She'd never understood his fascination with it, but all who worked for Bastan knew about it, and most were simply amused by his interest. So many of the jobs that Bastan hired people for involved acquiring another item for his collection.

"Not a sculpture then?"

Kevin shook his head. "Not a sculpture. This is some sort of art supply, from what I've heard. I think Bastan intends to move up in the world. He's probably thinking that he's learned enough to create his own art."

Someone hollered, and he glanced over, giving Sam a chagrined expression. "Back to work. The boss is in his back room. I suspect he wouldn't mind if you stopped by to see him. Anyone else he'd tell us to chase away."

Kevin hurried off, leaving Sam standing in the entrance to the tavern, looking around at the activity. It was busy, and she suspected that many of the patrons were people under Bastan's employ. Most of the time, that was how he maintained his business and his safety. He kept the tavern full of people who could watch over him. For the most part, Bastan's employees did so willingly. He was a reasonable man and a fair employer. Certainly, fairer than most found within Caster. And he was well connected. Many men worked for Bastan hoping to learn enough from him, and make connections of their own, that they could move on—and upward.

She noted a few familiar faces in the tavern, but not men that she knew personally. The rest were likely actual patrons.

Sam debated whether to sit and have a drink, maybe even get something to eat, but she had questions. That was the reason that she'd come here, hoping to learn something about what Bastan knew of her past and what he recalled of when she'd first come to him.

She made her way through the tavern, listening to the conversations at tables around her. Most were men making boastful comments, and others were little more than casual conversations, but a few were details about jobs. She heard a reference to slipping past the guards and into some of the different sections of the city, and Sam knew that likely meant smugglers. Even here, they should be careful speaking about jobs they'd taken on for Bastan where others could listen.

Once, she would have probably been sitting here

having a similar conversation. It was not uncommon for her to spend time at Bastan's tavern as she learned details of the task he had for her. Tray didn't hang around nearly as often as she did, something he'd once explained was because he felt less than comfortable around Bastan. It was a sentiment that she understood and had not pressed.

At the door, she paused and knocked briskly. She waited, listening for the sound of Bastan's annoyance, a familiar sound to her, but it didn't come. Instead, the door opened a crack, and his flint-gray eyes peered out from that crack. He hesitated, then pulled the door open, and drew Sam inside.

"It's nice to see you, too, Bastan," she said as he closed the door.

"That's what you have for me? You've been gone for, what... months? The last time you were with me, you had nearly died from a fall and were about to make a run at the university for your brother."

His gaze skimmed over her, seeming to take in her clothes. They were new and well-made. Sam had never had fabric quite so soft and had never worn anything that fit her nearly as well as the clothes she had been given during her time at the palace.

Bastan arched a brow, his appraising eye taking that in quickly. "Well. It seems as if you made a friend."

"It's not like that."

"No? Tell me, Samara, what is it like? It seems to me that you have moved on in the world."

"I found..." She caught herself before sharing that she had found her mother. That needed to come out differently. "I found out that Marin is working against the city."

Bastan took a seat behind his enormous desk, stacks of

books covering the surface, and a few rolled parchments that she imagined were art that he'd acquired. "How is she working against the city?"

Sam stood across the desk and resisted the urge to look around at all the art. It would only remind Bastan of the time she had broken into his office. She suspected that still angered him. "Do you remember the men who destroyed your tavern?"

"I remember my tavern burning, Samara. I have spent much energy trying to learn more about who was responsible. It is not easy to discover that secret."

"They're not from within the city."

"No. Were they from the city, I would have learned by now."

Sam took a seat, shifting on the hard surface. It was nothing like the comfortable and plush chairs that she had in the palace. Maybe she had grown too soft in the time that she'd been away. There would have been a time when the hard, smooth wooden surface of Bastan's chairs wouldn't have bothered her. They were all she had known.

"I'm trying to understand them better," Sam said.

"And if you do? Do you intend to share with me what you learn?"

Sam hesitated a moment before nodding. Bastan deserved that, even if there was nothing he could do. "Marin had a role in it."

His gaze narrowed, and the darkness in his eyes deepened. Bastan could be a hard man, and age had made him even harder. Sam had only known him for eight years— that she could remember—and she never wanted to be on the receiving end of one of his stares.

"How certain are you that Marin had a role?"

"Quite."

"And you? I know that she used you for some task."

"She tried to use me, but…" Sam didn't know how much of Marin's plan had been intentional, and how much had been accidental. She suspected that Marin intended the wasting illness from the Book of Maladies to be targeted toward the princess, but had Marin known that it would backfire on her and she would end up the recipient as well?

Bastan let out a long sigh. "What is it that you need?"

"Why do I have to need anything?"

He chuckled, clasping his hands together as he leaned forward on his desk. "You've been gone for a while. The fact that you returned tells me that you need something and that you think I'm the one who can help get it for you. What can I get for you that you can't obtain in the palace?"

He knew that she'd been in the palace. Sam doubted that was simply a guess. He was too well connected for something like that.

"Memories."

He frowned. "Memories?"

"I… I have discovered that my memories of the time when we first met are hazy."

"I never took you for the type to reminisce. You were always practical. It's a trait that I have always appreciated about you, Samara."

She shook her head. "This isn't to reminisce. I need to understand what happened to me."

"In saying that, I must assume that something

happened at that time that you don't fully recall. Is it something that I need to worry about?"

"Why would you worry?"

"I've seen these *augmentations* that you can do, Samara. I don't intend to be on the receiving end of one of them."

She shook her head. "It doesn't have anything to do with the augmentations. No," she corrected herself, shaking her head, "that's not quite right. It doesn't have to do with any of *my* augmentations."

"You don't intend to attack me for some perceived slight that occurred nearly a decade ago?"

"Bastan, you don't understand. My memories of you are... fond if nothing else. You took me in when you didn't have to. You gave Tray and me a place to stay. Who else would have done that?"

"Only because I saw that you had potential. I have an eye for things like that." He shrugged. "I wish I could say it was more altruistic than that, but I saw your raw talent and knew you had potential that could benefit me, and I intended to use it."

Sam laughed. "You can try to convince me that you had no other motive, but I've been around you long enough—and gotten to know you well enough—to be certain that you didn't have to help me nearly as much as you did. You paid more fairly than you pay most, and you never became overly angry when I didn't do the tasks quite as you instructed."

Bastan looked down at his hand. "You never were a great listener. Always too stubborn. Too much like me in that, I suspect."

"What was it like when Tray and I first came to you?" she asked Bastan.

"Like? You were small, even smaller than you are now. You were hungry and dirty, and I suspected you'd been on the streets for a while."

Sam didn't have a memory of that. "Why did you take us in rather than sending us off to one of the orphanages?"

Bastan shrugged. "I don't know. Pity?"

"I thought you said it was for cheap labor."

"There is some of that. You can do things when you're small that some of my other employees can't accomplish. People don't look sideways at a child, not like they do at a man creeping toward them. When you showed early success, I kept giving you more assignments." He spread his hands apart. "What can I say? I have an eye for talent."

"I'm having a hard time remembering much about that time," Sam said.

Bastan considered her a moment, his brow furrowing as he did, then he leaned back and shrugged his shoulders. "You had been through a lot. You had lost your mother. Your brother was young, though never quite as helpless as you wanted to believe him to be."

"I've never wanted Trayson to be helpless," she said.

"No? I think you enjoyed the fact that he needed you."

"I only wanted to ensure that Tray had everything he needed. I didn't want him to end up..." Sam closed her eyes, catching herself before saying too much.

"You never wanted him to be too indebted to me? Is that what you didn't want to say?"

"Yes. You have a reputation, one that's well-earned, and because of it, you create challenges for me. It was bad enough that Tray spent so much time with Marin, I didn't want to have him owe you as well. I didn't know what you would ask of him."

Bastan waved his hand dismissively. "Your brother was never in any danger from me. Once I saw how Marin latched on to him, it wasn't worth it to me to risk angering her. She has something of a temper."

Sam swallowed. What would've happened had Bastan attempted to make a play for Tray? How would Marin have reacted to that?

"Have you heard anything about her recently?"

"Only that she has not been seen. I think you know more about where she is than anyone else."

"I haven't seen her. I've been trying to learn…"

She had to be careful. She trusted Bastan to an extent but allowing him to learn what she was doing, what she knew, placed her and others in danger. He had his own agenda, one that wasn't always the same as Sam's.

"You've been trying to learn about this paper?" Bastan grinned. "You don't have to conceal that from me. I've seen enough from you, and about you, to know that you learning how to use that paper is valuable."

"That's just the problem. I don't want you thinking it's valuable."

Bastan shrugged. "That's how I operate. You've known that from the moment you set foot in my tavern. I haven't concealed that from you at all. You provide value, or you don't. When you don't, then you no longer have a place here."

"By 'you,' do you mean me? Do I still provide value? If not, do I no longer have a place here?"

Bastan smiled. "Samara, you will always have a place with me."

"That's not the same."

"Isn't it?"

"Does that mean that I'll always be valuable to you?"

Bastan smiled and held her gaze, saying nothing.

Sam sighed. She didn't know what she expected from Bastan but figured she had managed to get about as much as she would.

"Thank you."

She stood, and Bastan arched a brow at her in question. "For what?"

"For taking me in. I don't know that I've ever properly thanked you. So, thank you."

She headed to the door, and Bastan cleared his throat. "Samara, don't be a stranger."

"Don't worry. I plan on surprising you as often as possible."

"You know I always enjoy your visits."

Sam laughed as she pushed the door open and stepped back into the tavern.

4

STUDY PARTNERS

The inside of the university had a dark feel to it today. Alec had grown comfortable here in the months that he had studied within these walls. It was a different sort of comfort from what he'd had when training—and studying—with his father. With his father, there had been a practical application that required he study the effects of medicines that Alec chose. He was given freedom to practice as he saw fit. That gave him confidence in what worked and what didn't, confidence that few other students in the university shared.

Within the university, the method of learning was quite different. He attended lectures, and rarely was allowed to go and observe the direct care of people coming to the university for healing. Alec thought that a shame, and thought that were he and the others who studied with him granted that opportunity, they would learn much more.

Anxiety bubbled in his stomach. He tried to ignore it,

but it gnawed at him. It had been there for days, likely because he had not seen Sam in days. He often felt stretched when he didn't see her, a strange sensation that ate at his stomach, leaving him with a mild agitation.

Without her, he didn't dare attempt augmentations, even those he might try out on himself. She would know. That was something he hadn't realized before. He knew she had an awareness of it when he used her blood, but he'd not realized the augmentations caused weakness in her as well as him.

Tapping on his shoulder drew him out of his reverie, and Alec turned to see Beckah standing in the hall behind him. She clasped her hands behind her back and looked up at him, her curious eyes constantly seeming to study him, trying to figure him out. He was a puzzle to her, not the least because he was not highborn, as so many who came to the university were.

"Why are you just standing here?" Beckah asked.

"I'm not just standing here," Alec said. "I'm contemplating."

A hint of a smile played across her lips. "Why are you contemplating here in the hallway?"

Alec suppressed a laugh. Beckah had a way about her that amused him. She had a sharp tongue, but rarely did she direct it at him. Most of the time, she directed it at others within the university, masters who taught them, each getting targeted by the sharpness of her barbs.

"I'm thinking through the last lecture," Alec said. That wasn't entirely true, but a part of his mind was thinking through that.

She snorted. "You know that you're the only one who

spends time after the lecture trying to understand what you were just taught."

"I doubt I'm the only one."

"You're the only one who *questions* what we've been taught. I think it amused many of the masters at first."

At first. That, like so much else, had slowly faded. The masters that had once been intrigued by the way his father had taught him had increasingly become frustrated when he challenged their assertions. Often times, their book-learning was quite different from his experience. There were many times when things they had studied in their books didn't work when they tried them on living people.

"I don't mean to be disrespectful—"

"It just happens?"

Alec shook his head. It probably shouldn't just happen. He probably should be more respectful and should try harder to not put off the masters. He needed them if he intended to stay in the university to study.

"Did you come here just to give me a hard time?"

"Not at all. I wanted to see if you had any interest in studying this afternoon."

Studying with Beckah would be helpful. She had a knack for finding things within the library, and often, there were topics that he wanted to research but didn't always have the right way of looking at them. That was when Beckah was useful.

"I'd love to, but—"

"But you're going to see your friend again, aren't you?"

Alec hadn't been able to explain Sam to the others in the university. All he could say was that she was his friend. How could he describe that he was her Scribe and that together, they had magical abilities? None in the city —other than the few Kavers he'd met—believed in magic. Especially in the university, they felt that everything had an answer, if only one studied hard enough.

"I'll have you know that I haven't seen my friend in several days."

"Most of us gave up those we care about to come to the university."

"I don't think the university wants anyone to give up the people they're close to."

"The masters want our attention. They want our focus. We can't do that when we're distracted by things in our past lives."

Alec considered telling her how hard he thought that was, but she wasn't the only student within the university to feel that way. He knew that most had abandoned their former lives and considered their appointment to the university an honor.

Then there were others who didn't view it in quite the same way. They treated the university as a steppingstone, one that would give them greater political leverage in the future. Many of the city's leaders came from the university, and some of the least connected highborns attended the university simply to gain greater connectivity throughout the city.

"I'm sorry that I can't shut her out the same way others have shut out those they care about," Alec said. The brief flash of hurt that crossed Beckah's face had him shaking his head. "I'm sorry, Beckah. That's not what I intended."

"What did you intend? You know there are others who feel that you're too conceited?"

"Conceited?"

"You're aloof. You don't let anyone get close, and that strikes some as either arrogant or—"

Alec shook his head, trying to cut her off. "It's not arrogance. I don't feel like I fit in here the same as others. I'm not highborn."

"Highborn isn't the only requirement to be a part of the university," Beckah said. "And you've shown probably too often that you're certainly smart enough to be here." She cocked her head to the side and studied him a moment, the same playful smile on her face that he'd seen before. "Let me give you some advice. It would help everyone if you got to know people here. It would help if you were willing to be seen and weren't so standoffish."

Alec looked back at her and knew that she was only trying to be helpful, but it still hurt to hear. He wasn't trying to be aloof, but he didn't feel that he shared many commonalities with the highborn students at the university. In his mind, he was giving them the space they wanted, space that they probably preferred he maintain. Except Beckah was telling him that by giving them that space he made it worse.

"Thank you," he said.

Beckah scrunched her nose and frowned. "Thank you? That's all you're going to say?"

"I will see if I can do a better job of connecting," Alec said. There were a few of the other students he thought he could reach, but there were others who he would be unlikely to connect with. Some actually believed that he had no right to be at the university, in spite of the fact that he thought he'd proven himself.

"There you go again."

"What did I do this time?"

"Nothing other than Alec being Alec. You probably meant that to be sincere, but it comes off as sarcastic."

"I think with you, everything comes off as sarcastic," he told Beckah.

She smiled, taking that as a compliment that he had not intended it to be.

"If you don't want to study with me today, how about tomorrow?" Beckah asked.

Alec nodded. "Tomorrow would be better. I promise I will meet you tomorrow morning."

"Morning? You're going to make me get up to study with you during a free morning?"

"Isn't that what you—"

"I'm teasing you, Alec. You're going to have to get over yourself."

He could only nod in response. He wasn't really sure what she meant, but maybe he did need to get over himself. But he hadn't been spending much time with Sam. He'd been here. Studying. But could he have both? He enjoyed their time together and enjoyed attempting various augmentations. But in the end, if he had to choose...

He felt pulled between two different responsibilities. On one hand, he was expected to study and master the healing arts with the university instructors, and on the other hand, he was drawn to work with Sam, and felt the need—and desire—to serve as her Scribe.

"Tomorrow," she said. "I'll be there bright and early."

"I can't promise the same."

Beckah studied him, almost as if she couldn't decide

whether he was joking with her or not. Finally, she barked out a quick laugh. "See? That's better. You don't have to be quite so stiff." She laughed to herself, and then turned, disappearing down the hall, leaving Alec staring after her, uncertain what more to say.

5

A LIBRARY SESSION

Alec managed to beat Beckah to the library. His night had not gone as hoped. The attempt to reach Sam had failed. She had even given him access to her at the palace, but crossing the bridges leading to the section of the city where the palace was had been difficult. The guards had refused him, turning him away as soon as he had appeared, telling him that no crossings were allowed. Even with his papers, he wasn't granted access to Sam.

Instead, he had spent the night reading through his notes that he'd made during the week. He kept a neat journal, recording what the masters taught in class, and comparing it to what he could find in the library. Most of the time, they were similar, though occasionally, he had discovered discrepancies. When he found them, he wondered which to believe. The masters were not infallible.

Then again, the texts within the library weren't always completely accurate either. Alec had found references in the library that he knew to be inaccurate. Likely it was not intentional, but it made him question what he was taught. The masters based their talks and topics on information they had a particular understanding of, but there were things that even the masters had missed.

The library was empty. It was early in the morning, and most of the other students remained asleep after a long night spent in the taverns blowing off steam from the week. Even the librarian was absent, having shown his face when Alec first appeared, but then disappearing back into the stacks of books.

Alec leaned on his elbows as he stared at a page in one of the books he'd pulled out, reading about conditions of the heart. There were various treatments, many of which were consistent with what his father had taught him—and which Alec had seen firsthand to be effective—but some were odd. Alec didn't know what to make of the recommendation to give dorsalberry to women who were suffering from loss. The book made it seem as if that was a condition of the heart.

"You don't need to be sad that she didn't find you last night," Beckah said over his shoulder.

Alec looked up to see her smiling. She was dressed more casually today, wearing a practically shimmering blue dress that revealed a hint of her cleavage. A gold necklace hung low, a ring hanging from it that likely cost more than Alec's father's entire shop would have been worth.

"I'm not sad."

"Well, you're reading about heartache. It seems to me that would be more of a personal issue, don't you think?"

"Why would you think I suffered from heartache?"

"You're here already. You returned early last night.

And you didn't make it nearly as far as you intended into the city."

Alec studied her. "Were you following me?"

She shrugged. "Call it curiosity. I wanted to see who you've been meeting up with."

"You could have asked."

Beckah shrugged again. "Would you have told me?"

Alec doubted that he would have. That opened himself to more questions. Not only about why he was with Sam, but about her position in the city. Now that she spent time in the palace—training with her mother—she could no longer make the claim that she was lowborn. Not that Alec ever minded. She might view him as a highborn, but it wasn't the way he viewed himself.

"Who is she?"

"Like I told you. She's a friend."

Beckah snorted. "A friend? You're the son of an apothecary, and you're visiting someone on the palace grounds?"

Alec considered her for a long moment before answering. "If you followed me, then you would know that I didn't reach the palace grounds."

"Why do you think that's the only time I followed you?" She stared at him serenely.

If she'd followed him before, then she likely knew he had been on the palace grounds in the past. Most of the time, the guards allowed him to cross. That usually happened during the daytime. Last night was the first time since she'd gone to the palace that he had attempted to connect with Sam at night.

How much did Beckah already know?

Marin's betrayal had raised suspicion within Alec that

had never been there before. It was hard not to question when people all around him were deceitful. Marin's deception had cost Sam dearly.

"Are we going to study, or are you going to harass me about my friends?"

Beckah grinned. "You're getting better. Pretty soon, you'll fling it back at me."

"Fling what back at you?"

"All the crap I've been giving you. Listen, what do I care if someone in the palace is trying to make a connection to you already? You wouldn't be the first person to use your time in the university to make political connections. You might be one of the first to make a connection quite so high so early, but then again, I doubt there've been too many students who come to the university with your particular set of skills."

It might be better if she believed that he had simply gone to the palace to meet someone for political gain. As she said, he wouldn't be the first person to do so.

"I'm only trying to make sure I have a future."

She snorted. "Your future could be here if you wanted. You're clearly on track to be raised to master level. You might be the only other person in our class who can."

"Myself and Darnell?" Alec asked.

Beckah glared at him, and for a moment, he thought she might try to punch him. At that moment, she reminded him of Sam, in the way that she quickly was riled. He enjoyed tormenting her in much the same way. For some reason, being at the university had quieted him, especially after his rapid promotion. He was reluctant to say too much, not wanting to draw more attention to himself.

"Well?" Beckah asked.

"Well what?"

"What have you discovered?" She pointed to the section on the page that he was reading where it spoke about heartache. "I've been around you long enough to know that you must've found something. Otherwise you wouldn't have gotten that scrunched up look on your face that looks like you're constipated."

Alec blinked before he laughed. "Constipated?"

"Don't worry, it's not that I've been watching you there as well. I don't need to watch to know what a constipated face would look like on you."

"I'm not sure that I want to continue to study with you if you're going to insult me constantly."

Beckah ignored him. "It's almost like these authors have never met a woman before." She looked up at him, a playful expression on her face, and Alec could already begin to see where she was going to go. "Not like you. You seem to know all about women."

He cleared his throat. "That's not why I chose this volume."

"No? You didn't want to read all about heartache and the art of providing soothing elixirs to help ease a woman through such suffering?"

"Well, far be it from me to not offer something to someone who might be suffering."

"Such as yourself?"

Alec couldn't help himself. He laughed, the noise disrupting the silence of the library. The librarian appeared from between the stacks of books and shot him a hard look, silencing him.

"You're going to get us kicked out of the library. You're

quite loud. Maybe you should take your studies some-place else."

Alec stared at her, debating what he could say that wouldn't be taken the wrong way. With Beckah, it was never easy for him to know. "If you'd rather I study else-where, I'd be happy to do so." He gathered his books and prepared to stand up.

"You need to stop being quite so literal. I know you can have fun. I see it in you. You just have to relax."

It was surprising that she would tell him he needed to relax, especially as Sam had suggested the same thing. He found it difficult to relax here. Even entering the university had been a matter of passing tests that seemed determined to prevent him from joining. His connection to his father—an apothecary—placed him in an equally precarious situation. The university masters didn't care for the apothecaries attempting to push their way in to healing and had long questioned their abilities.

"And you need to recognize when I'm only kidding." He sat back, pulling the book back in front of him, and made a point of staring at the page. "Maybe you need some dorsalberry."

"And why would I need that?"

He shrugged. "Clearly, you're disappointed that I'm not spending as much time with you as you would like me to. Though I think that other treatments for your heartache might be more effective. In fact, if we were at my father's shop, I might suggest talun leaf, perhaps crushed and placed in a mixture of chaparral and weasel root."

She watched him, shaking her head. "Is that what you

read in that book? I'm not even familiar with weasel root or chaparral."

"You're not? I thought you considered yourself the only other person on the pathway to becoming a master."

She grinned at him. "Not Darnell?"

"Darnell would be lucky to pass this first year. He struggles remembering anything more than the basics of diagnosis."

This time, it was Beckah who barked out a laugh. As she did, she cupped her hands over her mouth, and the librarian poked his head out once more, sending his glare at both of them. Beckah made a playful expression, managing to somehow look both chagrined while pointing in Alec's direction.

When the librarian disappeared, Alec said, "Thanks for that."

"See? You have more fun in you than you realized." She grabbed the book from in front of him and pulled it over, quickly scanning the page. "This doesn't say anything about weasel root or chaparral. Where did you read about that?"

"Nowhere."

"So, it's something you learned from your father? Does it work?"

Alec shrugged. "I don't know."

"What you mean you don't know? I thought you had answers to everything."

"I don't know because I don't know anything about weasel root or chaparral. I made them up."

She started to laugh again, but caught herself, cutting off before she made too much noise. "Good. I'm glad that you think to make up your treatments for me. That seems like a good way to test ourselves, doesn't it?"

"How is that a good way to test ourselves?"

She grinned at him. "If you can tell that something was made up, then you must know the real treatment. Next time when we study, we'll pick topics, and if I convince you of a made-up treatment, I win. If you do, then you win."

"What's the prize?"

Her grin widened. "What do you have in mind?"

"Keep it up, and you'll need dorsalberry again."

She shook her head, smiling widely, and pushed the book back over to him.

6

THE MASTER PHYSICKER

A lec waited in the classroom, wondering why he was the only student there. The rows of desks were empty, his the only one stacked with books. There was no instructor here, and he frowned to himself, wondering if he had made a mistake.

There were plenty of traditions at the university with which he was not completely familiar. It wouldn't be the first time he'd made a mistake and ended up where he wasn't supposed to be.

His notebook—the running journal he kept with his notes, and then the notes of his notes—lay open in front of him. He studied it whenever he had free moments, hoping to uncover some nugget of information, some truth that might provide him a better understanding of his healing abilities.

When he flipped the page, he came across one that referenced something he and Sam had been working on before Alec's studies had become too consuming, and before Sam had been too caught up in what she learned from her mother.

How long had it been since they had studied together? Alec started ticking off the days and stopped when he reached double digits. Too many. He missed her. It was a strange thing to admit to himself, but he had grown accustomed to seeing her daily, and he had become accustomed to spending time with her, testing the various ratios of blood required to make particular augmentations more effective. Now he studied alone.

He told himself that his studies were important and that he did them so that he could one day help Sam even more, but when would that day come? How long would he be tasked with staying at the university, with learning various healing techniques, so few of which had anything to do with a real-world setting.

Most of the techniques the instructors taught were theoretical, which chafed Alec. It shouldn't; he knew he should simply accept what he was taught, and not question the knowledge the masters provided, but Alec had witnessed healing firsthand for nearly his entire life.

The door creaked open, and he looked up. Beckah poked her head in and grinned when she saw him. "Are you coming?"

He frowned. "Coming where?"

She giggled. "You really should learn to double-check our class assignments."

"What do you mean…" He pulled out another notebook, the one in which he kept his record of classes and where he was expected to be from day to day. It often changed, much as the speakers changed. They worked their schedules around the availability of the master physickers, and Alec had simply trusted that his notes were accurate.

As he flipped through the pages and settled on today, he ran his finger down the entries and realized that the ink was slightly off. He looked up at Beckah and saw her trying to suppress laughter again.

"You did this? You changed my journal?"

She shrugged. "I thought it would be funny to see what you would do. I didn't expect to see you sitting here quite so long."

Alec stared at the notes he had made, and there was only the subtlest evidence that she had done anything to them. It was actually quite impressive work. He hated admitting that, and he would never tell her that, but she had succeeded in modifying his writing in such a way that it actually looked somewhat like it had been done in his hand.

"Where are we really supposed to be?"

"The hospital. And it's Eckerd today. You're going to want to be there."

Master Eckerd was one of the most renowned physickers at the university. Of all the masters that Alec had met, Eckerd was the one who challenged him the most. He had a grasp of ancient texts and could often reference things from books he'd seen only once or twice before.

In that way, Eckerd reminded Alec of his father. Alec's father was not only a skilled physicker, but one of the finest minds he'd ever been around. His father would often read something a single time, and could then recite it back, typically unerringly.

He gathered his books and stuffed them into his bag, and hurried from the classroom, following Beckah.

She strode forward with her hands clasped behind her, her back tall and straight like every highborn he'd ever been around. Somehow, Beckah didn't make it offensive. She was an enigma to him but was fast becoming a friend. Within the university, he wished he had more such friends.

"You didn't tell me," Beckah said.

"Tell you what?"

"You didn't tell me how long you would have remained here before you'd have gone looking for the rest of the class."

Alec grunted. "I don't know. I probably would've waited a while longer."

"Why?"

"I trust my notes."

"Even when they can be tampered with?" she asked with a smile.

"No one has ever tampered with my notes before."

"Are you certain?"

Alec glanced down at his bag. Had she done something with his notes? She was determined to test him, to challenge him, but he didn't think she would go so far as tampering with notes that he made in class. Would she?

It was possible she might, but would she actually take one of his journals and change it?

It so, it would be subtle, and... No. Had she done that, he was certain he would've known. He looked over those notes often enough that anything unusual—and different from what he remembered—would have stood out. His memory was not quite as good as his father's, but that didn't mean it was poor.

"You haven't tampered with any of my journals."

She shrugged. "I made you think about it, didn't I?"

Alec shook his head and chuckled. If it were anyone else, and if he had a suspicion that anyone else might have tried that with him, he might have been more upset, but this was Beckah. She might compete with him, and she might want to test him, but she didn't want to harm him. At least, he didn't think she did.

"What's Eckerd teaching about today?" he asked.

"Something near and dear to your heart."

Alec frowned. "And what is that?"

She turned to the side, twisting just a little bit, and patted her chest, thrusting her breasts forward. "Heartache, of course." She laughed, and it carried down the hall, an airy sound that left Alec unable to do anything but laugh with her.

"Why would Eckerd be teaching about heartache?"

"Because I asked."

Alec shot her a look. "You asked?"

"Sure. I had to know if your techniques were accurate, didn't I? Isn't that how our game is going to go?"

"I'm not sure I know how our game is going to go. I think you've made it up as you go along."

"And I think you enjoy it more than you were letting on," Beckah said.

Alec fell silent, but he didn't deny the fact that he truly did enjoy their interactions. Beckah tested him, she challenged him, and for that, he was thankful.

They reached the door leading into the hospital, and she pulled it open.

The smell struck him first. There was always an overwhelming medicinal odor, one that was a mixture of the hundreds of different concoctions that had been mixed and used in the hospital. Beneath it, there was something else, a hint of something worse, something unpleasant, and it always twisted his nose, forcing him to try not to gag to keep himself composed.

He'd never had the same problem in the apothecary shop. Then again, in the shop, they only healed one or two people at a time. It was nothing like the hospital. Rows of cots were arranged here. On the cots, people with various ailments rested, some in much worse shape than others, all waiting for the master physickers to make their way to them. When Alec had first broken into the university, he had thought that the physickers cared more about money than they did about actually healing anyone. He still wondered if that wasn't partially true, but he'd seen the masters—including some like Eckerd, who truly seemed to care—make a supreme effort to use their knowledge to benefit the people of the city.

Today, like most days that he came to the hospital, almost all of the beds were full.

Those that weren't were being prepped, the sheets changed, and somewhere within the university, there were senior-level students coordinating the arrival of more sick and infirm people. If Alec remained at the university long enough, he, too, would take part in the screening process. Would he ever get to the point where he cared more about someone's ability to pay than he did about their need for actual healing?

A circle of students stood around one of the cots at the far end of the room. Eckerd, an average height man with a thick head of gray hair and a long, bushy beard, and eyebrows to match, stood near the head of the cot. His voice carried, booming over others here.

Beckah led Alec toward them, her demeanor changed now that they were in the hospital—and the presence of Eckerd.

As Alec approached, he heard Eckerd saying in his slightly nasally voice, "Can anyone give me their assessment as to this young man's ailment?"

Alec stepped closer and stood up on his toes, trying to peek over the shoulders of two of the students standing in front of him. Stefan and Matthias were slightly taller than Alec, and Matthias in particular was wider, blocking his entire field of view. Alec shifted to get a better view and managed to catch sight of the man on the cot.

He was a younger man with a shock of deep black hair, though it was thinning. His eyes protruded from his skull. The artery in his neck showed a bounding pulse, and the flesh on his arms seemed to sag.

"How fast is his heartbeat?" Alec asked.

Eckerd nodded. "A reasonable question. He has an average heartbeat, but it is irregular."

Alec glanced over at Beckah and saw her studying the young man with the same intensity that he had probably just shown. Was this the heartache that she had brought him to see? There was nothing physical about emotional heartache. And he didn't think this man's heart had anything to do with his symptoms.

Alec scanned the young man's skin again, letting his gaze drift down to his fingertips. There were small, purplish lesions at the ends of two of his fingers.

"Does he have any other sounds when you listen to his heart?" Alec asked.

The other students turned toward him, and Matthias glared at him. Matthias didn't care for the fact that Alec did well, and clearly felt threatened by him. Stefan on the other hand simply watched Alec with an interested expression. They had always gotten along well.

"What additional sounds would you be concerned about?" Eckerd asked.

Alec shrugged. "Sometimes with presentations like this, the blood will flow turbulently through the heart. That will create unusual sounds."

"Why would you suspect the blood to flow turbulently in a young, otherwise presumably healthy man?"

Alec pushed past Matthias and lifted the man's hand. "The tips of his fingers."

Eckerd stared at Alec blankly, leaving Alec to feel a flush work through him. Was he too presumptuous? His father had once described an illness that overwhelmed the body, and it had been brought on by an infection, but it was an infection found only in those who preferred to inject solpace juice directly into their arms. Alec had no reason to believe this man had done that and hadn't seen any marks, but it was the only similar illness that he could come up with.

"What about the tips of his fingers?" Eckerd asked.

Alec glanced around at the others and decided to push onward. He was a student, after all. He wasn't expected to have all of the answers. It was okay if he made a mistake, wasn't it?

"My father taught me about an illness that is self-inflicted," he started. Someone snickered, and Alec ignored him. "There are medicines that are addictive, and some men decide to administer them to themselves."

"Indeed? Your father knows of such addictive medicines?"

"I don't know if my father knows of the medicines, but he knows of men who have used them. They often end up harming themselves."

Alec stared at the man lying on the cot and felt a growing certainty that he was right. Not only was this man suffering from symptoms of an infection brought on by injecting himself, but he was suffering withdrawal from the substance he had been injecting.

"Solpace juice. That's what he did, isn't it?" Alec asked.

Eckerd made his way around the cot, and the other students peeled away, giving him space. When he stood across from Alec, he peeled back the sheets covering the patient, and Alec noted the injury on the man's feet. It was the kind of injury that was consistent with someone self-injecting and choosing somewhere that it wouldn't be detected.

"Impressive," Eckerd said. "I don't know that there are many masters who would have made the same diagnosis, certainly not without seeing more of the injured. Now, solpace juice is fairly caustic but gives a sense of euphoria when injected into the bloodstream. Many of the lowborns will make the mistake of injecting it into themselves, and think that in doing so, they can enjoy that euphoria. Few are savvy enough to know that the euphoria is temporary and is often times followed by severe pain. The pain causes the person to once more administer the solpace juice, and the cycle continues."

"Master Eckerd, why is his hair thinning?" another student asked.

"An interesting observation you've made. He suffers from an ailment that makes it appear as if his hair were thinning. It is a withdrawal from the juice he injected. You will see that his forehead is covered in a sheen of sweat as well. That is another symptom of his withdrawal. I think that if we were to do a full evaluation, you would see that not only does he have these symptoms, but there are probably others that we have not yet observed." He stepped away from the cot, and the students followed him as he made his way to one of the nearby cots.

Beckah elbowed Alec as he passed.

He shot her a hard glare, which she returned with a smile.

He followed Eckerd as the man reached another cot and resumed his lecture. This time, Alec stayed back, choosing not to speak up, not wanting to draw attention to himself. It was easier to remain silent, and easier to simply stay back, letting the others draw the attention of the master physicker.

Alec noted that Eckerd glanced at him from time to time, either waiting—or daring him to speak up. He didn't know if the fact that he didn't made him more of a target, or less.

7

A MERCHANT CARAVAN

Sam made her way through the Bolton section, keeping her canal staff clutched securely in her hand, separated into pieces. She didn't want to draw attention to herself and was careful to keep her cloak pulled around her shoulders. The day was cool, the breeze that gusted through the city attempting to tug at her cloak, and the air had an odd scent to it, one that had the stink from the canals, but mixed with something else that she couldn't quite track.

Why hadn't Alec come to her the night before?

She shouldn't be upset by it, but she thought they were going to work together, and that he would continue to come and help her understand her augmentations. Maybe he decided that his studies at the university were more important. Sam couldn't even be upset by that. They had both agreed that what he learned at the university was important. Discovering methods of healing could be applied in many of their attempts with augmentations.

Even though she knew that she shouldn't be upset, she

was finding it difficult to get over it. Alec was the only one who really understood what she'd been going through. He was the only one who understood the challenges she faced dealing with the discovery of Marin's deception. He had been the one by her side over the last few months, the one person she could truly trust.

Sam had known she couldn't trust Marin and had doubted Bastan's intent, but for so long, she had relied on her connection to Tray. She had done everything for him —and with him. Losing that connection, losing the bond, bothered her much more than simply learning that they may not actually be related. Alec understood that about her and understood how much Tray had meant to her. She needed him so that she didn't feel quite so… empty.

Movement up above caught her attention, and she pushed the thoughts away, quickly assembling her canal staff and flipping up to the roof.

Training with Elaine had helped there. Sam had always had skill with the canal staff, though perhaps not nearly as skilled as Marin. When she had begun attempting different augmentations with Alec, that had granted her even more skill. But it wasn't until she had begun training with Elaine that she truly began to improve.

When she landed on the roof, Sam tumbled into a roll, tucking her knees up to her chest so that she completed the roll smoothly and popped up onto her feet. She surveyed the roof, looking for signs of the movement she'd seen. There was nothing.

Sam frowned. There had to be something here. She hadn't imagined the movement, but whatever had caused it was no longer present.

Maybe it was best that she return to the palace. Perhaps she simply couldn't continue to work with Alec if it was so difficult to find a way to get together. She could continue working with Elaine, and the others whom Elaine wanted her to train with, and continue to hone her skills. Her mother seemed convinced that she didn't require augmentations to gain the agility that Elaine so often demonstrated. Given the shortage of easar paper, it would be nice not to have to rely on it, but she still struggled with the idea that she had skills and abilities that didn't require augmentations, that she only needed to tap them and learn how to use them. Even then, Sam thought herself far too small and petite to possess the power and agility that Elaine claimed was her birthright.

From her vantage on the roof's edge, Sam scanned the streets below.

The Bolton section was home to dozens of merchants. They had massive estates, many of them sprawling, stretching entire blocks. The merchants prided themselves on displays of wealth to the point where many had gardens and enormous shaped shrubs on display throughout the grounds. The buildings themselves were brightly painted, another garish display of their wealth, using bold blues and oranges, some deep reds and even a few vibrant greens, all an attempt to draw attention to their wealth. It was similar in many of the highborn sections, but in Bolton, it was more prevalent.

One of the merchants appeared from around the corner on the street below. He was an older man, thin, with a long beard that he'd slicked to a point. He wore a deep purple robe, the color flamboyant enough to signify significant wealth. The merchants in Bolton believed that colors like the purple he wore were a symbol of wealth, partly because of the cost involved in dying something so deeply colored. It took multiple washings to get a color as bright and vibrant as the merchant's robe. Then there was the jewelry he wore. Each finger was adorned by a massive ring, some twisted into strange shapes, others simple bands of gold or silver, all very expensive pieces.

When Sam had been working for Bastan, she had been tasked with acquiring rings like that. Bastan felt no remorse at taking from those with more, especially men like this merchant. He didn't necessarily believe in redistribution but did feel that not enough wealth flowed into Caster and other lower sections of the city. Bastan had done what he could to stimulate the movement of monies.

The merchant was trailed by nearly a dozen men.

Were they guards?

They were dressed in deep black clothing, and Sam imagined it signified their servitude to the merchant, but they carried themselves in a certain way, a posture of alertness, of awareness that wasn't typical of servants.

Most of the merchants were content with hiring the palace guards, content using the soldiers to protect them. Why would this merchant feel otherwise?

Unless they weren't there to guard him.

Had Sam read it wrong?

It wouldn't be the first time. She often struggled with understanding what highborns did, and the behaviors that were considered normal for them. There was a difference between what would be considered the norm in the more central sections of the city versus what was acceptable in the outer sections—the lowborn sections of the city.

Curiosity prompted her to follow.

She trailed the merchant from above, racing along the rooftops of the shops, and only jumping down to the street when the buildings transitioned from the row of shops that she could stay on top of to the line of houses. There wasn't any easy way to track from above the houses. She could attempt to navigate along the wall that surrounded most of them but doing that would likely allow others to see her.

Once down on the street, Sam disassembled her canal staff and hung it beneath her cloak once more. She pulled her cloak tight and buckled the belt around it, keeping it from fluttering as she walked. Movement would only draw attention, and she knew that if nothing else, she didn't want attention drawn to her. That was a lesson Marin had taught her, one that Sam had taken to heart, recognizing its value.

Given the number of men following the merchant, she half expected him to head into the outskirts of the city, to take the bridges that would lead him into the lowborn sections, parts of the city many considered more dangerous. For highborns, and those accustomed to some of the upper-class sections, perhaps it was dangerous. Instead, the merchant veered toward the palace.

That was odd, but equally odd was the fact that he passed unchallenged from one section to the next. Sam trailed from a distance, keeping her attention on the merchant, and soaring over the canals rather than taking the bridges. She had the appropriate documents to prove that she was welcome at the palace, but it was much more fun, and challenging, to jump the canals and travel that way. She was more accustomed to it, anyway, and it gave her a certain anonymity that crossing at the bridges did not allow.

When he crossed over to the palace section without being stopped, she knew that he must have permission.

Where had he come from? She had assumed that he had come out of one of the houses, but if that were the case, it was unlikely that he would travel to the palace with so many men of his own. More typical would be for palace guards to come to him and escort him. Sam had witnessed that in the past; it was how the princess had come to her attention.

Were the guards for his protection as he passed through other sections of the city?

She was forced to reassess her appraisal.

Maybe he wasn't dressed as he was to flaunt his wealth —at least not entirely for that purpose. Maybe he had come from someplace outside the city.

Sam had never ventured outside the city. It was dangerous enough inside the city, that leaving the borders of places she knew was not something she had ever been willing to risk. Part of that was her own reluctance, and part came from a desire to keep Trayson safe. She had needed to remain in the city in order to do that. She wasn't about to let Marin use him if she wasn't around.

Sam laughed inwardly. All this time she had spent trying to protect Tray from Marin, and it had never really been necessary. Marin wouldn't have hurt Tray, but she had used him to pull Sam closer to her.

The merchant and the men with him disappeared behind the walls of the palace. Sam watched for a moment longer before approaching the nearest guard, who watched her for long moments before waving her through. Sam passed through, but felt a moment of disgust at how easy it was for her to reach the palace now. It shouldn't be that easy for her. She was lowborn. There was no reason for her to be granted access to the palace.

She caught a glimpse of the merchant being welcomed into the palace, and Sam hurried back to her quarters. It would do no good for her to be caught watching. Better to hide her interest and hide the curiosity that tugged at her. She doubted Elaine would give her answers. But there might be others in the palace who would. Sam was determined to have those answers.

8

WHERE WE DIFFER

"I think we should continue our talking session," the physicker said.

Sam glanced over, clutching her arms around her. She hadn't seen Elaine since her visit to Bastan a few days earlier. There were questions she had and answers she needed. They were questions she should have asked before but had never considered them.

"I'm not sure it helped the last time," Sam said.

"Didn't it? You were observed visiting your old section of the city. I wonder why you felt the need to do that."

Had they been spying on her? That annoyed her more than it should have. "I felt the need to visit Caster because I don't recall what I should about my earliest years."

"And what did you discover?"

"Only that Bastan seems to care about me." She hadn't needed to visit him to recognize that, but it had been nice for her to hear it from him directly. "Oh, and I watched a merchant coming to the palace." She still hadn't discovered what that was about and was determined to do so. Eventually.

"Many merchants come to the palace," the physicker said, waving her hand dismissively.

"Not like that. Not with as many guards as I saw."

She frowned. "Guards?"

"And not palace guards. The merchant had his own guards."

"How do you know he had his own guards?"

Sam chuckled. "I've seen them enough to know."

The physicker shook her head. "Let's get back to Bastan."

"Fine."

"You said he seems to care about you. Did you doubt that he did?"

Sam leaned back in the chair, staring at the ceiling. She hadn't noticed before, but beams crisscrossed the ceiling, giving it an even more decorative appearance than others within the palace. Just what sort of room had the princess given her?

"In Caster, it's hard to believe that there are others who care about your well-being. I know that there are, but most of the time, I feel—felt—as if I was on my own."

"But you weren't, not really."

"I wasn't," Sam agreed.

How much of her background did the physicker know? Had Elaine and the princess shared what Marin had done, in addition to wiping her memory? Did they tell her about the way she had used Trayson in her plan?

For Sam to get any benefit from these sessions with the physicker, she would have to share everything, wouldn't she?

Doing so was difficult for her. She'd been through quite a bit, but she had also told herself that she handled it well. She didn't need the help of others. She was strong, and the time she'd spent alone in Caster had only made her stronger.

"I had my brother with me," Sam said.

The physicker tapped her quill on her mouth as she often did, seemingly lost in thought. "What can you tell me about your brother?"

"You know that he's not actually my brother."

The physicker looked up and held her eyes. "Is that what you believe?"

"I believed Tray was my brother for the last ten years of my life. No, that's not quite right. I've always believed Tray was my brother. Now, I've been told he's something else, and that he was used to keep me close."

"Does it change your feelings about him?"

"It changes nothing. He's my brother. I would do anything for him."

"Is that part of what she planned?"

Sam didn't know what Marin had planned, or why she had used Sam to connect to Tray. There was no question that she had been used, just as there was no question that Tray had been used. Neither of them had known the truth about the other, which made it all the worse.

Tray didn't deserve that, not from someone he thought cared about him.

Though from everything Sam had seen, Marin *did* care about Tray. She'd made a point of helping him, getting to him in a way that allowed him safety. She never put him in a dangerous position, not as she willingly did with Sam.

"It doesn't matter," Sam said.

"It doesn't matter because it doesn't change your opinion, or doesn't matter because it's happened? Or does it no longer matter because you've moved on?"

"It doesn't matter," she said again. "Besides, I don't even know where he is. Since I've learned of what happened, I've lost track of him. I've searched, but haven't managed to find him." That bothered her more than anything else. "And it sounds like Elaine is looking for him."

"What would you say to Trayson if you were to see him?" the physicker asked.

Sam sighed. She'd thought about what she would say to her brother, and how much to tell him, but every answer that came to mind felt wrong. She couldn't tell him about the way Marin had used him, not without admitting that their relationship was not real. She thought that he would react the same way she had, and that he would want to remain connected to her, but what if Tray didn't want that?

What if he would use it as an excuse to separate from her? He'd felt oppressed by her, and though she'd only intended to help him, to protect him as best she could, she had driven him away. With his increasing size from his Theln bloodline, she had to admit that he probably didn't need her protection. Even if she had augmentations, she might not be able to do much to help him anyway.

"I would tell him how much he means to me," Sam decided. That seemed the best answer. After all, wasn't that all that mattered? Tray deserved that much from her.

"Tell me about your brother."

"What's there to tell? I imagine he's much like any other brother."

"Yet from all reports, you have a particularly close relationship with him. Is that not a fair assessment?"

"We've been close. When you think you've lost your parents, it brings siblings together."

"And Trayson believes that he lost his mother as well, doesn't he?"

Sam swallowed. Thinking of it always gave her a lump in the back of her throat, one that was uncomfortable, and unpleasant, and left her feeling like there was nothing she could do to keep from losing him. "We both thought we lost our mother."

"But in reality, his mother was there with him the whole time, and he didn't know it. How will he react when he learns the truth about Marin? When he learns that his own mother betrayed him?"

That was the question Sam knew least how to answer. Not only would Tray learn that his mother still lived, and that they did not share the same mother, but he'd also learn that his mother had been there all along, hidden in plain sight, keeping an eye on him and keeping him safe, but also using him for her own needs.

Her using Tray was different, though. If she'd used Sam because she was angry at Elaine, there was a certain sensibility to it. But Marin had used Tray for a very different purpose. Maybe it had been because she thought to protect him by bringing him close to someone she suspected would have Kaver blood, but maybe there was another reason to it.

Could Marin have feared something happening to Tray if he were discovered? Could she have sought to conceal his Theln connection by keeping him close to Sam?

Short of finding Marin and asking her, Sam doubted she would get those answers.

"I don't know how he'll react," she finally said.

The physicker made another note in her journal, leaving Sam wondering what observations she'd made. With Alec, he would let her read what he'd documented. He had such a keen eye that she had appreciated the opportunity to see what observations he might make. There was rarely anything she could add to them, but every so often, she could. She was always pleased with herself when she managed to add to what he'd observed. She doubted this physicker would allow her the same liberties with her notes.

"I like to think that Tray will understand what was done. I like to think that he won't react with anger."

"You worry about his reaction to Marin?"

"Not Marin, but me. I don't know how he will take it."

"Why do you fear violence?"

"Because of who he is. What he is."

"And what is that?"

She considered the physicker for a moment, noting the thick the jowls and the curious intensity in her eyes. How much should Sam trust this woman? She knew very little about the physicker and hadn't been able to reach Alec at the university in several days. She suspected Alec knew this master, but maybe he didn't. From what Alec had shared, the masters took turns instructing, but not all worked with the entry-level students. Maybe this woman didn't work with students at Alec's level.

It was difficult for her to find trust. She wanted to, but now, more than ever, she struggled with it. How could she trust these people that she didn't know when she had been lied to?

"He's a young man," Sam answered. "He's still trying to understand where he fits in the world. He's often rebelled against my desire to help him, which has gotten him into trouble in the past."

"Such as when he was imprisoned?"

"That would be a good example." But Tray hadn't been the one rebelling then. That had been her taking Marin's assignment. Tray had been caught by chance. An accident. And held because they had thought him a Theln sympathizer.

"That's when you first came to the notice of the princess, I believe."

"It wasn't intentional. I was trying to find a way to reach Tray."

"You thought that you could reach your brother and break him out of prison?" the physicker asked, cocking a brow up as she did. The movement created a rippling effect on her face, and the fat shifted amusingly.

"I was willing to do whatever was necessary to help him. You know what they do to thieves."

"I thought you said your brother wasn't a thief."

"He's not. But he was found helping me when I was doing something I probably shouldn't have been. And they believed him a Theln sympathizer." Would the physicker reveal any knowledge of the Thelns?

"Do you have a brother?" she asked the physicker.

The physicker shook her head. "No brother, but I have a sister. She's a little older than I am. Why?"

"What would you do if her life was in danger?"

"I would pray for her," she said.

Sam waited for her to laugh or make some sign that she was speaking in jest, but she didn't. "Prayer won't help in many situations. Sometimes, you have to take matters into your own hands."

"In a situation like that—if my sister were foolish enough to find herself arrested—I doubt I would determine that risking my life to save her and risking ending up in prison alongside her would be the appropriate course of action."

Sam met the physicker's gaze and forced a smile. "I guess that's where we differ," she said. "When Tray was captured, I was willing to do whatever it took to free him. If that involved breaking into the prison and risking my life, I was more than happy to do it."

The physicker studied her for a few moments, tapping the pen on her cheek, before turning and making a few notes in her journal. The pen scratched along the surface, and Sam stared at her, wondering again what she was documenting, and what notes she made on the page.

After a while, the physicker looked up, an ink stain on her cheek. "Let's talk a little more about your brother."

Sam sighed but nodded. She wouldn't refuse, not if this had a chance of helping, though she didn't know exactly how it would. Maybe she would never get those memories back.

9

FOLLOWING THE KAVER

S am kept her distance as she followed Elaine through the city. She moved quietly, staying to the rooftops, maintaining a position behind her so that Elaine wouldn't realize she was being followed. Would her mother even notice?

They passed through a section of the city that Sam had never been in. It was a merchant section, and much like most of the merchant sections, massive estates occupied its center. Warehouses lined the waterfront, and barges stopped at them, loading and unloading before moving on.

For a moment, Sam thought that Elaine would stay here, but she didn't. She moved on, heading toward an outer section.

As she went, Elaine turned quickly ahead of her, and Sam lost sight of her.

Kyza!

Here she thought she could keep up with Elaine, but the other woman was quick.

In the time that she'd been training with her—and others—she had struggled to keep up. It angered her that there might be more that she could do—more that she could be—that was hidden from her, stolen by what Marin had done. All Sam wanted was to have that part of her mind unlocked.

She meandered, making her way through the merchant sections as she spiraled back toward the center of the city and the palace. Now that she had documentation, she didn't need to worry about reaching the palace, though she preferred to jump, taking her canal staff and leaping across the water. One thing her training had done was improve her jumping. Working with Marin had begun to help, but she had never managed to draw out the same capabilities that could now, training with Elaine and Thoren—a man assigned to train her with the staff—and others who worked with her at the palace.

As she neared the center of the city, she caught sight of another merchant trailed by a dozen guards.

Two such sightings in just as many days? What was going on?

She decided to follow, keeping a safe distance. She imagined what Alec would say if he were with her, but Alec had been busy—far too busy for her. He would have warned her not to follow and would have told her that doing so would only get her into trouble.

She realized they were not continuing toward the center of the city as the other merchant had but heading away from it.

Where were they going?

The merchant was dressed far too formally for one of the outer sections. He would be too easy to identify as a merchant, and certainly better-dressed than the lowborns found in these sections. There had to be a reason for his coming out here.

Curiosity drove her forward. She stayed in the shadows, wishing that she had her cloak, but since training in the palace, she'd left it behind. There was something almost deceptive about wearing a cloak like that, and Elaine had preferred that she dress for the palace. She had thought that the merchant was out of place, but with her clothing, she would be just as out of place as he was.

He reached an outer section that she wasn't familiar with. In the distance, she could see the beginning of the swamp, the stink of the water carrying. It was a smell that she had noticed when they first reached this section, but she hadn't known what it was. Sam rarely came to these sections, rarely spending much time so close to the swamp. Caster was nearer the steam fields than the swamp, and even there a certain odor hung over everything.

She stayed near a building as the merchant came to a stop at the end of a road. He waited, and after a while, a man came out of one of the nearby buildings, dragging a heavy cart with him. They spoke softly, and Sam wasn't close enough to overhear what they were saying. She needed to get closer, but she didn't want to risk being seen.

The merchant handed over a bag of what Sam suspected were coins and took the cart from the other man.

He nodded toward his guards, and they started back toward his section.

It was nothing more than a simple transaction.

Even though it was probably nothing, there was strangeness about the transaction that still struck her. Why come all the way out here? Most of the time, merchants preferred to have others come to them, especially someone as well-to-do as this merchant obviously was. And why so many guards? Did he worry about the part of the city he visited? It was possible. She had no idea what was in the wagon.

There was something she didn't fully grasp. Sam didn't know what it was, but she needed to understand, so she continued to follow the merchant, staying close.

They crossed a canal bridge, and Sam gave them space, not wanting to follow too closely. She jumped instead, soaring over the water and landing on the other side. When she did, she heard the sound of fighting.

She froze, holding on to her canal staff. Without any augmentations, she wasn't sure that she could risk joining in any confrontation, but she needed to know what was taking place.

The timing was odd. It seemed far too coincidental that it would happen while she was following the merchant.

Could it be that someone had attacked the merchant? With nearly a dozen guards, such an attack would be suicide, unless whoever was risking the attack had come with even greater numbers.

It wasn't uncommon for fights to break out in some of the outer sections of the city, but it was uncommon for people to attack merchants. Doing so risked the attention of the city guard, and even Bastan knew better than to do something like that. He was careful. He had no problem stealing from merchants, but he had no interest in attacking them openly. It was better to keep others from realizing what he was doing.

Sam crept forward, keeping her staff ready, and rounded a corner, expecting to see the attack, but when she reached it, it was already done.

What had happened?

The dozen guards were down, and most of them weren't breathing. Dead.

The merchant moaned, and Sam raced forward, reaching him. "What happened?"

He looked up at her, a question in his eyes.

"What happened?" Sam demanded.

"An attack."

"I see that. But why? What were you transporting?"

"For. The palace."

"I'm with the palace."

The merchant stared up at her, but his eyes became glassy.

He took a gasping breath and then no more.

Kyza!

Sam stood and looked around, searching for the direction that the attackers would have gone. The cart was missing, so whatever it was the merchant had was valuable, but who would have risked taking something from a merchant who was transporting it to the palace?

She used her staff and jumped to the nearest rooftop, searching for signs of activity. It was still early in the evening, certainly not late enough that she would expect the streets to be as empty as they were, though an attack like that might be enough to drive everyone back inside.

The people in the outer sections were smart enough to recognize when the streets were dangerous.

If that were the case, then all she had to do was find movement.

As she raced along the rooftop, she thought she saw them.

They were heading back toward the swamp.

Could the man the merchant bought the goods from have sabotaged him?

It would be underhanded, and yet, not completely unheard of. There were plenty of people who were foolish enough to attempt a double-cross, especially in the lowborns sections.

Sam was forced to jump down to continue following them and used her staff to leap the canal, tracking the sense of movement. When she reached the street, she looked for signs of movement but saw nothing.

Once again, she climbed to the roofs. From here, she scanned the streets. There had to be something, anything, that would help her understand what had taken place, but she found nothing.

As she continued to search, she tried to see through the growing darkness, wishing for an augmentation that would allow her to see more clearly. If she had some sort of augmentation, maybe sight or hearing, she would be able to see more than the shadows.

But there was nothing. Even the sounds in the street were quiet.

There had to be someplace they were going. She decided to retrace her steps, going back to where the merchant had made the initial transaction. When she reached the street, she found the building the man had come out of, but it was empty.

She swore under her breath. Bastan had buildings like that. Empty shells. Being the owner of multiple properties made him appear reputable. He would arrange meetings nearby, in the open, and then manage to disappear through one of his buildings.

It was possible that there were buildings connected, but she wasn't willing to search through them, especially not at this time of night and in a section that she was unfamiliar with.

Sam stepped back out on the street, listening. Wind gusted, and she felt the evening chill coming on, once again making her miss her cloak. She made her way toward the edge of the section, toward the waterfront that would lead out to the swamp. Beyond here, it was pitch black. She'd visited the edge of the city a few times, and had seen the swamp, and had smelled the putrid odor that radiated from it. There was no way of crossing the swamp. Barges would often drift out, heading away from the city, but be forced to return. From what she'd heard, it was difficult to navigate, if not impossible. More than a few barge captains who thought to venture through the swamp were lost. Sam had a hard time finding sympathy for men like that. All it took was one look at the swamp to know it wasn't a place that anyone should go. It was imposing, almost as dangerous as—

A splash caught her attention, and she turned, looking toward the north. The sound had come from there.

What was it?

Sam raced along the shore, looking to see if she could

find any sign of movement, but there was nothing. Just the splash.

When she reached where she'd heard the sound, she stared into the darkness. As she did, she realized that there was movement out on the water. It was too large to be any sort of creature. The swamp was rumored to be the home of strange animals, and the eels that Sam knew to be in the canal water had to be found in the swamp, too.

As her eyes adjusted, staring into the darkness, she realized what it was that she saw.

A barge.

It wasn't a large one, but it moved swiftly, heading out and away from the city, venturing into the depths of the swamp.

Could that be the merchant's attacker? Could they have risked heading out across the swamp?

If so, why would they have come this way? Unless it really had been the same man who had traded with the merchant to begin with. Unless he really had double-crossed him.

Sam continued to gaze into the darkness until the shadowed form of the barge faded from view. When it was gone, she turned back, heading toward the palace. She had to tell someone what she had seen, but who? Elaine was gone, and she didn't know anyone else in the palace well enough to share this with. If Alec were still accessible, she would have shared with him, but he was gone, too.

Maybe she needed to find Bastan. But what could he do?

She remained unsettled as she meandered through

several sections of the city, before realizing where she was heading.

Caster.

It was almost as if her feet carried her of their own volition.

She wound her way to Bastan's tavern and slipped inside. She nodded to familiar faces that she came across before knocking on the back door.

"He's not there," Kevin said.

She turned. "Where is he?"

"Out."

Sam frowned, staring at Kevin for a moment. "That's all you're going to give me?"

"I'm not at liberty to share anything more than that."

"Come on, Kevin. Tell me where he went."

"It's an assignment that he hasn't involved me in."

Sam took a seat at one of the tables, and Kevin stared at her for a moment before heading into the kitchen and returning with a tray of food. She smiled at him as she dove into the tray of food that he offered. She wasn't about to turn it down; Kevin was a good cook. The palace might have good food, but there was something about the cooking in Bastan's tavern that simply tasted like home.

When she was nearly done with her meal, the door to the tavern opened and Bastan entered. He surveyed the inside of the tavern quickly before his gaze settled on Sam, and he made his way to her table, taking a seat across from her. "All of a sudden you are visiting more often."

"I saw something I thought you should know about."

"What did you see?"

"I'm not really sure."

"Why should I know about it?"

Sam shrugged. "I'm not really sure."

Bastan leaned back in the chair and took a swig from the mug of ale that Kevin brought him. "You're not giving me much to work with here, Samara."

"I followed a merchant."

"Whose job?"

"Nobody's job. I just thought it odd that a merchant would have nearly a dozen guards with him." Bastan's brow furrowed. "I trailed him into one of the outer sections, one that abuts the swamp."

"Why would a merchant venture there?"

"I don't know. But when he headed back toward his section, he was attacked. All of his guards. Him. Dead. Whatever he bought. Gone."

Bastan stiffened. "Did you see what happened?"

"No. It happened too fast."

He arched a brow at her. "Too fast for you?"

"There are things that I can't do, Bastan."

"I wasn't implying that there weren't. I'm just saying that you are incredibly capable, Samara. What *did* you see?"

"That's just it. I didn't see anything. I tried to track where the man's cart went. I followed it back to where the merchant had purchased the goods, but there was no one there. Then I spotted a barge out in the swamp, but I couldn't tell who was on it."

He was silent, watching her for a moment. "Does this have anything to do with Marin?"

Sam shook her head. "I don't think so, but…"

"But what?"

"There was another merchant who went to the palace

the other day, and the physicker I've been meeting with dismissed it when I asked about him."

"Why have you been meeting with a physicker?"

"The princess and Elaine think the physicker can help me recover my memories. They believe that if she can, it will unlock something within me."

"Do you think you need that?"

"I've lost ten years," she said.

"Have you? I've known you those ten years. You haven't lost anything."

Sam stared at him, trying to decide if it was some sort of joke or not, before realizing that with Bastan, it wasn't. "Fine. I didn't lose those years, but I lost the years before that. Does that make you feel better?"

"A little."

Sam glanced down at her tray and used the remaining hunk of bread to mop the gravy before stuffing it into her mouth. "Will you see what you can find out?"

"Now you would direct me?"

"I'm not directing you, but if there's activity happening in the outer sections, it impacts you."

"I don't control all of the outer sections."

"You control enough of them."

Bastan watched her for a long moment before nodding. "I'll see what I can find out, but if it doesn't have anything to do with Marin and what you're after, I can't promise that I will have much to share with you."

"Anything you can discover is more than I have now."

Bastan watched her for a moment before standing. He tapped the tabletop once, hesitating as if he wanted to say something, then meandered through rest of the tavern, stopping at several of the tables before disappearing into his office.

Sam turned her attention back to the food, finishing off her meal. She hadn't thought the merchant incident had anything to do with Marin, but could it?

And if it did, what would Marin be after?

10

A STUDY GROUP

Alec sat in the library, poring over the book that he'd pulled off the shelf, but his mind wasn't on his studies. He wanted nothing more than to see Sam, to share with her what he'd been learning, but she had not come to the university. That had been their agreement and one she hadn't fulfilled. When he'd tried going to her, he had failed.

The other tables in the library were all full of students, and he was thankful that he had his own space, a booth that he could stay in, where he could be left alone with the books he'd borrowed.

A figure appeared in front of him, and Alec looked up, expecting Beckah, but it wasn't she. It was Stefan. He was a tall man and had a long face and gently sloped eyes that made him look like he was always a bit sad. "What are you studying?" Stefan asked.

Alec glanced down at the book. "Our last lecture was on healing broken bones. I thought I would review the various types of splints that we've been taught."

Stefan smiled. "Do you need to study the splints? I thought your experience with your father had given you hands-on training."

It had, but there were different types of splints, for different types of injuries. Alec thought about the author and imagined he had a sort of fascination with injury. He described various fractures with a loving sort of detail.

"The things I learned while with my father haven't always been applicable," Alec said.

Stefan nodded to a chair and waited for Alec to give him permission before he took a seat. "No? I think from what I've seen, the things you know always seem to have some sort of applicability. It may be nontraditional, but it definitely seems to connect with the different masters. Especially with Eckerd."

Alec glanced down at his book. "I got lucky with Eckerd. I noticed the spots on the fingers and recalled something my father had once taught me."

"You don't have to downplay it with me. I don't have a problem with you being the smartest student the university has seen in a generation."

"I'm not the smartest person in a generation," Alec said.

"No? That's the way I hear you described by many of the masters." He looked over at the book and shook his head. "Your father studied here?"

"Apparently. I didn't discover that until recently."

Stefan started to laugh before he seemed to realize that Alec wasn't joking. "You didn't know that he had studied here?"

"No."

"And I suppose you didn't know that he was once

considered the brightest mind in his generation," Stefan said.

That Alec didn't have a hard time believing. His father was a natural with healing, and his near-perfect memory made him even more skilled. "I didn't know anything about my father's training, or his time at the university. It's not something he talks about often."

"I've been looking through the old rosters, and every time I come across your father's name, there is another comment about how smart he was, or all the things that he knew, or even the fact that he managed to discover a new way of treating a specific injury."

There was a lot there for him to work through. "You've been reading through the rosters?"

Stefan shrugged. "Maybe a little."

"Why?"

"Most students have some connection to someone in the university. I thought I would see what yours was. Then when you said your father was an apothecary, I thought that maybe he wouldn't have any connection to the university, but he does."

"What about you? Do you have a connection to the university?"

Stefan flushed. "My grandmother. Master Helen."

Alec couldn't help himself, he started to smile. "Master Helen is your grandmother?"

"She is, but that doesn't mean I get any sort of special treatment," he said.

Alec wasn't surprised. Helen didn't seem the sort to give anyone special treatment. She was well-known for being quite difficult. Alec had little experience with her so far, but the longer he stayed at the university, the more likely it would be that he would have some exposure to her.

"I think, if anything, I'm a bit of a disappointment to Grandma Helen. She would much rather have someone like you in the family than me."

"I'm sure that's not the case," Alec said. "I'm sure she's just happy that you're here, and that you're willing to study."

"You really haven't had much time around Master Helen, have you?"

Alec shrugged, grinning. "No. I really haven't. Tell me more about your time with Grandma Helen, and what I should expect."

Stefan grinned. "You know, you're nothing like your reputation."

Alec's smile started to fade. "What reputation is that?"

"I don't know. Most people think that you're too studious to have much of a sense of humor."

Alec chuckled. That was exactly what Beckah was working with him on to change. She wanted to ensure that he didn't come across as too uptight and that he didn't come off as unapproachable. He still wasn't certain why she cared, but was glad that someone at the university cared about him, and cared about making certain that he fit in.

"I've tried to hide it. I don't want to overwhelm everybody with how amazing I am."

"And humble, too."

"It's not easy to be humble when you're as..." Alec shrugged, flushing slightly. As much as he wanted to come across with the same sort of cocky arrogance that he could have around Beckah, it just didn't fit him around someone like Stefan. It didn't fit him at all. He *was* studious. There shouldn't be anything wrong with that, but he felt as if that tendency of his predisposed him to getting mocked by the other students.

"Don't worry about me," Stefan said. "I'm just happy there's someone here who can challenge some of the masters. Grandma Helen tells me that, too often, the masters will just go on dumping on us what they've done for years, and often they stop studying, and when they do, they stop learning."

"I think I would like your Grandma Helen," Alec said.

Stefan shrugged. "She's not as bad as most claim she is."

"No? I heard a rumor that Master Helen made one of the junior students spend three straight weeks in the library trying to find an answer to a question that didn't have an answer."

Stefan grinned. "You got to admit, that's actually sort of funny. So many of the students are determined to impress the masters that they don't stop and think of whether or not there actually is an answer to the question. With healing, there still are questions without answers."

"I am quite aware of that. My father loved nothing more than to make me look up illnesses that he knew had no known cure. I think it gave him a twisted sort of satisfaction."

"Either that, or he wanted you to get used to searching for questions that needed an answer."

"Isn't this nice, two young students sitting at a table, getting along."

Alec looked up and saw Beckah approaching. She carried a stack of books, and he skimmed the titles, recognizing several of their most recent topics. He wondered what she would test him with this time.

"You know, comments like that make me realize that you're probably one of the two smartest students at our level," Alec said to Stefan. "I realize there are others who wish they could be at our level, but they have to work too hard at it, and they just really aren't as smart as they think they are."

Beckah took a seat and stuck her tongue out at him as she did.

She grabbed the book from Stefan and pulled it toward her, turning it around so that she could look at the page. She scanned it, grinning slightly at Alec as she did, and made a face at him. "Why are you reading this?"

Alec only shrugged. "I've got to stay ahead of you, don't I?"

Beckah grinned. "You do have to stay ahead of me, but I don't see that happening. Especially if you keep grabbing books like this, those that have no bearing on what the masters are asking of us."

"The masters aren't asking anything of us. All they want is for us to study. They've made no demands other than that."

Stefan leaned toward them and lowered his voice. "There's a test at the end of the year. That's how they determine whether we progress."

"What kind of a test?" Alec asked. He glanced from Stefan to Beckah and realized that both of them seemed to already know about the test. If they had family that were a part of the university, it made sense that they would know about it. That put him at a disadvantage.

Even more than he already was, given that he came from his father's apothecary.

"It's not one you have to worry about," Stefan said. "You've already proven that you deserve to be here. I think even Master Eckerd will vouch for you, and he vouches for no one."

"What happens if we don't pass the test?"

Beckah and Stefan shared a glance.

"Do they ask us to leave?" Alec asked.

Beckah shrugged. "Nothing quite so terrible as that. Most of the time, they give the students longer to prove themselves. But there's a stigma to it, and if you are one of the slower students, you'll never progress far."

"I don't know what that means," Alec said.

"That means that you would never be considered for full physicker level if you fail your first time. It means that any connections you hope to gain from your time at the university will be limited."

Alec glanced down at his journal containing his notes. He wasn't entirely certain what he wanted from the university, but now that he was here, he wasn't ready to leave just yet.

He'd already invested himself, planning to devote himself to his studies, and had been almost fanatical about it, but maybe he hadn't done enough.

Beckah watched him, a worried expression on her face. "What is it, Alec?" she asked.

Alec forced a smile and shook his head. "Nothing. Let's... continue with our studies."

11

NEITHER ALIVE NOR DEAD

The lecture hall was dimly lit when Alec arrived. There was a medicinal odor in the air that seemed determined to mask something else, though he wasn't entirely certain what it was. A single lantern was set at the front of the room, and he realized a cot was there, as well, with a person lying on it.

He paused as he entered, glancing around the room briefly before his gaze settled on Beckah. Her eyes were fixed straight ahead, and Alec wondered if he'd missed an announcement, but their instructor for the day hadn't yet arrived.

He turned his attention back to the figure lying on the cot, looking to see any signs of why it was there. Often times, there were easy ways to determine what the masters wanted from them, but he couldn't tell from here in this case. Was there an injury they were asked to assess? They had been studying injuries so it wouldn't be surprising for their instructor to bring someone with an injury to them, but it was unusual to bring patients to class.

Alec took a seat, not able to determine anything from a cursory glance. "What do you think we're expected to see today?" Alec asked.

Beckah shook her head and raised a finger to her lips. She tipped her head toward the far corner, and Alec looked over, realizing that their instructor was already here.

Master Carl was a heavyset man, with an enormous gut that flowed over his pants, forcing him to belt them below his stomach. He was a stern master who was widely considered one of the brighter minds at the university, but he could be difficult and seemed to take particular joy in tormenting the students.

After a few more minutes ticked by, Master Carl looked around and stepped forward. He clasped his hands behind his back, marched toward the cot, and stopped next to it. He slapped his hand down on the side of the cot, the sound drawing all eyes that might have been ignoring him before.

"Now that we are all here," he began, his gaze lingering on Alec, "we can talk about something a little different today. I understand that Master Eckerd demonstrated ingestions to you. Today, we will be discussing something else. Now, I need you all to gather around."

He stepped to the side and waited for all of the students to join him at the cot.

When Alec did, he realized the person lying there was not alive.

He wasn't the only one to pick up on that. Someone gasped, though Alec couldn't tell who it was. Others took a step back. Alec remained close to the cot, trying to study the body, wondering what Master Carl would have them learn from this person. There had to be a reason for him to have brought the body to them. It was unusual enough that an instructor had a cot in one of the lecture halls, but even more unusual was bringing in a lifeless body.

"What can you tell me from initial observations?" Master Carl asked.

No one spoke.

Alec looked at the body. It was an older man, possibly close to his father's age. Dark hair was cut short and neatly groomed. The man had a trace of a beard across his face. He didn't have any appearance of someone who was ill, nothing like so many who presented to the university. Surprisingly, he looked rather hearty. Were it not for the fact that he clearly did not breathe, Alec would have believed him sleeping.

As his father had taught him, he let his gaze go from studying his face to looking at his neck, and then on to his hands. Master Carl had made a point of referencing the solpace juice injection that they had seen with Eckerd, so Alec wondered if there was a connection there. Maybe that was part of the point, a reason that he had shared that. He noted nothing unusual about the hands, other than that his nails were trimmed and clean.

Alec found himself staring at the man's nails for long moments. Unlike the last man, this one had the look of a highborn. His appearance was nothing like the other man's. Where that man had a shaggy and unkempt look to him, this man was well-dressed, and his clothing finely appointed.

"No one has any observations about how this man

might have perished?" Master Carl looked at each of the students and held his gaze on Alec the longest.

The master clearly wanted some response and seemed to expect something from Alec in particular. He knew that he'd gained something of a reputation, but hoped that it was a good one, not one where he annoyed the masters. He understood they cared little for his father's work at the apothecary. They viewed that as beneath someone who had trained at the university.

Beckah elbowed him, and he resisted the urge to look down at her.

"Surely, one of these excellent students has some idea about what happened to this man. It can't be that none of you has an opinion, can it?"

Alec stepped forward and took the man's hand, ignoring the annoyed glares from several of the students, Matthias among them. Beckah followed him to the edge of the cot, watching him assess the man. Alec first confirmed that there was no heartbeat by placing the tips of his fingers on the inside of the man's wrist feeling for a pulse, but there was none. He double-checked it by going to his neck, reaching for the larger artery there, but once again, there was no pulse.

He couldn't shake the fact that this man seemed too healthy to have died at a fairly young age. Alec tipped his head down, listening for breath sounds, but there were none. With no heartbeat and no movement in his chest, he hadn't expected any.

"What are you doing?" Beckah asked in a whisper.

"Trying to figure out what claimed him."

"Why are you reevaluating his heart and lungs? You can tell he's not alive."

Alec glanced over, ignoring the watchful eyes of the others around him. Master Carl simply gazed at him through slitted eyes. "Because he's either recently dead, or he isn't completely dead."

It felt odd to say that last thought, but Alec had been around people who had died before, and there was a change to the complexion of the skin that occurred almost immediately following death, a sallow appearance that this man simply didn't have. Even the texture of the skin on his hands was more rigid than what Alec would have expected.

"Not completely dead?" Matthias asked with a hint of derision.

Alec glanced over. Matthias had a bright mind, and he immediately wondered if he'd missed something that Matthias might have picked up. If he had, Alec had little doubt the man would throw it in his face and make certain that the others were fully aware of Alec's folly.

"It doesn't make sense," Alec began. "I've been taught to look for inconsistencies, and to avoid expectations."

"Expectations?" Matthias snorted. "You're questioning the expectation that the man is dead when you can see that with your own eyes?"

Master Carl leaned forward, placing his belly up to the edge of the cot. It shifted the weight of the cot, sending it into Alec's thighs. "What would your assessment be if not death?" Master Carl asked.

Alec shook his head. "I don't know. He has no pulse, though it could be too faint for me to detect."

"And he's not breathing," Beckah added.

"You're not helping," Alec said out of the corner of his mouth.

Beckah shrugged.

"Like I said, either he's recently dead, or something happened to him that put him in a suspended sort of state."

There were a few snickers around the table. Master Carl silenced them with a single gaze. "We deal in what can be observed, not what can be imagined. Are you really suggesting that something magical might have happened to this young man?"

Alec squeezed his eyes shut. Were he any other place —were he with Sam even—he would question whether the easar paper had been used and whether it was responsible for somehow holding this man in a state like this. That was the only magic that Alec knew, but it wasn't beyond his understanding of what was possible with easar paper.

"I'm not suggesting anything," he said with a frustrated sigh. "Only that what I see doesn't completely make sense."

Master Carl grunted. "Back to your seats, students." He waited as they all took their seats, and Beckah gave Alec a nervous glance. His heart pounded, and he realized that maybe he'd overstepped himself one too many times. Perhaps this was the time that he should have simply remained silent and let the master teach as he had intended. Why did he feel the need to speak up? Had he already begun to think that he knew so much more than the others? It wasn't that the others here were not smart— Alec knew that they were—and he'd become far too comfortable with speaking his mind.

"Now," Carl continued, "we will talk today about mimickers of death. There are many that give an illusion of death, and when dosed in such a way, they can create a believable corpse."

"Is that what happened with that man?" Matthias asked. "Was he given something that mimicked death? Maybe some sort of magical mimic of death."

Master Carl offered a hint of a smile. "As I said, there are many things that mimic death. In this case, we believe he was administered foxglove, a plant found on the plains of one of the southern sections that, in adequate doses, can slow the heart. There are stories of men who used foxglove to fake their own death, before awakening and escaping."

"Will he awaken?" Beckah asked.

Alec had heard of foxglove in passing, but it was a leaf used for other reasons. His father had explained foxglove and how it was used to help with a racing heart. Just a small amount would help slow it and settle the heart of someone suffering from such an ailment. Alec had never had the opportunity to administer it, but he supposed that if it was possible to use foxglove to slow a racing heart, it could also slow a resting heart, couldn't it?

"He may awaken," Master Carl said. "Your magic-chasing student was correct in that. He does not appear as one would expect of someone who is deceased."

It was small consolation to Alec to be granted that much of a compliment. He didn't feel he'd observed anything useful. He felt more like he'd made a massive mistake in speaking up.

"Today, we are going to work with foxglove," Master Carl said. He pulled a jar off the shelf and set it on the table at the front of the room. "A small amount is all that's necessary. Nothing more than a pinch, and you'll be able to feel its effects firsthand."

"What if we use too much?" Beckah asked.

"There is a reversing agent," Master Carl said.

"Why don't you give it to that man?" she went on.

"Finding the reversal agent is difficult. Thistle root only grows in a few places. Even then, it must be carefully harvested. It is fragile and has been known to break before it can be fully used."

Alec's gaze went to the man on the cot. If thistle root worked to help reverse the effects of foxglove, was there any at his father's apothecary shop? His father often carried medicines that weren't found any other place in the city. It was one of his father's gifts, an ability to harvest what others could not, and for a moment, he wondered if he might be able to help this man.

"Pair up and test the foxglove. Don't use much more than a pinch unless you wish to end up like him."

Beckah grinned at Alec. "Will you be my partner? We'll see if we can stop your heart."

"I'm not sure you really want me for your partner."

"Why? Because you believe in magic? You wouldn't be the only person in the city to believe in it." She leaned forward and lowered her voice conspiratorially. "You might be the only person at the university, though."

"Great."

Beckah took the jar of foxglove as it was passed around the room, and took an entire leaf, setting it on the table between them. She passed the jar to Stefan, who had paired with Matthias.

Alec looked at the leaf. It had serrated edges and deep

green coloration. The surface was practically velvety otherwise.

"I suppose you've worked with foxglove before," Beckah said.

"I haven't worked with it. I know of it. My father used it for other purposes than what Master Carl describes."

"So, something other than faking your own death?" Beckah asked with a smile.

Alec grinned. "I can't say that my father ever was asked to help somebody fake their own death."

"Did he ever poison anyone?" she asked, turning toward the man lying motionless at the front of the room.

"I find it hard to think of my father attempting to poison anyone. He's always been so focused on healing."

"Isn't it interesting how medicines can so quickly turn into poisons? Think of what we've learned. How many of these treatments have other uses and can be used to harm as quickly as they can help."

"It's all about moderation," he said.

She peeled off a strip of the foxglove and stuffed it into her mouth. "Monitor my heart. I would hate to have it stop and not be able to restart."

Alec took her wrist and pressed his fingers over the artery, feeling her pulse. He couldn't help but be impressed that she so willingly had taken the foxglove. She knew the risks and had seen what could happen, the same as he had. Master Carl had not given them any instruction about how much was too much to take. Only a pinch. If she mistakenly took the wrong amount, she could be the one lying on a cot, her heart rate undetectable, and her breathing stopped.

"Interesting," she said. Her voice had taken on a sleepy quality to it.

Alec could feel her pulse slowing. It happened quite rapidly. "We should have documented how much you administered."

"He said only... a pinch."

The lids of her eyes started to drift closed, and she swayed in her seat. Alec hurried around to the other side of the table and helped her slide down in the seat so that she wouldn't fall. She was still awake, and she fought to keep her eyes open, but he could see her fighting through the effects of the foxglove.

"How do you know if your pinch is different from his pinch?" Alec asked. "To be safe, we should have a way of maintaining consistency."

Beckah took a deep breath, and her eyes popped open. She shook herself and sat up. "Well. That was interesting."

Alec took her wrist, noting that her pulse had rebounded. The effect of the foxglove was short-acting. If that was typical, then why did the man remain so sedated?

Alec looked to Master Carl and saw him speaking softly to a pair of students near the front, Jason and Sarah. Both were minor highborns, and both were of moderate ability from what Alec had seen.

"It's your turn," Beckah said.

Alec turned his attention back to her and tore off a narrow strip of the foxglove. He hated taking much more than that, hated the idea that he might end up incapacitated as the man at the front of the room apparently still was, if he wasn't dead by now.

"What is it?" Beckah asked.

Alec popped the leaf into his mouth. It had a bitter

quality to it and was strangely meaty. "How is it that the man has been out for so much longer than you were?" He could hear his voice slurring and felt his heart slowing.

"What? I couldn't understand what you said."

Alec sighed and reached for his wrist, pressing his fingers to it, feeling the slowing heartbeat. It was down to a dangerous level. Had he taken too much?

Panic set in, and he tried to will his heart to beat faster, to force it to speed up, but nothing he tried worked.

The effect hadn't lasted long for Beckah, and he hoped it would be equally short-lived for him, but he felt his mind fogging even more; with each passing moment, it became increasingly difficult for him to think clearly.

Much longer, and his heart would stop.

What would Alec do then?

"Why isn't it wearing off?" he asked. The words sounded strange, even to him. What must they sound like to Beckah, or the other students?

He continued to feel himself drifting and hated that he did.

Then his heart stopped.

Alec felt it stop, was aware of that moment, and knew fear unlike anything he had ever known in his life. He was going to die. Worse, he would die, and Sam would never know.

That was his last thought before he knew nothing else.

12

UNDERSTANDING THE PAST

Sam hurried through the courtyard, having heard word that Elaine had returned. She hadn't known the woman had been gone but hadn't seen her in days. All of her training had been overseen by others, those with skill, but not much more than that. If Elaine was back, she had more training ahead of her, but she also had questions.

She came across Elaine near the massive rear door to the palace.

The woman was covered in dirt and had dark circles under her eyes. She was slightly taller than Sam, but otherwise had the same slight profile and dark complexion as Sam.

"Samara. Is there something I can do for you?"

A dozen different questions raced through her head, but none of them seemed fully appropriate. "Where have you been?"

Elaine gaped at her a moment. "I know you feel a certain entitlement here but trust me when I tell you that

I have greater responsibilities than accommodating your needs."

Sam stepped back, feeling almost as if she'd been slapped. "My needs? I think my needs have been ignored for nearly a decade, don't you, Mother? And how have I ever come off as entitled?" Sam didn't know whether to be offended, outraged, or a mixture of both. Both seemed appropriate, but she was willing to remain cautious.

Elaine took a deep breath. "Yes. You have been treated poorly. You live, when so many with your gifts do not. Excuse me if I struggle to feel as sorry for you as you would like."

"What happened?"

Elaine blinked. "What happened was that I attempted a maneuver outside of the city and was nearly overwhelmed by the Thelns. The other Kaver with me did not make it back."

Outside of the city? She'd followed Elaine and lost her in the darkness. Could *she* have been the one on the barge rather than whoever had attacked the merchant?

"You lost a Kaver?"

"There aren't many Kavers left. Those who do remain don't have their Scribes. Often, the Scribe is the first one targeted, as without our Scribes, we are limited to how much we can do."

"But you've been teaching me to function without my Scribe." Sam had barely managed, but that wasn't the point, was it? Elaine had tried to prove to her that she didn't need her Scribe, or her augmentations, to effectively use her abilities. Sam tried but thought that she had only tapped into the barest edge of her abilities. She certainly didn't have anything quite like what Elaine had demonstrated when they were sparring and working together.

"I've been teaching you to function without a Scribe because at some point in your life, it's likely you will not have a Scribe available to you. If you continue to follow this path, you will need to be stronger than you would be otherwise. You will need to be strong enough to manage without having a Scribe with you."

"What exactly happened?"

Elaine shook her head. "It was an ambush. With the Thelns, it often is. We continue to suppress them, keeping them from the borders of the territory we control, but they continue to attempt to disrupt the protections we placed long ago."

"What kind of protections?"

"The kind that you may learn if you continue to develop. If that's all, I have a report to give," she said, beginning to turn away from Sam.

"Who was my father?" Sam blurted.

"Your father?" she repeated slowly. She hadn't turned back around and stood with her back to Sam.

"Yes. The man who fathered me. I presume that Kavers can't do it alone."

"Your father was an amazing man."

Was. Sam didn't miss that particular word, which meant that her father was no longer.

"What happened to him? Was he a Kaver or Scribe?"

"He was neither. He was a man who helped save me when I was young."

"He saved you?"

"It's nothing quite like that. He protected me when I still was learning my abilities, concealing me from an attack that sought to overpower me. It was before I truly understood what I was capable of doing. Without him, I would've been killed, and you would never have been here."

"Why won't you tell me his name."

"His name no longer matters."

"What? It matters. How can it not? He was my father. I'd like to know where I came from."

"For his safety, I can't tell you that."

Sam took another step back. "He's... He's alive?"

Elaine inhaled deeply. "He lives."

"Does he know about me?"

"I couldn't tell him about you. Doing so put him—and you—in danger."

"Danger? Like the kind of danger that happened when Marin tried to kill you and managed to somehow abuse my memories in such a way that it made me forget my entire childhood? Forget you? The kind of danger that comes from living a life on the streets in Caster, trying to stay ahead of the palace guards, avoiding notice so that I can stay alive? That sort of danger?"

"No. That's the kind of danger that kept you alive. What I refer to is an ancient battle, one that has waged between the Thelns and the Kavers for many years. If I had not hidden you—and him—you would have been a target."

"You're not hiding me now."

"Because they know about you now. You *are* a target. Regardless of anything else, you will remain a target. *That's* why I am training you."

"Why only now? If I have this ability, why wouldn't

you want me to use it? Why wouldn't you want me to be able to protect myself, and help others?"

Elaine fixed her with an unreadable expression. "Because I didn't want another one to die."

"Another what?"

"Another child of the Kavers," she said softly. "Too many have been lost over the years. It was a mistake getting pregnant. I knew it, but I loved your father."

"Loving him doesn't mean that you abandon him when he's in danger."

"Abandon? Is that what you think I've done?"

"I honestly don't know what I think," Sam said. Some of the anger had been extinguished, partly because she struggled with Elaine's rationale. "Why not keep your Scribe safe, use augmentations on the Scribes?"

"Scribes have some capacity to receive what you refer to as augmentations, but they don't have the same innate gifts that allow them to use them the same way."

"That's not the only reason, though, is it?"

"No."

"Are you going to tell me what it is?"

"I fear that telling you will leave you believing you need to do something dangerous."

"I think I've done a few dangerous things."

"Which is exactly my concern."

"At least tell me why I need to be concerned about Alec," she said.

Elaine glanced back at the door to the palace, before settling her gaze on Sam and shaking her head. "Scribes are particularly attuned to the dark magic used in the Book of Maladies. You've seen that yourself."

"You mean when the princess was attacked?"

"Yes. Such as then. Scribes, by their very nature, are at risk. Thelns capture all Scribes that they can and use their abilities. Why do you think so many Scribes have been lost?"

"I don't know! I don't know much about the Scribes, other than my own. Alec doesn't seem particularly at risk, but I don't want him to be in danger."

"He won't be, not if he stays at the university. The university was established as an option to counter the Theln magic."

"What of you? Don't you worry about your Scribe?"

Elaine fixed her with a hard expression. "Every day." She started to turn before catching herself. "Continue your studies. Continue to work with the physicker and see what Helen can uncover. She is a skilled physicker, and we have much faith in her ability to uncover what you need to know."

Sam swallowed and nodded. What else could she do?

She was caught up in something different from anything she had ever imagined. When she learned from Marin about the Thelns, she had begun to fear their ability to hurt her. That had been bad enough, especially when she didn't think there was anything she could do to counter their power. They had poison that could kill her. Somehow, she and Alec had managed to overwhelm it. She had survived, and they had pushed out the Theln attack in the city before it became anything greater.

And they had done it untrained. Shouldn't that have given her a chance to get the attention of the princess sooner? Shouldn't they have brought her in, and offered to help her learn her abilities sooner than they had?

Instead, they had not come to her until Sam had begun tracking the princess.

Sam watched as Elaine disappeared behind the door into the palace. She wanted to help, but it seemed as if those who she could help didn't want her help.

All she could do was devote herself to her training.

And she needed to find Alec. She felt empty having not seen him for so long. They'd already learned that they needed to stay better connected, and when they weren't, both of them felt off.

Maybe she needed to discover another source of easar paper, as well. That way, they could continue to practice. Elaine had not revealed her source of paper and had bristled the few times Sam had attempted to find out where it was stored. She knew it was in short supply, but there had to be a way to replicate the process, didn't there? If the Thelns could manufacture it, why couldn't they?

If they could find the secret to creating the paper, maybe they wouldn't have to rely on the source of it outside the city, stealing from the Thelns and attracting even more of their attention. Already, it seemed as if the Thelns were focused on the city, and as she considered what Elaine had shared with her, she thought it might be more than what the Kavers could withstand.

Had Sam developed enough skill to face them?

That might be the worst part.

She didn't think that she had. Luck would only carry her so far, and it was possible that she wouldn't continue to have the same luck.

And then what?

13

THE TRAINING CONTINUES

S am spun her canal staff, and it whistled through the air with the movement. She'd gotten faster with it over the last few days and managed to strike Thoren twice during their spar. Each time she had, she'd grinned with a vicious excitement, hoping to get past his defenses. He might not be a Kaver, and might not be enhanced, but he was still wickedly fast with the staff, and she considered any time that she managed to get through his defenses a victory.

Thoren spun, and Sam twisted to counter. As she did, she discovered he wasn't where she expected, and she swung at empty air. His staff smacked on her arm, then her back, and she staggered forward, dropping her canal staff.

Sam cursed under her breath, hating losing the staff, but it was better losing to Thoren than to Elaine. At least Thoren didn't seem to take the same satisfaction in beating her that Elaine did. He was mostly interested in working with her, and teaching, and she appreciated that about him.

"You have to get up quickly if you fall," he said.

"I'm trying, but I don't think my hand will work."

Thoren grunted, and his staff caught her on the backside again.

Sam swore again to herself and scrambled forward, grabbing her staff and swinging it around in a low arc.

Thoren jumped, easily missing her attack, and swung down at her, pinning her staff to the ground. "If you're too slow grabbing your staff, you'll be easily defeated."

He lifted his staff, letting her grab hers, and she jumped back to her feet, stepping into the ready posture that he had demonstrated for her. He waited, letting her attack first, and she feinted forward, before stepping back, slipping back again, and whistling her staff around in a short arc that caught him on his shoulder.

His grunt was the only acknowledgment she had that she'd gotten to him.

He spun and managed to sweep the staff out of her hands.

Sam jumped toward it, not wanting to let it get too far from her. Thoren was nothing if not annoyed if she failed to learn from her lessons.

She grabbed the staff and came up in a roll. As she did, she brought it back around, reacting to movement in the air that signaled his staff neared her. They connected with a sharp snap that reverberated throughout the practice grounds.

Thoren chuckled. "Good. You're getting better at anticipating. Elaine suspected that you would have an ability similar to hers," he said.

"And what ability is that?"

"There aren't too many who can anticipate and react to attacks. If you're anything like Elaine, there's a subtle sensation she seems to manage that allows her to react even when she can't see the attack coming. If you have anything similar to that, you will be skilled with the staff."

Sam could only nod. She wanted to be more effective when fighting with the canal staff, but so far, she didn't feel as if she had anything near Elaine's ability. Her mother managed to flip and leap, leaving Sam staring after her, struggling to react.

"Now you need to work on your aerial response."

"My aerial response?"

"You're fighting with the staff. That does not require that you remain on the ground. There are times when it's better to get above the action so that you can gain a different perspective."

To demonstrate, Thoren planted his staff into the hard-packed earth and flipped up, balancing briefly at the peak before dropping back down. He did it again, this time, spinning in a lazy circle, suspended high over her head as he did.

Sam was reminded of how Elaine had used the staff to flip over her, but what Thoren was demonstrating was somehow a little different.

"You have to be careful with this technique, as you are placed in a precarious position with it, but it can be advantageous."

Sam jabbed her canal staff into the ground and flipped up, attempting to hold her position.

Her momentum carried her up and over, leaving her to tumble to the ground, her breath forced from her lungs as she hit the hard ground. She got up slowly and tried again. This time when she flipped, she tried to hold her balance, trying to maintain a connection to the position and managed to remain in place for a heartbeat at most. It might've been even less, but she had succeeded.

"Good. That is something you need to practice. It's all a part of balance. If you manage to succeed in acquiring a sense of balance, you can use it to your advantage." He kicked his legs up and suspended himself vertically, his head facing down, and bounced on the end of his staff.

Sam would not have expected the staff to support his weight in such a way, and it flexed slightly, but not nearly as much as she thought it would. He hopped again, and when the staff came down, it flexed, and as it straightened, Thoren flipped up, pulling his staff from the ground and swinging toward her.

Sam had barely a chance to react. She brought her staff up, protecting her head moments before his staff would have collided with her skull.

She flipped the ends of her staff, catching him on the wrist, and he grinned at her.

"Good. Always remain alert."

"It seems to me that balancing like you're trying to demonstrate would put me in a difficult situation. If someone hits the staff while I'm suspended like that, wouldn't I fall?"

"Everything comes back to needing to maintain awareness of your surroundings. You need to keep your eyes open, observe everything, and anticipate ways you may need to react. Once you manage that, you will be truly difficult to stop." He tapped his staff on the ground, a gesture that Sam had discovered meant the lesson was over and bowed at the waist toward her. "You should practice. We will meet again tomorrow."

Thoren left her alone in the practice yard. Sam attempted the flipping several more times, but each time, she managed to hold herself upright for only a moment, never much longer than that. She wasn't certain if that meant progress, or if she should simply abandon her attempts. She'd found that when something didn't connect for her, a technique that she struggled to master, leaving it for a while would often give her a chance to let her mind approach it differently. Maybe this was one of those times.

It was also possible that she simply needed rest. She was exhausted from working with Thoren, and her body ached from dozens of injuries, most of which would take time to heal. How would she fare if she had augmentations?

Yet she understood the need to master fighting without the benefit of being augmented. They had variable durations, depending on the ratio of blood used by both Scribe and Kaver, as well as the technique used in recording the planned augmentation. Thankfully, Alec was nothing if not diligent in how detailed he was with his documentation, recording the amounts of blood they used, and making diligent notes about the various ways they had tried to use it.

After a few more attempts to improve on the technique Thoren had shown her, she broke down her staff and tucked it away.

She glanced up at the sky, noting the position of the sun. It was still early in the day. Days like today, she had few other responsibilities. She no longer had to want for food, clothing, or her overall safety, not as she once had. The princess had assigned her various tasks, but most of them revolved around learning to fight, and there were precious few that involved her using her mind, or trying to master the other skills of a Kaver, though Sam wasn't exactly sure what they were. Maybe they didn't involve her in such studies because they didn't think much of her capacity.

More than anything, she wanted to see Alec. They had been separated for long enough. Since running into Elaine days ago, she hadn't seen her again, either. Sam suspected she left the city once again, getting the sense that she did so frequently, which was probably part of the reason that years had passed without Sam gaining her attention.

She grabbed her cloak from where she'd hung it near the entrance to the yard and slung it over her shoulders. She departed the palace grounds, reaching the bridge and nodding to the soldiers monitoring it, before getting waved through. As she always did, she contemplated simply jumping the canal. That might be more enjoyable to do, giving her a chance to flex her skills with the staff, but taking the bridge was a more surefire way of remaining dry and not drawing anyone's attention.

The Forlain section adjacent to the palace was comprised entirely of highborns. It was a section with countless massive estates. Sam had always avoided it in the past because when traveling through this part of the city, it was difficult to avoid notice. Now, she had the proper paperwork that made getting between the sections quite easy.

Sam hurried along the street, heading toward the next

section of the city, and decided she wanted to jump the canal. Marin had demonstrated jumping the canals with minimal run up, and had done so without any augmentation, a skill that she thought she should work on, as well. It was not always straightforward for her, and usually she required more of a run before she could leap, but Marin had done it with only a single step. If she was to confront Marin, she would have to learn to mimic what the woman was capable of. Then again, if it were up to Elaine, they wouldn't allow her the chance to confront Marin.

She backed up two steps and lunged forward, leaping at the last possible second, stabbing her staff into the middle of the canal and flipping up and over the water. She teetered on the edge, nearly falling in, but caught herself and pulled the staff free.

Her heart pounded heavily in her chest as she collected herself. She didn't need to jump the canals, so why was she risking it? She had no desire to end up in the water, and no desire to face the damned eels, bloodthirsty things that they were, regardless of what the physicker claimed.

Yet there was a certain thrill in jumping the canals, one that she didn't get from anything else that she did.

She continued along the waterfront, heading toward the university section. She could see it from where she was now, barely two sections over, which meant two more canals to jump. At the next one, she challenged herself by taking only a single step and pushed off with even more force than she had before.

She landed barely a foot within the shoreline.

Sam grinned to herself and hurried on, racing toward the university. She was determined to see Alec tonight and determined to do so dry. The next canal—the one with the university on the other side of it—was one of the widest in the city. Strangely, according to the map that she had in her head, the university was situated toward the center of the city, rather than closer to the palace as would otherwise make sense. The canal around the palace was wide, but not nearly as wide as what was found around the university.

She'd attempted to jump this before and failed. And she'd attempted to jump it with augmentation and succeeded. Did she risk it now?

If she did and failed, she would have to go to Alec sopping wet. She suspected even with her papers that the university would not grant her access. The alternative was taking her papers to the guards, but that meant admitting that she needed her access, that she needed the connection that she now had to the princess. That meant that she had truly allowed herself to become highborn.

Lowborns didn't use papers to travel between sections —certainly not to the university section. They were forced to travel at specific times and given only very specific access.

Sam stared at the canal, watching the eddying current. There were only a few things that made the current move like that.

She shivered. How could others claim there were no eels in the canal? Sam had *felt them*. And she had no interest in joining the eels or becoming their snack, but she wanted to see Alec, which meant that she would have to use the stupid bridge and the papers that the princess supplied to her.

Sam marched along the bridge, reaching into her cloak

for the documents that she'd been given. She swore under her breath, hating that it came to this, hating that *she* had come to this, but recognizing that what she did was necessary if she wanted to see her Scribe. How else could she do it?

The guards blocking entrance to the university section glanced at her, taking in her cloak and the staff barely hidden beneath it. The staff was not new, but the cloak was, so different from the one she'd long ago taken from Marin that seemed to shed the shadows. This one bore the crest of the royal family. In the light, the crest glittered, taking on an undulating sort of pattern. Maybe the guards wouldn't even ask her for the papers.

The nearest guard, a man with a wide face and a neatly trimmed beard, watched her through slitted eyes. He held his hand out, saying nothing to her, and took her documents without a word. He scanned them before holding them back out and waving her through.

She entered the university grounds and hurried forward, trying to ignore the same feeling she had every time she used her new-found connections—the feeling that left her feeling like a fraud.

In the distance, she caught sight of a familiar form. Alec? She almost called out to him before catching herself.

He was walking with another woman. She had deep brown hair and the straight back and fine clothes of a highborn. She looked up at him familiarly, and Alec smiled at her, the grin on his face more open and welcoming than any he'd had for Sam in quite some time.

What was she doing?

She shouldn't feel guilty and shouldn't feel jealous of Alec having friends at the university, but she couldn't help that she did. It wasn't that he was only supposed to have her as a friend, but here she'd been working and training, feeling isolated at the palace, while he was busy making friends, and possibly more, within the university.

She watched for a while longer before she turned away, ignoring the moisture on her cheek that was *not* a tear as she headed back across the bridge.

14

FOXGLOVE TOXICITY

Alec awoke with a pounding headache. He was lying on the cot and realized that he was in the hospital, other beds all around him with injured people. A woman with a medium length gray jacket made rounds nearby and stopped at cot after cot before reaching his.

"Good. You're awake."

Alec took a deep breath. "What happened?" he asked. His mouth felt thick, and his tongue dry. His head pounded, almost like he had had too much to drink.

"A training accident, from what Master Carl tells me," the junior physicker said.

"I only took a pinch."

"Indeed. Only a pinch. But was your pinch greater than your body can tolerate?"

He felt like an idiot. "How many others ended up here?" he asked. It had to be more than just Alec, didn't it? He couldn't have been the only person to have mistakenly over ingested the foxglove.

"Only you. It happens from time to time with the foxglove lesson, but it is rare. You're lucky you woke up."

"Lucky?"

The physicker shrugged. "Some don't."

Alec tried to sit up and realized that he wasn't wearing anything beneath the sheets. Could he have died during the training? Why would Master Carl have let them try it were that the case?

"Where are my belongings?" He cared less about his clothes than he did about his books and the journals that he kept. Those were his most valuable possessions within the university.

"Everything you had is beneath the cot," the woman said.

"Can I return to my studies?"

"You may return, but I would caution you to not exert yourself too much. Foxglove can linger in the blood-stream. You will find that there will be some strange side effects."

Alec looked over at the physicker. He decided to ask her the question that had come to mind when he was in the session with Master Carl. "Why does it seem to last longer with some than others?"

The woman shrugged. "Foxglove is unpredictable. That is what makes it dangerous for so many. With some, the effect is short-lived."

"Like most of my class?"

"Yes. Most will have some effect. They'll notice that their heart slows, and they may even pass out, but in others, the effect lingers. We have not been able to deter-mine what predisposes one person to such effect over another."

"What is it that would keep someone in a perpetual slumber?"

The woman grinned. "Stories of men using foxglove to fake their own death are nothing more than that. Stories."

"But Master Carl had a man in our room who he claimed was suffering from foxglove poisoning."

Her brow furrowed for a moment. Then she shrugged. "It's possible that Master Carl does have someone like that. If he does, I can't say that I know anything about it. It's something that he might have kept to the masters."

Alec realized that he wasn't going to get anything else from her, and waited for her to depart before reaching beneath the cot and grabbing his belongings. As she promised, everything of his remained there. There were his books, and thankfully, his journals. He grabbed his clothes and began to dress quickly, not wanting to be left in a state of undress were someone else to appear.

He started out of the hospital ward, leaning on an occasional cot for support. It was difficult for him. As she claimed, he was weaker than he realized.

Alec made his way out into the hallway and toward his room. All he wanted was rest. He hoped he could be granted that, though worried that perhaps he wouldn't awaken if he did fall asleep.

Staggering down the hall, he finally reached his room. Once inside, he fell onto his bed and simply lay there, his mind racing. Why had he been affected this way? There was little doubt in his mind that Matthias, and probably some of the other students, would give him a hard time about what had happened. They'd probably taunt him about it.

As he lay on his bed, staring up at the smooth ceiling,

he tried to think about foxglove. Something troubled him about it. The physicker in the hospital hadn't realized that Master Carl had someone who had been poisoned by foxglove. It could simply be that Carl was more senior than she was at the university, but he wondered if maybe there was something more to it. Were they concealing something from Alec?

There was a knock, and Alec sat up, looking at the door. Who would come to his room?

He managed to stand but doing so was difficult and required strength that he didn't have yet.

He pulled the door open, and Beckah stood on the other side, wearing a deep blue robe, the belt cinched around her waist. Her expression softened, and she let out a relieved sigh when she saw him. "I went to check on you in the hospital, but you weren't there. They told me you were released."

"I'll be fine," he said.

"Fine?" Beckah asked. "You nearly died."

"And it's something I'm sure others will be talking about," Alec said.

"Only because they're worried about you."

He turned back to look at her. "Worried about me? I think that's an overstatement. They might be interested in what happened, and they might have questions about why I can't even handle a little foxglove, but…" Alec sighed.

"You were right," she said. "We should have been monitoring how much we were administering to every-one. The dose was different. What was a pinch for you was not the same as a pinch for me."

Alec hadn't even thought he'd taken a full pinch. He'd torn a strip along the edge of the leaf, which shouldn't have been enough to incapacitate him, certainly not when Beckah had taken a similar-sized sample and had done reasonably well.

"I don't think it matters," he said.

"Alec—"

He shook his head and cut her off. "Listen. I was wrong. I got too hung up on feeling like something was… unusual, and I made a claim I shouldn't have."

"You're still worried about that?" she asked.

"I don't think anyone else is going to let me live that one down."

She shrugged. "You're not from the same section of the city as most of us. People's beliefs are different elsewhere in the city."

Alec closed his eyes, resisting the urge to contradict her. It had nothing to do with which section of the city he was from. Had he been asked even just several months ago what could have caused the state of the man they'd seen in the lecture hall, he never would have leaped to the possibility of some magical cause. That was because of his time with Sam.

Yet there *were* magical things in the world. Alec had seen firsthand the way that different powers could manifest, using something as simple as his own blood to write on paper.

No, it had nothing to do with his beliefs, and more to do with what he'd experienced. But he couldn't speak of it to anyone. He had to keep that concealed, otherwise Sam and Elaine, and the other Kavers who studied in the palace would be in danger. Alec didn't want to be responsible for that.

"What's bothering you?" Beckah asked.

"I'm bothered by the fact that I made a fool of myself."

"How did you make a fool of yourself? You offered an answer."

"An answer that Master Carl thought was ridiculous."

"He's not the only one who thought it was ridiculous," she said. She smiled, and Alec couldn't help but smile along with her. The easiest thing for him to do would be to tell her and admit what he was capable of doing, but he didn't dare do that without having Sam's permission, because they were really a team. It was not his decision, but *their* decision.

"It still doesn't make sense," Alec said.

"What doesn't make sense? You saw—and experienced —the way that foxglove works."

"I did, and I also saw how quickly you recovered from your dose."

"And you didn't recover that quickly. You were out for nearly eight hours," she said.

Eight hours? He'd not been told how long, nor had he asked when he awoke in the hospital. The other man—the one who had been poisoned by foxglove—had been out at least that long.

There was a way to test it, but that meant he had to find this thistle root.

Not only that, but he had to find the man to test it on.

"I've seen that look in your eyes before," Beckah said.

"You've not seen any look before."

"Sure I have. You have a look to your face that tells me you intend to do something you think is stupid."

Alec shrugged. "Maybe you have seen that look on my face before. But that doesn't mean I will do something or that it's stupid."

"No? What do you intend to do then?"

"I want to know why I had the reaction I did and why that man remains unconscious. Unless he's regained consciousness in the last eight hours."

Beckah shook her head. Alec was not surprised by that but had the man awakened, it would have changed his thinking a little bit. He would have had no choice but to accept that what Master Carl told him was accurate. That it was just an overdose of foxglove.

And why shouldn't he believe that?

"I'm going to visit my father," he said.

"You know what time it is?" she asked.

He shrugged. "Does it matter? My father will be happy to see me." He hoped that was true. But given the hour, his father might not even be in his shop."

"Good. I have wanted to visit one of the famed apothecary shops found in that section of the city."

Alec looked at her askance. "Famed apothecaries?" he asked. "There's only my father's shop."

"That makes it easier. I don't have to visit quite so many."

Alec sighed and shook his head, but had to admit to himself that having company—especially Beckah—would make the trip across the city more palatable.

15

IN THE APOTHECARY

"This is where you grew up?" Beckah asked in a hushed tone.

Alec glanced over. She had grown increasingly quiet the farther they got away from the university section and approached some of the outer sections. With each bridge they crossed, they went farther and farther away from the center of the city, and closer to a place that Alec had long considered home. He still considered it home, even though he hadn't resided there for many months.

"This is where," he said.

"You're practically lowborn," she said before clamping her hand over her mouth. "I mean, it's a nice merchant section."

A hint of a smile crossed his face. "Practically. We never considered ourselves that when we were here, but the more I've gotten to know other people in the city, and other sections of the city, I've come to realize that I really was practically lowborn."

Sam wouldn't see it that way. Sam saw herself as

lowborn and saw anyone else anywhere near the inner sections of the city as highborn. It was an endearing quality about Sam that he'd always been amused by. She tended to pay more attention to things like that than Alec ever did, though in her defense, she had never been anything other than a lowborn. He had the advantage of being raised in a place where he might have been viewed as between classes, but he was much closer to highborn than he was to lowborn.

"Why would your father choose this section to establish his apothecary?"

"I don't know. Maybe he likes the people. Maybe he liked the access."

"Access? What kind of access do you get all the way out here?"

"You know, there are other sections of the city."

"I know. You can go far beyond this, and you get deep into those lowborn sections. Kyza knows what would happen to you if you weren't careful there."

"Nothing will happen to you there. I've spent a lot of time all the way out in Caster, and rarely did I feel threatened."

"You're a strange man, Alec."

Alec shrugged as he turned down the familiar street toward his father's shop. He glanced at the nearby buildings, wondering who might still be awake. Mrs. Rubbles had a lantern lit, so he suspected she was awake, but no other shops were. Even his father's shop was darkened.

"Which one is yours?"

Alec led her to the apothecary and knocked on the door. He waited but doubted his father would be there. He tested the handle and found it locked. Thankfully, since his last visit, his father had given him a key. Alec fished it out of his bag and unlocked the door, pushing it open to the soft tinkling of the bell over the door, and stepped inside.

Beckah hesitated and watched him for a moment before following him in.

Once she'd joined him inside, he closed the door and locked it. He didn't want someone entering the shop while they searched for the thistle root.

"It's so dark," Beckah said.

Alec fumbled forward, trying to use his memory of the new shop's layout, thankful that it was somewhat similar to the one he'd grown up in. This one was different, but it was similar enough that he was able to find his way to the tables in the middle of the shop. He suspected he would find a lantern there.

He did. Alec fumbled a moment until he managed to get it lit, casting a soft orange glow over the room.

Beckah's eyes widened as they adjusted, and she peered around, holding her breath. "This is an apothecary shop?" she asked.

"It is. This is the kind of apothecary shop that my father runs. I don't know what others might be like." He hadn't actually ever been to any other apothecary shops. What need would he have?

She stopped at one of the shelves, and her hand ran along the row of jars there. "All of this is medicine," she said.

Alec laughed softly. "Yes. What did you think we would have?"

She glanced over at him. "I never expected you to have the same capabilities as they have in the hospital."

She tapped one of the shelves and lifted the jar. "They don't even have some of these in the hospital, do they?"

"My father has unique sources for various things. I don't think many at the university have the same access he manages."

Beckah continued along the row of shelves, stopping at a few before continuing on. Every so often, her breath caught, and she muttered something softly to herself, though he never was clear what that was. She slowly made her way through the shop before coming back to the center and leaning on one of the tables.

"It seems I've underestimated you," she said.

"How so?"

"Well, when you've spoken of the things you've seen and done, I think part of me has always believed that maybe you weren't entirely honest."

"Everything I've said has been the truth."

Beckah grunted. "Yes. I can see that now. What I'd like to know is how your father managed to obtain such supplies. Some of the things here are obscure, things that the masters would love to have access to."

"As I said, my father has a unique ability to acquire various medicines. I think he takes a strange sort of pride in being able to find things that the university believes impossible to source."

"Such as thistle root."

Alec shrugged. "Things like that," he agreed.

"Well?" she said.

Alec arched a brow. "Well what?"

"Does he have any?"

Alec hadn't looked yet, he'd been preoccupied

watching her explore the shop. "Why don't we take a look?"

Alec walked over to one wall. He wasn't certain if his father even had thistle root here. But if it was going to be anywhere, Alec suspected he would find it along this row. This was where his father stored a variety of roots, though Alec didn't have the entire row of plants memorized, not as his father did.

Most of them had labels, and the labels were really for Alec's benefit, not so much for his father, who had no need for labels as he was often the one who had collected them. Alec scanned the row of roots before finding what he sought. He pulled it out and glanced at the jar. The root was a deep black and strangely twisted. There were small forms along the edge, and he had no idea how it was used to counteract the foxglove.

"He has some?" Beckah asked.

"He has some, but now that I have it, I'm not sure exactly how we would use it to counteract the foxglove."

"Wouldn't it just be ingested the same way as the foxglove?"

"Not necessarily. Sometimes, with different treatments —and especially with roots like this—they have to be crushed, pulverized into a powder before they are effective. There are some that need to be juiced, squeezing out the oils from within them to make them effective."

"If your father has these here, wouldn't it make sense that he might have some record of how it would be used?"

"Oh, my father keeps meticulous records. It's just that finding anything within his records is a matter of patience and perseverance." And most of them had been destroyed in the fire.

She smiled. "How can they be meticulous, but also require patience?"

"Come with me, and I'll show you."

Alec led her toward the back of the shop, behind the counter where his father often did most of his accounting and nodded to a row of thick bound books. There were over a dozen, each written in his father's hand, each detailing knowledge he'd accumulated from several months of treatments.

"My father has an organization, but it's one that fits with his mind. He remembers where and when he saw something before and can find it in his notes. Without knowing when he treated a particular ailment, it's not always possible to know—or find—what he did for that person. This is all since the shop was rebuilt."

Beckah reached for one of the books and glanced up at Alec, seemingly waiting for permission. He nodded. It wasn't that there was anything secretive in any of his father's books. They were records, no different from the records that were kept at the university, only they were records of his father's preferred treatment attempts.

"This is... amazing," Beckah said, looking up. "He's detailing the symptoms, what he has come up with as a diagnosis, and whether the treatment worked. Can you imagine if the journals at the university were anything like this?"

Alec chuckled. "That might be part of the reason I have had such a hard time at the university. I understand the master physickers have a different way of documenting, but it's hard when it's so different from what I grew up learning."

"How much of this were you a part of?"

Alec flipped the book closed, noting the date scrawled across the front. "This one? Not much. These are since I left for the university."

"Any of these?" she asked, waving her hand toward the other volumes.

Alec crouched down, looking at the volumes that she'd indicated. "Some of these I had a hand in." He grabbed one of the books and flipped toward the end, pointing to his notes.

Beckah leaned over the page, reading what he'd written. "You sound like him, you know that?"

Alec chuckled. "I don't think I sound like him."

"Well, you document like him. Does that make you feel better?"

He shrugged. "He trained me. It's his style I'm using."

"And the first thing you showed me was a case of diarrhea?" She wrinkled her nose as she said it, and Alec grinned.

"You wouldn't believe how much diarrhea comes through here."

Beckah pulled her hand off the book, and Alec laughed. "That's the side of healing that I'm not quite sure I'm ready for. I am great with the theoretical aspect of it, being able to work through a problem and come up with a solution, but applying it—especially when it's disgusting —isn't something I am certain I'll excel at."

She turned her attention back to his father's books. "You don't think there's any way to search through these books to find where your father might have used thistle root?"

"Short of asking my father, or searching through each section? No."

"He had to have indexed it in some fashion."

"His indexing is by year. He documents because that is what he's always done, but he never needs to reference his notes because he remembers every treatment he's ever administered and every patient he's ever treated. His records are mainly for... me, I guess. So, he only compiles indexes annually. And after the fire..."

"But you studied them, didn't you?"

"I did study some of them, but it's one thing to observe and record symptoms, and another to look back and try to find where my father might have documented something from years past."

Beckah stood and tapped her chin. She had a slight hunch to her shoulders, and leaned over the table, peering at the book, unmindful of the fact that she was shoulder to shoulder with Alec. She smelled of flowers, mostly lilacs and roses, both of which were used at the hospital for various healing concoctions.

"What other way would you have of searching this?" she asked him. "I think you're right. Searching through all the volumes here would be far too difficult, but if there was another way to do it, perhaps somehow triggering your memory of something related to where you might have seen a reference to thistle root."

"I came across it once, but..."

Beckah bit her lip. "To have come across it, wouldn't you have likely been reading about foxglove?"

"Maybe," he agreed. Alec tried to think about when he would have read—or written—about foxglove. There was a time a few months ago, when one of their neighbors came into the shop, complaining of something in their chest. His father had taken a listen, done a brief exam, and ultimately chose to administer foxglove.

"Grab me that one," he said, motioning toward one of the volumes on the nearby shelf.

"This one?"

He shook his head. "The one next to it."

Beckah pulled the book off the shelf, and Alec opened it and started flipping through the pages. As he did, he remembered seeing many of these ailments. The descriptions took him back, practically putting him in front of the patients he and his father had treated so long ago, and he recalled them vividly.

He suspected that, more than anything else, was the reason his father documented in this way. It was easy to recall a diagnosis and to recall what they tried. It was much more difficult to remember all the different faces and people they'd seen over the years, though his father would have managed even that.

Alec turned the pages, feeling the thick paper in his fingers, reminded of the easar paper. Not for the first time, Alec knew that his father would have interest in the easar paper, and he could only imagine what his father would do were he to get his hands on it, enough to document all of the ailments. Would he ever consider creating a record of healing, one that was similar in some ways to what the Thelns had with their Book of Maladies?

About halfway down the page, he came across the cluster of symptoms that he remembered. His finger paused, held just above the surface of the page, and he traced down, looking to see if there was reference to thistle root here.

"Did you find what you're looking for?"

"I found what I remembered of foxglove," he said. He looked up, meeting her gaze. "There was a man who came into the shop, and he had been complaining of pain. My father determined that it was from his heart and gave him foxglove." He tapped the page, the marker where his father had documented the need for foxglove.

"Any reference to the root?"

"Unfortunately, not. It's only about the foxglove, the dose needed to slow the man's heart. My father never intended to stop his heart, and hadn't worried about that the fact that he probably wouldn't have been able to slow it enough to stop it without significant amounts of foxglove, anyway."

"Well. It seems that since we have no way of learning from books, it's time for an experiment."

Alec shook his head. "I don't think I can take foxglove again. The last time—"

Beckah smiled. "Not you. I wouldn't put you through that again, even if I thought that was a good idea. You're clearly sensitive to it."

"Thanks."

"And sensitive about many other things as well, it seems. I'm only suggesting that we take the thistle root and see if we can't figure out the best means of administering it."

Alec picked up the jar, noting the amount of root inside. There didn't seem to be an enormous amount, though he didn't know how much was necessary to counteract the effects of the foxglove.

"Where? Back to the university? If we get caught taking foxglove out of Master Carl's supplies..." Alec didn't even want to think about what the master would do.

"Why would we have to go back to the university when we have a full apothecary around us?"

Alec looked around his father's shop, realizing that her suggestion made a certain sort of sense. They could test thistle root and determine the best means of administering it, and then could return to the university, and attempt to find Master Carl's patient.

"I'll get the foxglove and thistle root. Maybe we start with swallowing it whole to begin with."

Beckah lifted the jar and stared through the glass. Alec could practically see her mind working, trying to decide if she'd made a mistake volunteering herself, as she noted the thorns on the side of the root. "I'm not sure I like this idea so much anymore."

Alec smiled. "Well, it was your idea."

16

THE TEST

They laid out a row of foxglove leaves on a small table that Alec pushed up next to the cot along the back of the wall. He'd carefully removed the thistle root from the jar, and cut off a few small sections of it, uncertain whether it was harmful to handle. Some of the various medicines his father collected were caustic and would be dangerous if handled without gloves on.

"This would be much easier if my father were here," he muttered.

"If you think he'll return, we can wait until morning."

"I don't know with him. There are times when he disappears for days, even weeks."

"Why does he disappear?"

Alec shrugged. "Harvesting. That's usually what he's up to when he disappears. There's no one else who can collect everything that he needs. I think that bothers him."

"He thought he'd have you with him?"

Alec nodded. "He thought I would one day join him. Father and son running the apothecary shop together."

"Is that what you wanted?"

"For a while."

"What do you want now?" she asked.

It seemed a loaded question, one that Alec didn't really have a good answer for. What did he want now? He wanted to continue to learn and study at the university. He wanted to know what it meant for him to be a Scribe, and how he could best use those, but that required him to have more time with Sam.

"I want to help that man if I can."

Beckah nodded once. "Me, too." She grabbed an entire leaf of foxglove and put it in her mouth and swallowed it.

"Beckah—"

"Better find an antidote."

Her eyes grew heavy fairly quickly, and she blinked at him, looking through half lids. "This might have been a mistake."

The words were thick, and Alec wasn't sure that he heard her correctly but agreed that she'd probably made a mistake. She was impulsive, and if he failed to find some way of helping her, she might not survive.

Alec grabbed one of the cut ends of the thistle root and handed it to her. "Chew this."

She opened her mouth slightly, and Alec shoved the small finger of thistle root into her mouth. She chewed on it, and her head began to bob.

He didn't know how long the thistle root took to work —if it even would in this manner.

She stopped moving, and he quickly grabbed another section of the root and crushed it beneath his knife. The effect would be much like chewing it, but sometimes cutting it like this—pulverizing it—helped release various healing compounds from the different roots.

A few more moments passed before he managed to get her to take that into her mouth. "Swallow."

Would she obey? She seemed confused enough that it was possible she wouldn't. Thankfully, she managed to maintain enough focus to chew on the root and swallow it.

Alec waited, watching her.

He grabbed for her wrist, feeling her pulse. It slowed dangerously, dropping into a range where he knew she wouldn't last long if it persisted like this.

"Beckah—" he said.

He had to do something different.

The juice of the root seemed more likely to be effective than anything else, but he couldn't exclude that the pulp might have some beneficial properties as well. Maybe they hadn't used enough. After the first dosing, she hadn't gotten any worse, but she hadn't gotten any better. After the second dosing, she had definitely not gotten any worse, but she still hadn't woken up.

Alec cut off a longer section of thistle root. If this worked, they wouldn't have much remaining. It might be enough to help restore the man at the university, but he would leave his father with no supply. Was that dangerous?

Alec pulverized the section of root and slipped it into Beckah's mouth. He had to force her to chew and then stroked her throat to encourage her to swallow. She did so, but reluctantly.

It was all he could do. He sat back, waiting. If this worked, he hoped she would come around quickly.

"Beckah?"

She didn't react. Was this what he looked like when he'd succumbed to the effects of the foxglove? With Beckah, at least he had the hope of an antidote, but at the university, they hadn't had any thistle root. They had simply put Alec in the hospital until it wore off.

Would he have to get Beckah to the hospital? He had no idea how long she might be in this state. Or if she'd ever come out of it.

She took a quick breath of air and sat up suddenly, looking around the room as she blinked her eyes. "That was unpleasant," she said.

"Which part?"

She licked her lips before glancing over to the cutting board where he'd diced up the thistle root. "Probably that most of all. It has a particular aftertaste that lingers. It is *not* pleasant."

Alec laughed in spite of himself. "Your heart seemed to have stopped, much like the man at the university. I don't know if the thistle root made a difference, or if it simply wore off."

"I took enough foxglove that it should have taken longer to wear off."

"I don't know. When you took a pinch of it when we were in class, it worked immediately, but it also wore off very quickly with you. This time might have been similar, but the greater dose could have extended the duration of the effects."

Her gaze drifted down to the foxglove leaves. "There's only one way to test."

Before he could stop her, she pinched off the end of

one of the leaves and stuffed it in her mouth and began chewing.

"If the thistle root is truly an antidote, then this shouldn't affect me," she said.

Alec smiled to himself.

"What is it?"

"Only that I wonder if we could have tested this differently. If the thistle root prevents the foxglove from working, then we could have gone about this in reverse."

Beckah barked out a laugh.

"Anything?"

She shook her head. "I'm not feeling anything yet. There's a slight burning in my throat, but I don't know if that's the thistle root or the fact that I've now taken two doses of foxglove. It could be that all I'm feeling are the effects of the different ways I've tormented myself this evening."

"This time, you seemed to take about as much as you did at the university."

"Yes. I pinched off the end of the leaf just like I did there."

"There, you began to succumb to the effects fairly quickly."

"Right." She grabbed her wrist and felt her pulse. "There's no slowing. Nothing beyond the usual."

"That means it worked."

Beckah grinned. "Didn't you think it was going to work?"

"I wasn't about to risk myself the way that you so willingly have done."

She waved her hand. "I wasn't in any real danger. You were here with me."

Alec shook his head, unable to believe that she would so willingly place herself in harm's way. "Now we need to go back and find where Master Carl left that man."

"That means breaking into the hospital," she said. "Is that something you're ready to do?"

He was tempted to tell her that it wouldn't be the first time he had broken into the hospital, though the first time had been with some urgency, looking for his father. But back then, he was completely oblivious to the workings of the university. Now, they had some right to visit, though it was rare for first-year students to spend much time in the hospital without having the masters there with them.

"We won't be breaking in so much as we'll be investigating a treatment response," Alec said.

Beckah laughed again. "I think I like this Alec. Maybe dying was good for you."

"I don't think dying is good for anyone."

She hopped up off the cot and pointed at the thistle root. "Are you going to grab that, or should I?"

Alec stuffed it back into the jar and tucked it into his cloak, before following her.

As they reached the door, he paused and turned back.

"The lantern?" she asked.

"Not just the lantern. I need to leave a note for my father that I took the thistle root. I should also let him know that we used a few of the foxglove leaves. He likes to keep a tight inventory."

Beckah waited as Alec hurried to the back of the shop and scratched a quick note on a piece of his father's paper. On it, he explained what he'd been through, and the fact that they were testing thistle root as an antidote for foxglove and apologized for taking the last of his supply.

Alec extinguished the lantern on his way out and joined Beckah at the door, closing and locking it behind him. It felt strange leaving the shop this late at night, and stranger still that the shop itself no longer felt quite as much like home as it once had.

17

INTO THE MORGUE

The inside of the hospital was darkened. At this time of night—practically the middle of the night—no lanterns were even lit. Any physickers who were on duty had long since retired for the evening, and Alec suspected that whoever was here wouldn't wake up unless they made too much noise.

"We need some light," Beckah whispered.

"Do you know of any way to produce light that won't get us caught?"

"You and your fears about getting caught all the time."

Alec looked over, but she was nothing more than a blur of darkness. "In this case, I think we're both equally concerned about being caught here."

She shuffled off into the darkness, and he heard a soft clunking sound before she returned. She lifted her cloak, and a faint light shone out. "See? We can try this."

"We can try, but even that much light is probably enough for someone to notice us."

"Probably, but it's not enough for us to be caught by

anyone monitoring the halls. That's what I'm more concerned about. If they find us in here, there's not much we'd be able to do to convince them that we didn't know where we were. The smells alone should have steered us away."

She started off between the cots, flashing the lantern briefly at each patient before hiding it away again. She made her way quickly around the hospital, after making a circuit of the hospital, she returned to stand next to him. "He's not here," she whispered.

"Where else would he be?"

"What happens if the foxglove doesn't wear off?" she whispered.

"I suppose you die."

Beckah nodded. "And if that's what happened to him, I suppose they'd take him with the rest of the bodies."

Something about that troubled Alec. Master Carl had brought him to the classroom, making a point of demonstrating that someone could have an appearance of death, but not actually be dead. "Could he still be in the lecture hall?"

Beckah shook her head. "I don't think so. I stopped by there before coming to your room. There wasn't any sign of the cot or the patient."

"Why did you stop by there first?"

"I thought I could find something out about our patient, but..."

"What if Master Carl took him somewhere?" He asked.

"Master Carl wouldn't keep a cot with a nearly dead man someplace hidden, would he?"

Alec shrugged. "I don't know what Master Carl would do. I don't have much experience with him. All I know is that he didn't seem too impressed with me or my obser-vations."

"That's only because he doesn't know you yet. You'll impress him soon enough." She grinned at him.

Alec shook his head. "I don't think that anything I do will impress Master Carl, especially if I make the mistake of breaking into his classroom."

"It's not going to be his classroom."

"That's even worse," Alec said.

"We could check the morgue," Beckah suggested.

"I don't know where to find the morgue."

"It's a good thing you have me." With that, Beckah hurried down the hall, leaving Alec watching her back. She moved confidently, her back straight once more, striding with a purpose that compelled him to follow her. How could he not when she seemed so determined?

She reached a set of stairs that angled down. It was a hidden stair toward the back of the university where few people would ever come unless they had a reason. He hurried after her, trying to keep pace, not wanting to have her disappear into the darkness of the stairs. There weren't any lights shining here, and it would be all too easy for him to lose sight of her.

When he caught up to her, he grabbed her arm, and she took his hand.

Alec didn't draw away but felt a hint of guilt at the fact that he didn't.

"The morgue is below ground?" he asked.

"Way below ground. Moisture used to be a problem until the engineers managed to seal off the walls."

Alec ran his hand along the wall. It was damp, and he could only imagine the difficulty of trying to suppress moisture seeping through the walls, especially the further underground they got. The pressure from the canals could continue to build, and he could easily envision seepage through the cracks in the foundation of the university.

"This has the potential to be quite disgusting," Alec said.

"There's potential, but it gets better the farther down you go."

Alec glanced over at her. Every two dozen steps or so, there was another lantern, each one flickering faintly, but enough to give light for him to make out her features. "You know this for sure?"

"I might have ventured this way in the past."

She hurried down more steps, and Alec had no choice but to follow her.

The stairs continued down, changing directions every so often, heading deep beneath the ground. The walls were stacked stone, and faint cracks traced through the rock, leaving a hint of dampness in the air.

Surprisingly, the farther they went, the less that scent of dampness was present. It faded before disappearing altogether.

Alec touched the wall and realized that it was dry here.

Beckah noted what he did and nodded. "Like I said, the engineers managed to secure the lowest levels of the university. They're less concerned about higher up, for some reason."

The stairs ended, and she led him to a door along a narrow hallway. Alec half expected the door to be locked, but Beckah opened it and stepped inside.

The appearance of the morgue assaulted him first. The

inside of the room was simple. Solid stone surrounded him from floor to ceiling. Metal cots were arranged in rows, and bodies were set on top of them. There were dozens here.

Then he noticed the smell. It was overwhelming. The foul stench of decay filled his nostrils, and it was obvious that no attempt had been made to preserve the bodies. How long had they been left here, rotting? The walls didn't allow any moisture through, but that didn't prevent decay of the bodies.

"You've been down here before?" Alec asked.

"I've had to come," she answered.

"What possible reason would you have to come down here?"

Beckah turned away from him, ignoring the question.

"Beckah?"

She sighed. "I've come down here to assist in the post-mortem evaluations."

"I don't understand why you would do that."

"You don't? What better way is there to learn the body than to study it? I've been given access to use the morgue to continue my studies."

"How were you given permission?"

"We've already talked about how everyone has a connection to the university. I'm no different."

Alec waited, thinking she might expand on that, provide him some details, but he was mistaken.

"Now. Let's see if Master Carl's patient is here."

Beckah made a circuit of the morgue, much like she had in the hospital above. She moved quickly, with a comfortable stride, and stopped on the opposite side of the morgue to wave Alec over.

When he joined her, he realized that she'd found the man. He looked no different than he did before. His skin still had decent turgor to it, and there were none of the typical signs of death present. Alec once more checked him for a heartbeat but found none. There was no pulse present in his wrist, or in his neck when he reached for the primary vein there.

"Well?" she asked.

"He doesn't look any different than he did before."

"By that, you mean he's still nearly dead."

Alec shrugged. "The foxglove didn't have a prolonged effect like this. Whatever poisoned him has lingered longer."

"Unless he is actually dead."

Alec bit his lip, trying not to breathe through his nose. "Yes. Unless he is actually dead."

"There's only one way to see if your theory is correct." She held her hand out to him, waiting.

Alec pulled out his jar of thistle root and fished out a long section. Then he changed his mind and pulled out all that was remaining. If it was to have any chance of working, he needed to use as much as possible. With Beckah, a small cutting hadn't been enough. He'd needed much more to have any effect.

Taking out his folding knife, he sliced up the thistle root, smashed it into a pulp, and stuffed it into the man's mouth.

"Now what?" Beckah asked.

"Now we wait."

"How long do we have to wait?"

"With you, it took a bit of time to take effect, but once it did, you became fully conscious quickly. If it's going to work on this man, given how long he's been in this state, it will likely take much longer, if it's going to work at all."

"Well, if it's going to work, it had better happen before morning."

"Why before morning?"

"That's when they begin to incinerate the bodies."

Alec looked at the man and wondered if he somehow had to get it into the man's digestive system. He stroked the throat, trying to force the thistle root down into his stomach. Would it make a difference?

And if it didn't, what did that mean?

It meant that he hadn't been poisoned by foxglove, or if he had, it had been in such an amount that it stopped his heart permanently.

"This... is a little anticlimactic."

"You were expecting it to happen rapidly?" Alec asked.

"I don't know. I was hoping he'd sit up, look around the room, and thank us for saving him."

"What if he didn't want to be saved?" Alec asked.

"Why wouldn't he want to be saved?"

"Not all people want to live." He'd seen that often enough in his time with his father and recognized that there were plenty of people who had no interest in living. Some had traumatic events happen to them and became depressed, others simply lost the will to live. His father had often tried various combinations of medications, but rarely had he ever been successful. It was one failing of the types of medications his father knew.

"I don't know how much longer we should stay here," Alec said. More than that, he wasn't sure how much longer he could tolerate being in the morgue. The stench was nearly unbearable.

"What if he wakes up?"

Alec watched the man and shook his head. "If he wakes up, it will seem as if the foxglove wore off. Probably nothing more than that. But if we're caught here, especially this late at night, there will be other consequences."

"None of the masters care that we're here. All they care about is that the bodies are properly disposed of."

"I think that if they find us here in the middle of the night, they'll have different opinions about whether or not we should be allowed to be here."

Beckah looked around, and a sly grin crossed her face. "As in how they might think we're into some pretty strange things?"

"I'm not interested in finding out what the masters might think of us," he said.

Alec checked the man's pulse again, waiting to see if there might be any sign that the thistle root took hold, but nothing had changed.

Beckah gave him a strange glance before nodding and leading him away from the morgue. Alec followed her, wanting nothing more than to get out of there, feeling surprisingly uncomfortable around all the bodies. Considering the amount of time he'd spent with his father, time spent healing, it surprised him that he should be uncomfortable around death.

Maybe it was the fact that nothing had been able to be done for so many of these people. The physickers had failed them. Or maybe, it was something else. Either way, he was relieved when they closed the door behind them and started back up the stairs.

18

SEARCHING FOR MARIN

S am jumped canals here with ease, no longer paying attention to how much space she gave before making the leap, simply reacting. At one canal, as she flipped up, she felt the staff begin to wobble beneath her. Sam pressed up, balancing briefly, before realizing that she was doing just as Thoren had taught her.

She kicked, carrying herself over the canal, landing once more on the solid shore. This side of the canal was protected and had dozens of shops, most of them barely highborn. A merchant section. It was situated between the lower sections of the city and those that were traditionally considered the upper-class sections. She wasn't far from the section where Alec's father had his shop.

Sam didn't remain there very long.

She hurried along the edge of the canal, ignoring the scents here, and paying no attention to the barges pushed along the canals. There had been a time not so long ago when she would have avoided the barges, not wanting to draw their attention, but what did it matter anymore?

Now she had papers in hand and could easily use those to hop on one of the barges and take that toward the palace.

She passed another couple of canals before finally landing in Caster.

After months away, she had been here several times in the last week.

She wandered along the street, making her way toward Marin's house, deciding on impulse to take a look at it. She had already examined the woman's house herself after Marin had disappeared, so a return wouldn't matter. How could it? Marin was far too clever to leave anything incriminating behind.

The building was one of the oldest in the Caster section. It was well-constructed and as fancy as anything found here, nice enough that she half expected someone to have attempted to move in since Marin had been absent. But the entire complex had an air of disuse to it.

Sam paced around the outside of the building, circling the perimeter carefully before using her canal staff and leaping up to one of the neighboring rooftops. From there, she crouched, waiting.

There was no movement.

She watched it for a few long moments, ready to disappear if she saw any sign of someone within. Knowing Marin, she would likely keep her home monitored by someone. Maybe even Tray. Then again, had she kept her home monitored, Sam expected that Bastan would have been aware and would have said something to her. That he hadn't mentioned it suggested there had been no sign from Marin.

Sam slipped down from the rooftop and crept toward the building's front door. In times like this, she wished she had an augmentation. She wasn't sure what she would use in this circumstance, but Alec would probably have had an idea. He could make her small, small enough that she wouldn't be noticed. Maybe he had some way of turning her into a wisp of smoke, though Sam wasn't sure that she cared for what risks might be involved in something like that.

If she only had her cloak, the cloak that she'd once taken from Marin, she would be able to hide. Instead, she was forced to rely on her own stealth.

It had been months since she had needed these skills. Now that she did, would they be rusty, or would she fall back into her familiar patterns?

Making certain there was no one moving along the street, she hurried forward and reached the door front door to the building. When she tested the handle, it was unlocked.

Sam frowned as she slowly opened the door and went inside. That was not typical for Marin. As far as she knew, Marin was the only one who lived in this building, the woman having bought out everyone else, and she was a stickler for keeping her door locked. Sam doubted that anyone else would have broken in and left it unlocked.

Had she hurried away so quickly that she hadn't taken the time to secure it?

That didn't fit with what Sam knew of Marin.

The entryway was quite nice for anyplace in Caster. The walls had evidence of fine craftsmanship, though it was aged and more ornate than was common these days. Even the lanterns on the walls were nice, though she had no idea how long it had been since the lanterns had been lit. No one but Marin lived here for as long as she could remember, and she had never lit them.

Sam crept up the steps, keeping her feet light, not wanting to disturb the silence within the building. When she reached Marin's door, she paused a moment, listening for sounds on the other side. There were none.

She forced the door open. Unlike the door out to the street, this one was locked. It took a bit of effort, no longer carrying the lock-pick set Bastan had given her, but she managed to pick it open and stepped inside.

As she had suspected, the room was empty, though not completely so. There was a cot along one wall, and the shelves that had stored Marin's collection of books remained, though none of the books were here. Had Marin come back and collected them? Had she sent someone else after them, possibly Tray?

She made a slow circle of the room and stopped in the center, looking around. There was no evidence that Marin had been here in months.

The wind rattled the window. Below her, something thudded.

Sam froze. Was that the wind, too?

It has certainly been windy enough when she had come here, but she didn't think that sound was the wind. How could it be so gusty all of a sudden? It hadn't been nearly that gusty when she had been up on the rooftop, and if she had felt it anywhere, that would have been the place.

That suggested there was another answer.

Was there someone else in here with her?

She thought she'd been careful and had paid attention to activity on the street around her, surveying the area around Marin's building, looking for evidence that anyone else might have been watching, and she hadn't seen anything—had she?

There hadn't been anything obvious, nothing that would have told her she had been spied but was it possible that she had missed something?

Sam hesitated, listening, and the rattling came again. This time she was certain that it wasn't the wind, but there was no questioning that the window had rattled and that whatever had caused it was leading to a building pressure.

Below her, she felt a thudding again.

She'd felt something similar in the past, hadn't she?

Sam approached the window slowly, taking a closer look, but didn't see anything that would tell her why she was feeling the pressure here.

A growing unease built within her chest, and she wanted nothing more than to get out, but Marin's room was on an upper floor, and the only way out was through the window or back down the stairs.

She wasn't sure what to expect, but she was prepared for an attack.

Sam assembled her canal staff and flicked it at the window. It was no longer the time to worry about making too much noise.

Glass shattered and sprinkled the street far below.

Sam listened, waiting to see if someone noticed what she'd done, but she heard no one.

If she had rope, she would have an easier way of getting down. All she had was her staff. It was far too high for her to jump from here, too high to use her canal staff for support.

What choice did she have?

The thudding increased, and Sam recognized heat behind it.

Why would there be heat?

Not just heat, but a *familiar* type of heat.

Thelns. They had used some sort of explosive to destroy Bastan's tavern, and they had done something similar at Alec's father's shop.

If the Thelns were here, and if they had observed her, did they know that it was she, or did they think that she was Marin? They look similar enough that it was possible they'd made a mistake.

Sam licked her lips, her mouth suddenly dry.

If the Thelns were here, and if she had no augmentations—and no Alec to assist her—she was in a dangerous position. Even her training with Thoren wouldn't have prepared her to face the Thelns.

And now she had blown out the window glass, revealing herself.

Heat continued to rise, and the stone of the building began to tremble.

Sam had to get out of here. The building would explode, and if she was in it, there was no augmentation that would save her.

Closing her eyes and taking a deep breath, she raced toward the window and jumped.

The jump carried her out the window and sailing into the street. She clutched her staff, trying to spin as she jumped, and jabbed down with the staff, needing to find a way to balance. She wasn't certain that it would even work, and if it did, didn't know if her staff would support her or if it would flex and snap.

The wind whistled around her, and she reacted the way she had when training at the palace practice grounds, facing Thoren.

She kicked up, twisting in the air and spinning around.

The change in perspective gave her a chance to survey the street, however briefly.

Two massive men emerged from the door into Marin's home. A third, a massive man with eyes that were nearly black, stood in the middle of the street, watching her movements.

Still airborne, Sam flipped her staff around and swung it toward him.

A hint of a smile played across his face, and he reached up for the staff.

Kyza!

She jerked it away and pushed the tip down, into the ground along the street, not wanting to give him an opportunity to grab her only weapon.

When it touched down, she felt the staff flex, and for a moment, she feared it would snap. Thankfully, the staff pressed back up, and she was able to carry the momentum upward and rotated one more time before landing on her feet on the street.

Sometime later, she would have to give herself a chance to celebrate what she had just done. Never before had she managed to dance with the staff like that, and the fact that she had jumped out of a second story window, with only her staff for support, should be reason for celebration.

The large man in the middle of the street lunged toward her, and she scrambled backward.

She held out the staff, preparing to flick it at the man,

to use the length and speed that she could generate with it to attack.

As he had before, the man casually reached toward the staff.

Sam jumped back and almost bumped into one of the other two men.

She spun around, frantically trying to react, and dipped the staff toward his feet before twisting it up, catching him between the legs.

Once again, she felt a sort of whistling in the air, one that told her to drop, and she rolled onto the cobbles, flicking the staff around an arc as she did. Even if she didn't catch any of the attackers, she hoped to prevent them from chasing her, to at least give them pause as they threatened to attack.

If these men were Thelns, Sam doubted she would have any way of overpowering them. She struggled with even a single Theln when she had her augmentations, and to attempt to face three of them without any sort of augmentation would be suicide.

Sam darted toward an alleyway, one that she knew would lead her toward a rooftop that she could jump on, and hopefully escape that way, but one of the men blocked her way.

She tipped her staff into the ground and flipped up, soaring over his head. When she landed on the other side of him, she swung her staff toward his back with two sharp cracks that struck him, sending him staggering forward.

She needed to thank Thoren when this was over—and if she survived.

She continued forward, racing toward the alley, and to safety, when she heard a soft peal of laughter.

"I suspected you would make the mistake of coming here," one of the men said, his voice thick with gravel. Sam had heard a similar voice before, and there was no question this man was a Theln.

As she reached the alley, she flipped up, climbing to the nearest rooftop. She paused, then turned around and noticed that the Theln hadn't directed the comment to her. Another stood in the middle of the street, watching the Thelns with a wary expression. At first, Sam thought it might be Marin, and if it was, she was determined to let them have her.

But it wasn't Marin. It was Elaine.

19

RESCUING A KAVER

Sam scooted forward on the rooftop, wanting a better vantage to see what Elaine might do. Had she followed Sam here? Or had she followed the Thelns? As she stared, she saw a cluster of men a street over lying on the ground, none moving.

Another merchant?

Had *Thelns* been responsible for the attack she'd seen?

If so, they'd been back in the city far longer than she'd realized. And it meant that whatever protections Elaine claimed existed to keep the Thelns from the city had failed.

How much longer before they attempted another attack on the princess? How much longer before they dared breach the palace? With what Elaine said about the Kavers dwindling in numbers, there might not be enough of them left to stop the Thelns.

Kyza.

"The only mistake I made was not destroying you outside of the city," Elaine said, casually gripping her staff.

She was dressed in a flowing gray robe that seemed to catch the wind and swirl around her, reminding Sam of the one she used to have.

The massive Theln grunted. "Nearly dying wasn't enough?"

"Did I nearly die?"

The Theln laughed. "You're a fool coming here. You against three of us? Do you believe in yourself so much that you think you can take us on?"

"Yes."

Elaine jumped into the air.

The suddenness of it was jarring. She flipped high into the sky, clearly augmented, and swung her staff around in a vicious, whistling arc.

She caught one of the Thelns who had been approaching from behind her, a man she shouldn't even have seen, but was somehow aware of him. The force of her strike sent the man staggering, his skull crushed. Sam doubted he would rise from that injury.

That left only two Thelns.

Elaine might have augmentations, but the Thelns had a different sort of magic, one that Sam still didn't fully understand. The larger of the two had seemed casual with his movements when he had reached for Sam's staff, but when facing Elaine, the movements were anything but casual.

He reached forward, his hand fast as a snake attacking, and snatched her staff.

Sam's breath caught, but Elaine went with it, following the movement, holding on to the staff, and swung her feet toward him, kicking him as she did.

She managed to get her staff free, and flipped up into

the air once more, coming down and striking not the large Theln, but the one trying to sneak up from behind. She caught him twice, once on the leg, buckling him, and the second on the back of his neck, sending his head flying toward the cobbles with a sickening crack.

The large Theln grinned at Elaine. "You will make a nice prize," he said.

"Is that what women are to you? A prize?"

The Theln grinned. "One with attitude as well. You most definitely will make an excellent prize."

Elaine lunged at him, flickering her staff as she did, swinging it in an arc and whipping it down at the last moment, catching the Theln on the arm. Somehow, he ignored the force of the attack and simply shook it off. He grinned at Elaine and moved so quickly that Sam had a hard time tracking him.

He reached toward the staff, and this time when he grabbed it, he shook it, flinging Elaine free.

She went soaring, colliding with the building near Marin's.

Sam tore her attention away from the fight, realizing that she hadn't paid any attention to what was happening to Marin's building. The power that she had detected was still there, pressing away, building gradually, leaving the heat haze in the air.

The building was going to explode. Sam knew that deep within her, certainty that she couldn't overcome.

Elaine lay motionless, the Theln having thrown her violently, leaving her unable to get up.

Sam watched, feeling helpless.

What could she do?

There was nothing. She didn't have augmentations,

not like Elaine did, and even with them, she hadn't been able to overpower the Theln. Maybe had Marin not wiped her mind, suppressing some part of her that gave her Kaver abilities, Sam might be able to do something, but those were lost to her. She was still too slow. Maybe she'd always be too slow. All that would happen if Sam got involved would be her injury. She would be tossed around even more violently than Elaine.

But Sam needed to help Elaine—her mother—otherwise, the woman would be carried off by the Theln. She wasn't about to allow that to happen. If nothing else, she thought she could provide a distraction, and give Elaine a chance to get up and maybe get away.

Sam crawled toward the edge of the roof. If she timed this right, if she managed to coordinate it with the pending explosion, she could grab Elaine right before the building exploded, and use that distraction to prevent the Theln from chasing them. He had to know that it was coming, but maybe he had a resistance to the heat and fire. She knew so little about the Thelns other than what they were capable of doing and the violence they brought with them.

The heat became unbearable. Her hair felt as if it vibrated, attempting to stand on end.

She had to act. She knew it, though wasn't sure if she could be fast enough—or strong enough—to do so.

Sam took a deep breath, collecting herself, and jumped.

For the second time today, she jumped from a high level, unmindful of the fact that all she had was her eight-foot-long canal staff. It was long enough to help support her, but she would feel a severe jarring when it stuck.

Sam braced herself.

The staff plunged into the cobbles and flexed.

The Theln kicked, catching the staff as it flexed. Sam pushed up and twisted her body in the air, angling so that she went flying toward the building where Elaine had collapsed. She held tightly onto her staff, knowing the way the Theln would try to disarm her, and tumbled to her feet near her mother.

"You have to get up," she said.

"Samara?" Elaine asked, barely opening her eyes. "What are you doing here?"

"Trying to save you. Now get up."

"You shouldn't be here. The Theln—"

"I know what he can do. I was already here, anyway."

She scooped her arms underneath Elaine, trying to get her to move. Her mother was only slightly larger than Sam but seemed to weigh quite a bit more. Was that because of the augmentation? She could envision a situation where having increased weight would be an advantage, especially when facing a much larger Theln. It was something she would have to talk to Alec about. If she survived.

"You need to run, Samara. Don't let him reach you."

Sam felt a whistling that reminded her of when she sparred with Thoren, though this seemed to press against her, much like the pressure building within Marin's building.

She rolled, flipping Elaine with her, and managed to move her moments before the Theln crashed into the wall.

Sam smacked him twice with her staff, doubting that it

would do anything, but feeling a twisted sort of joy that she managed to hit him.

She forced Elaine to her feet, thrusting her in front of her, and they staggered down the street.

"We won't outrun him," Elaine said.

"We don't have to outrun him. We have to outrun the explosion."

Elaine glanced at her. "Explosion?"

Sam dragged her down the street. As she did, the heat continued to rise, and she felt the pressure tingling under her skin.

"We can't leave him in the city," Elaine said.

"We can't beat him, either."

Just then, an explosion thundered from Marin's building.

Rock and debris and dust sent both of the women flying forward. Sam held on to her mother's hand, keeping a tight grip on her, and they went sprawling across the cobbles.

Thoren's comment about getting to her feet stuck in Sam's head, and she scrambled forward, dragging Elaine with her. She managed to stand and hazarded a glance back.

She tensed, fearing that the Theln might appear from the rubble, but she saw no sign of him.

"Come on," she said to Elaine.

"We need to get back to the palace," Elaine said.

"Not yet. You're injured, and we need to make sure that you can handle the journey."

"I think I can—"

She wasn't able to finish, and her eyes fluttered before she collapsed.

Sam swore under her breath. Somehow, she would have to carry Elaine. Elaine had used her augmentations during the fight, but Sam didn't have the necessary augmentations to ensure that she could carry her easily.

It didn't seem quite fair.

20

THE EASAR PAPER

The tavern smelled of smoke from the distant hearth, mixed with the savory scents coming out of the kitchen. Sam barely managed to hold on to Elaine as she staggered into the tavern. If she had to go much farther, she would drop her.

Every so often, Elaine would groan. She writhed in place, resisting Sam as she clutched her against her. Sam couldn't lift her and had been forced to drag her as they made their way down the street to the tavern.

Kevin reached her as they entered. He cocked a brow and waved her in, scooping an arm underneath Elaine to help Sam.

"Is he here?" she asked.

"He's here. He's—"

Sam ignored him and shuffled toward the back of the tavern, one arm still around Elaine, though Kevin had taken over most of the lifting at this point. She banged on Bastan's door with her foot, no interest in being discreet.

The door opened, and he shoved his head through. "What is—"

Sam nodded toward Elaine. "I need your help, Bastan."

Bastan glanced from Elaine to Sam before shaking his head. "It's not a good time, Samara."

"I'm sorry to interrupt one of your meetings. I need your help."

Bastan glanced over his shoulder before stepping into the tavern and closing the door behind him. He made his way across the tavern toward the kitchen, motioning for Sam to follow.

Sam did, but looked back at his office, wondering who he was concealing. There was something going on in the office, something that Bastan intended to keep from her, but maybe now wasn't the time to push him.

The kitchen was a coordinated sort of chaos. Four cooks worked near the oven, shoving food from place to place. The servers stepped in, grabbing plates or ale, before heading back out into the tavern. Bastan crossed the kitchen and led them to a door along the back wall. He pushed it open and hurried through and down a series of steps.

"She needs help, Bastan."

He paused at the bottom of the stairs. "Like you did when you fell?"

"This is different. This is…" How much did she tell him? Did she admit that this was a Theln attack again? He'd faced it before and had nearly come up on the wrong end of it, his tavern destroyed. Bastan being who he was, had quickly rebuilt, but would he be eager to bring such danger upon himself again? "Yes. It's like me when I fell."

"I'll send word to the university and get your friend to join us."

"That will only work if we have"—she glanced back at Kevin, lowering her voice—"more of the easar paper."

Bastan's face tightened, and she realized that he was going to be forced to admit something that he did not want to.

A comment made by Kevin the last time she'd come to the tavern came to the front of her mind. Bastan had been seeking supplies—art supplies. That meant paper. "You have more of it, don't you?"

"I have a few sheets."

"Why? You can't use it."

"But you can, Samara. I'm not foolish enough to believe that isn't valuable in the right circumstances. You might think that we are done working together, but I don't."

Bastan continued down the short hall and pushed the door open. When Sam reached him, she set her hand on his arm, and Bastan turned and looked at her with his hard, gray eyes.

"I don't think I'm done working with you," she said.

"No? You've avoided me for the last few months."

"After all the years we've worked together, you think a few months matter?"

Bastan slowly began to grin and then nodded. "Good. Otherwise I would be compelled to find some way to force you to work with me."

Sam punched him on the shoulder, and Bastan shrugged it off as they entered the room. Had she her augmentations, he wouldn't be able to so easily shrug it off. A threat like that from Bastan was meaningful. It was more than likely that he would find some way to force her assistance. It was entirely probable.

"What happened?" Bastan asked.

"She was attacked."

"Did you see the attacker?"

"He's a larger man. And she's tiny."

As Kevin helped her to a cot, Bastan glanced from Elaine back up to Sam. "You're tiny, but I've seen you face down much larger men."

Sam shrugged. "With the help of the paper. Otherwise, there's not much I can do."

Bastan turned to a nearby desk and wrote a note on a slip of paper, folding it neatly and placing the wax seal across the edge. "Take this to the university. Ask for Alec," Bastan said to Kevin.

"University? You're sending me for a real physicker? You know they won't come to Caster."

"Not a physicker, but a student."

"Looks like this woman needs more than a student," Kevin said.

"Which is exactly what she will get," Bastan said.

When Kevin hurried from the room, Bastan turned his attention back to Sam. "Are you going to tell me what really happened?"

Sam sighed. "She's like me."

"I can see that."

"No. She's able to receive augmentations, the same as me. But that wasn't enough to escape the attack."

"I thought your augmentations… One of them was in the city, wasn't it?"

Keeping it a secret from Bastan was not anything she wanted to do. It was better for him to know the truth, especially as he had been such a help to her when she'd needed it—most recently when she had nearly died from a fall while trailing the princess.

"Three, actually."

"And where are they now?"

"I think two are dead," she began. She nodded toward Elaine. "And the third was much larger than the others. Even with her augmentations, she was no match for him."

"Where were they?" Bastan asked. "It must have been near for you to have brought her here."

"Marin's. I was looking to see if there was anything I could discover when I realized they were approaching."

"They came after you?"

"I don't know if they came after me, or if they came after Elaine, or whether they thought they were finding Marin, or even if they were the ones who attacked the merchant." She hadn't had the opportunity to see if the men she'd seen in the street were like the others. "There was another attack, Bastan. In Caster. I saw the bodies down in the street."

"Not in my section. There shouldn't have been."

"There was."

His brow furrowed, and irritation flashed across his face. "And here I thought my attempt to watch the merchant movements had been effective in preventing more attacks like that."

"You did that?"

"After what you told me the last time."

Sam frowned. Could that be why the attack was in Caster this time? That seemed unlikely, but maybe the Thelns had come after Bastan for meddling.

"You have to be careful."

"I'm always careful."

"I'm not kidding, Bastan. If the Thelns have returned, and they intend to attack…"

"You don't have to worry about me."

"I'm not."

He smiled. "Tell yourself whatever you need." She glared at him, and he ignored it. "Do you know why the Thelns returned to the city?"

"I think they constantly attempt to attack the city," Sam said. "Elaine, and others like her, fend them off."

"How many are there like her?"

"I don't know. I know only of Elaine."

Bastan watched her, his head tilted to the side as he considered her. "Just Elaine?"

"I understand one of them died outside of the city, if that's what you're getting at. I never met her."

"Her? Are these people with augmentations always female?"

"I don't know. Like I said, I've only met Elaine."

"And Marin."

"And Marin," Sam agreed. "Marin told me nothing about them, other than the fact that I was descended from someone with some abilities. She was no different from anyone else in her attempt to keep that knowledge from me."

"Maybe there was not an attempt to keep it from you, but to keep you safe."

She shrugged. "I think I'm safer now that I understand a little bit about how to use my abilities, don't you?"

"Honestly, Samara, I would prefer if you knew nothing about these abilities. It seems to me that since you've learned, you've been placed in much more danger than you ever had been before."

Sam crossed her arms over her chest. If Bastan were closer to her, she would've hit him. She was of half a mind to assemble her canal staff to smack him from the other side of the room. "You put me in more danger than anyone else ever did."

Bastan shook his head. "You were in danger, but none that I couldn't help you with. You were never so far gone —or isolated—that I couldn't lend a hand if it were needed."

"Like you did with Tray?"

"Had you given me more time, I would've gotten Tray free."

That wasn't what he had told her at the time, but she didn't want to argue with Bastan about that. "Instead, Marin managed to get him free."

Bastan grunted. "Unfortunately, she did."

"Unfortunately? You would rather have left Tray stuck in that cell, tormented by the guards, in danger of dying?"

"You were in the prison, however briefly it was. You know the prisoners are treated well. And your brother was never in any danger. My resources were clear enough on that. Had he been in real danger, I would have gone after him myself." There was an edge to his voice, one that made Sam question why Bastan would act so fiercely on her behalf.

"If you were going to help Tray, you could have done it long before I had to intervene," Sam began.

Elaine moaned. It was the first sound she had made since they had brought her down to this room.

Sam hurried over to her and took her hand, thinking

that Elaine might open her eyes, but the woman only moaned again.

Bastan approached and stood on the other side of the cot, looking down at Elaine. "She's quite lovely, albeit smallish."

"Smallish? Don't let her hear you describe her that way," Sam said.

"Does she have a temper like you?"

Sam glowered at him. "I don't have a temper."

"I thought maybe it was a trait of those with your particular ability. I thought maybe you all got angry quickly. Marin certainly has a temper. And yes, Samara, even you have something of a temper."

"Careful, Bastan, or you'll get to see exactly how much of a temper I have."

Bastan grinned. "I've seen your temper from time to time. Now, if you will excuse me for a moment, I'm going to check on the status of a few items and then will return."

Bastan slipped out the door, leaving Sam alone with Elaine.

She looked around the room and decided that it had to be a different room from the one that Bastan had brought her to when she'd fallen. This was simpler. Walls were boarded up, and there were no decorations here. The cot appeared otherwise unused, and she noted a few crates in the corner but nothing else.

There were other rooms along the hall, but Bastan had chosen this one, almost as if there were some particular reason behind it. Was there something unique about it? Or was it simply an empty room?

She turned her attention back to Elaine and watched her mother taking steady breaths. At least she breathed easily. Alec had taught Sam a few things about healing, and she remembered him telling her to first check to ensure the person was breathing, then check for a heartbeat, and then begin looking for wounds. Since Elaine still breathed, and she'd been breathing since Sam rescued her from Marin's property, she had to assume that she also had a heartbeat. Any wounds that she might have were not visible.

"This would have been easier had you not gotten hurt," Sam said to Elaine. "No, if I'm honest, this would've been easier if you had found me years ago. It would've been nice to know where I came from."

Sam watched Elaine, thinking that she might open her eyes, or that her breathing patterns might change, but nothing changed for her. Strangely, it was easier for her to talk to Elaine with her unable to answer back. As she stood there, looking down at the woman who was supposed to be her mother, she found that emotions bubbled to the surface that she had not expected.

Anger was foremost among them.

Sam had spent the last decade of her life thinking that she was little more than a lowborn, that she deserved nothing from life, that she had to go out and take what she needed if she was to survive. That was the way—and the mindset—of the lowborns. She had never believed that she deserved anything more. And maybe she still didn't. Maybe she really *was* nothing but a lowborn, and still needed to go out and take what she was owed.

It was hard for Sam to believe that Elaine had not known about her, especially considering some of the conversations they'd had since being reunited. Elaine was interested in training her, but that seemed about it. She was more focused on spending her time outside of the city, either fighting the Thelns, or serving the princess in whatever way that she did.

Why hadn't she fought that much on Sam's behalf?

If she had, what would have been different for her?

Sam wouldn't have known Bastan, and she wouldn't have developed her abilities to sneak around, finding her way into places she really didn't belong. She never would have gotten to know Marin, though that wouldn't have been all bad. But, more than anything, she never would have known Tray. Whatever else might have been different, she couldn't imagine a life without Tray being a part of it.

She really needed to find him.

"Why won't you work with me?" Sam went on, looking at Elaine. She seemed so peaceful as she rested, but did she deserve to be peaceful, did she deserve to have that, when Sam could not?

"I need to learn how to use my abilities. I deserve to know this."

"You are learning."

The soft-spoken words startled Sam, and she jumped back a step.

Elaine didn't open her eyes, but clearly, she was able to answer and was much more alert than Sam had expected.

"You abandoned me," Sam said.

"I did not abandon you. You were... lost."

Lost. Sam didn't think that she'd been lost. How hard would it have been to find her if Elaine had looked? Marin had known where to find her, which suggested to Sam that Elaine should have been able to discover her as well. Instead, she had seemingly assumed that Sam was dead.

Maybe she should have stayed dead to Elaine.

She didn't really feel that way. She had to admit a certain thrill as she learned the staff with Thoren, and she had to admit an edge of excitement as she realized that her Kaver abilities were not entirely tied to the easar paper. If she didn't have to rely on the paper, then there had to be other things that she could do, other abilities that she could work, and perhaps she would be able to face the Thelns even without augmentations.

Yet even Elaine had come at them with an augmentation. The speed she'd used to attack couldn't have been anything other than an augmentation—could it?

Unless that was what she had wanted Sam to learn.

"Did you know they were there?" Sam asked.

"They entered the city. I lost them."

"How did you find them?"

"Pressure."

At first, the comment seemed strange, something that Sam was not meant to understand, but the more she thought about it, the more she thought she understood the pressure that Elaine meant.

"Their explosions?"

"Not. Explosion. Their magic." Elaine still seemed weak, and her words were clearly draining what little energy she had.

"I don't understand."

"You. Shouldn't. Untrained."

Elaine's face twisted, and it seemed as if something hurt her, and her breathing quickened.

"What is it?" Sam asked.

"Stomach," Elaine grunted.

Sam took her hands and squeezed them, trying to find a way to soothe Elaine, but feeling inadequate. There was nothing she could do or say that would help put her at ease. She stroked Elaine's hair, brushing it away from her face, and realized that sweat had beaded on her forehead.

She was fighting something awful.

"Did he hit you?" Sam asked.

"Staff. Hit."

Sam thought back to what she'd seen during the fight. When the Theln had grabbed Elaine's staff, she'd held on, until he ultimately flung her off and she flew against the wall of the building. But had her own staff hit her in the process? The Theln had reached in, moving so quickly that Sam had a hard time tracking it, but it was possible he had done more than simply throw her against the building.

The Thelns liked poison, didn't they?

The first time Sam had confronted them, she'd been chased by a man who was eager to poison her. The Thelns thought their poison universally fatal to Kavers, but why should that be when Scribes could heal them?

Unless it had something to do with the Book of Maladies.

"Do you think you could have been poisoned?"

"Possible," Elaine agreed.

Sam paced around the table, wringing her hands. She needed Alec to get here. He had saved Sam when she'd been poisoned, and she thought if anyone could do something to help reverse the effects of a Theln attack, it was Alec.

"Need to. University."

"You're too sick to go to the university. I brought you to someone who will help."

"Who?"

"A man who has helped me many times," Sam said. "A man by the name of Bastan."

Elaine moaned. Sam smoothed her hair again, brushing it off her forehead. It didn't seem like the gesture made much of a difference, but she felt the need to do something for her mother.

She lost track of time. Elaine had stopped speaking, and Sam didn't feel comfortable yelling at her anymore about the past. Not now, knowing that her mother might have been poisoned and might be dying before her eyes. She didn't want her angry words to be the last thing her mother ever heard from her.

After a while, she heard the door open and looked over to see Alec walk in. Relief swept through her, but it faded when she realized he wasn't alone.

The woman she'd seen with him before walked in behind him.

SURGERY

The hospital was as busy as usual today, and Alec kept his hands clasped behind his back as he looked over the line of students in front of him, peering over the cot. They were with Master Eckerd again, and he made a point of speaking quietly, almost as if he didn't want to reveal too much to the people near him.

The patient here was fairly young, certainly younger than many of the patients that were often seen at the university and had dark brown hair that reached her shoulders. Her skin was deeply tanned, and he wondered if she spent significant time working outdoors or if she naturally had a darker complexion. There were many people within the city with darker complexions, though most were lowborns, which fit with their tendency to work outdoors. Most of the highborns had pale skin and preferred to maintain that by remaining inside and keeping covered. It was another way to maintain division between the classes.

"What do you see about this woman?" Master Eckerd asked.

Alec couldn't see anything unusual. Her eyes were closed, and she breathed regularly, but she hadn't moved in the time they been there. There were many ingestions that could lead to such a coma, and many of the medications used by the university as sedatives would also induce something similar.

"Has she been administered anything?" The question came from Matthias, who stood across the cot from Alec and shot him an amused glare as he asked the question.

"An excellent question," Master Eckerd said. Matthias flashed a satisfied smile at Alec. "But as far as we can tell, she's not been administered anything."

"Nothing from the university?" Alec pressed.

"There has been no need. She has been motionless since she arrived."

Stefan took one of the woman's hands and raised it to examine her nails, then pulled back her sheet to look up her arms.

Master Eckerd chuckled. "This is not a self-inflicted injection, either."

Stefan shrugged. "I only thought—"

"You thought that I would have another person who had indulged in solpace juice?"

Stefan looked down.

"Master Carl was teaching us about foxglove," Matthias said.

Master Eckerd's gaze narrowed. "He was teaching first-year students about foxglove, was he?"

No one answered immediately, so Alec nodded.

"Well then, if you've learned about foxglove, see if you think this might be a similar ingestion."

Matthias pushed one of the other students—Karen—out of the way. She was short, nearly the same height as Sam, but dressed in much more formal clothing that Sam wouldn't be caught dead in. She wore a floral-patterned dress that reached to the ground, and a heavy gold locket hung from her neck.

"He might want to be careful. He'll upset his girl-friend," Beckah whispered.

Alec's eyes widened. "She's his—"

Beckah shook her head. "Not her. Nanci."

Nanci was a taller woman, who dressed nearly as formally as Karen, but didn't wear the same gold chain, or any other sign of the highborns. Alec had rarely spoken to either of the two women.

Matthias grabbed the patient's wrist and checked for a pulse. He moved up to her neck, feeling the artery there, before leaning his head down to her chest to listen.

Beckah laughed before covering her mouth.

Master Eckerd arched a brow. "You find this woman's illness amusing?" he asked.

Beckah shook her head. "I'm sorry, Master. It's just that Matthias can clearly see that she's breathing. And she has a bounding pulse. I can see it in her neck. His exam is more for show."

Master Eckerd nodded once. "Wonderful observations." He tapped Matthias on the shoulder, forcing him to step back. "Yes. You can see her breathing, and her pulse is readily visible. This is not foxglove."

"Probably good," Matthias muttered. "I hear the other patient given foxglove didn't make it."

Master Eckerd frowned again. He looked over at Alec before turning his attention back to the woman. "Yes. Well, can anyone tell me any other observations here? We have decided this is not foxglove. We have decided this is not solpace juice. What else would you question?"

"Have there been any signs of fever?" Beckah asked.

"No fever. Any other questions?"

Everyone fell silent, most simply staring at the woman, waiting for Master Eckerd to explain what had happened. Alec didn't want to answer. He had suspicions, but after what had happened with Master Eckerd the last time, he didn't want to speak up and hesitated saying too much, otherwise he ran the risk of getting taunted again. It was bad enough that someone—likely Mathias—had left clippings of leaves at his door.

"None?"

Beckah elbowed Alec, and he shot her a look before taking an unintentional step forward.

"Mr. Stross. What would your assessment be?"

"He probably thinks some magical spell was placed on her," Matthias said.

A few of the people on the other side of the cot— including Karen and Nanci—laughed.

Alec took a deep breath. "Has she had any injury?"

"You can see that she hasn't," Matthias said.

Master Eckerd watched Alec. "Assuming no visible injury, why would you ask?"

Alec took another step forward. He was already committed, and now, it was too late to step back. He slipped his hands under the woman shoulder and tipped her, looking at her back and up to her head. There was no sign of any injury. Had there been, he suspected that Master Eckerd wouldn't have chosen her as an example.

His father had once used a similar example.

"The people who brought her in. Did they mention any previous injury?" Alec said.

Master Eckerd smiled. "Is that the path you would like to go down?" he asked.

"I just thought I'd ask," Alec said.

Master Eckerd came around the end of the cot and pointed to a spot on the back of her head. "She was seen slipping near the canals after stepping off one of the barges about a week before she was brought to us. There is no visible injury, but her husband claims she hit her head and had been complaining of a headache for the last week."

"Wouldn't you see signs of an injury sooner than this?" Matthias asked.

"Not if she had internal bleeding. There are some injuries that take time, and bleed slowly, before becoming incapacitating," Alec said.

Master Eckerd watched him a moment. "Yes. There are many hemorrhages inside the brain that will lead to swelling. We have tested this with mice and have seen similar effects."

"Is that what happened to her?" Beckah asked. She looked up at Alec, a curious expression on her face.

"Unfortunately, there is little we can do to determine that. Given the history that we were given, it is entirely likely that is the cause of her symptoms."

"What can be done?" Stefan asked.

"There are no medicines that will reverse this," Master Eckerd said. "At this time, it's mostly a matter of waiting to see what will happen, but we can also attempt to remove some of the pressure."

"Pressure? That means—" Matthias said.

Master Eckerd nodded. "Yes. That means she will be taken to surgery. Mr. Stross, as you seem to have diagnosed her, I would ask if you would be interested in attending the surgery."

Alec made a point of only looking at Master Eckerd. It was uncommon for first-year students to be allowed into the surgical suites. They were reserved for upper-level students and physickers only. For him to be given that opportunity was more than an honor; it was unheard of.

"I would be happy to," Alec said.

"Good. We will take her now. The rest of you will go with Physicker Terrence, and he will review the remaining new patients with you."

Terrence walked up to Master Eckerd. He was a junior physicker and looked older than his likely age. He was thin, with a narrow beard, and nodded to Master Eckerd. "Are the students ready for me?"

"They are."

"Good luck," Beckah said to Alec. "And you better be prepared to tell me all about it later."

"I'll tell you what I can," Alec said.

She elbowed him as she moved away from the cot and joined the line of students at the next bed. Alec watched them until Master Eckerd cleared his throat.

"Are you ready?" Alec nodded. "Good. I will need your help wheeling her out of the hospital and into the surgical area."

Alec assisted Master Eckerd as they pushed her down the hall. They took a route he'd not taken before, and the hallway was wide, practically cavernous as they made their way through it. Enormous double doors opened up off the hall, and Eckerd nodded toward them and turned the cot to go through.

A master physicker—as designated by the jacket she wore—much older than Master Eckerd stood on the other side. She had gray hair pulled into a tight bun and stepped forward to welcome to Master Eckerd. Two junior-level physickers, a man and a woman, stood behind her. Both were older than Alec.

The other master glanced at Eckerd but said nothing. Eckerd pushed the cot toward the middle of the room then addressed the rest of us. "Today, Master Helen and I are going to try to relieve some swelling in this woman's head," Master Eckerd said. "This will require us to remove a piece of her skull bone, which means a steady hand. Physicker Abigail has been chosen to assist. Physicker Jeremy is here to observe."

Alec stood at the back, suspecting that as a student, he had little right to be too close to the activity. He preferred to be up close and would prefer to watch what Eckerd did, but was simply thankful that he was allowed in here at all.

He watched as Master Eckerd and Master Helen prepared for the procedure, and was impressed by the way they moved efficiently, both masters using balsping oil on their hands, a liniment that had a sharp, pungent odor, but was widely known as an effective antiseptic. They used the same oil on the woman's scalp, scrubbing through her hair. Physicker Jeremy remained nearby and stepped in to remove the liniment container.

Master Helen procured a scalpel and stood back,

waiting for Eckerd to signal her. He nodded, and she leaned forward and made a sharp incision, cutting into the woman's scalp. She worked quickly and had a steady hand.

Alec couldn't help himself, and crept forward, watching as they peeled back a layer of skin, exposing the bone. He'd seen injuries where the bone of the skull was revealed but had never imagined cutting into the scalp to reveal it. His father was skilled with medicines but had never attempted any surgeries. That was the role of the university, and his father had never shown any desire to offend them by overstepping his place.

Master Eckerd took a shiny hammer and a sharp, spike-like instrument off the table next to the cot. Placing the spike against the exposed bone, he gently tapped the hammer against the spike, then moved the spike to a new spot, tapping again. Working quickly, he formed a circle in the skull, and with one final tap, Alec could see the center mass separate from the rest of the skull.

Alec heard gagging and looked up to see Physicker Abigail looking ashen, her face pale.

"You can step out if you're going to be sick, Abigail," Master Helen said.

Abigail clenched her jaw and shook her head. "I'll... I'll be fine."

"If you vomit on our patient, she will get an infection in her head, and there will be no way she'll survive this."

Abigail paled even more before nodding and hurrying from the surgical room.

"Alec, step into Abigail's place," Master Eckerd said.

Eckerd glanced over at Master Helen who looked at him with an unreadable expression. Alec hurried around the table and stood where Abigail had been. From this vantage, he could see a little better. He saw the way Master Eckerd held the instrument, and the way he made a series of movements that lifted the bone free. From there, the brain matter was visible.

"What do you—" Master Helen began.

Blood began seeping from the hole in the woman's skull.

Eckerd breathed out. "Ahh. Excellent."

"Why excellent?" Alec asked. He knew that he should be quiet, that he was here only as a courtesy, but he couldn't help himself. It was the same tendency that always seemed to get him in trouble. He couldn't keep himself silent when he was curious about something.

"There are times when the blood is deeper. Other times, when we don't cut in the right place."

"How did you know where to cut?" Alec asked.

Master Helen frowned. "There were slight discolorations of the skin." She turned her attention to Master Eckerd. "Did you need to bring a chatty student into the surgical suite?"

Eckerd glanced up and met her gaze. "He has diagnosed both solpace injection as well as her injury."

"Her injury? Three masters examined this patient before—"

Eckerd nodded. "Exactly. You now can understand the reason I decided to have him join me?"

Master Helen grunted but said nothing else. She took a towel and began dabbing at the blood seeping from the woman's wound, saying nothing as she did.

"You were able to make the diagnosis?"

Alec turned to the other junior physicker beside him.

Jeremy had a plain face and was of average height. Alec was a few inches taller than he and wondered what the young man was be able to see. It was difficult enough for Alec to see the patient from his vantage. If he were any shorter, he would not see anything.

"I only asked about injury," Alec said. "There can be a delay in swelling following a head injury."

"How is it that a student knows this?"

"My father is an apothecary in one of the middle sections of the city."

He knew that wasn't a perfect answer, especially considering how few people at the university cared for apothecaries, but honesty was the only way he was going to not be overlooked.

"Your father must be an impressive apothecary for him to have taught you that diagnostic skill."

"He is. He trained at the university."

"An apothecary trained in the university? Why did he leave?"

The masters were simply waiting, holding pressure against the woman's skull, soaking up the blood. Alec heard them talking quietly to each other, but they weren't speaking loudly enough for him to hear. The surgery must have been completed, and Alec wondered what they would do next. Now that the section of skull had been removed, where did that leave the woman?

"I don't know why he left. I only learned recently that he had trained here."

"An apothecary hid that he'd trained at the university?"

Alec shrugged. "He didn't think it necessary. I think part of him thought it was better to conceal that than to make it widely known."

"Imagine the rates he could have charged had he shared that he trained at the university."

Alec chuckled. "My father was never very concerned about how much he could charge."

"Seems like a wasted opportunity to me. Why wouldn't you take an opportunity to make as much as possible?"

He didn't need to answer. Master Eckerd spoke up, looking over at Alec. "Tell me, Mr. Stross, if you weren't able to reach the swelling, what would you do?"

Alec glanced over and saw the physicker looking at him, a deep frown pulling the corners of his mouth, before turning back to Master Eckerd. "If I opened up the skull and there was no way to reach the swelling?"

"Yes. What would you do?"

Alec had no surgical experience. He had stitched wounds closed, but that was the extent. Anything greater than that his father had always sent to the university. Was Master Eckerd asking him a question about a technique that he assumed he would have read about, or learned from his father?

No. Eckerd would've known that Alec had no experience, and the first-year students rarely ventured into the surgical section of the library. Alec hadn't even considered it, mostly because there was more value in learning various medicinal treatments. He was much more interested in finding various combinations of medicines and liniments that might produce a response. There were few illnesses that required cutting.

If Master Eckerd didn't expect him to know some mysterious surgical technique, what was he getting at?

Maybe it was something as simple as how to find the area of swelling.

Alec thought about what he knew of anatomy, having studied that for years, and thought about how everything in the brain was interconnected. There seemed to be a way that you could evaluate for pressure, and Alec imagined looking into a patient's eyes, or possibly in their ears with the right type of implement, but neither of those would give the origin of the swelling.

"Couldn't you simply look into her throat?" the other physicker asked.

Master Eckerd looked over at the man with a hint of disgust. "Throat? Perhaps you need to review your anatomy, Jonas."

Master Helen had given some idea, suggesting the discoloration on the skin would reveal where the injury had taken place, but it seemed like even that missed something.

"I think if you tried to use an instrument within the brain cavity itself, you would run the risk of damaging the tissue," Alec said.

"You would," Master Eckerd agreed.

"You would need some sort of flexible device to run along the inside of the skull, and use that to allow whatever blood is there to run along it, or, if it's hollow, through it."

Master Eckerd considered him a moment. "Good. Come over here."

Alec blinked but did as he was instructed and made his way over to Master Eckerd.

"Use balsping oil on your hands first."

Alec turned to the jar of oil and used the section of cloth that was lying on the table next to it to apply it to his hands, rubbing it in. He was familiar with the oil, having used it when stitching people up. His father had always claimed that application of the oil inhibited infection, but he'd never had any way of proving that. It was simply something his father had taught him. Other things his father taught him were verifiable, and he could apply them to illnesses, or injury, and test whether they were as effective as his father believed.

The oil tingled on his skin and created a coating.

"Take the krashole," Master Eckerd said.

Alec shook his head. "I'm not sure what that is."

Master Helen reached for a thin, long rod. As she held it up, he noted that it was flexible, bending in her hand. "It's named after the master who created it," she said, handing it to him.

Alec took it from her and studied it. It was hollowed out along the length of it, and he marveled at the skill that must've been required to make such a thing.

"Now, you put a slight curvature into the krashole, and you slide along the inside of the skull."

"You want me to do this?"

"Would you prefer Jonas have the opportunity?"

"I don't want to take an opportunity from a physicker," Alec said.

"Perhaps I was mistaken."

Master Eckerd reached for the instrument, but Alec pulled back.

"No. I'll do it."

Jonas glared at him, but Alec ignored it. He had been invited into the surgical suite, and he needed to take advantage of that opportunity. How often was it that a first-year student was given the opportunity to perform surgery, and brain surgery at that?

Eckerd smiled tightly. "Now. You will slide this up along the inside, moving slowly and feeling for any change in resistance."

Alec followed his instructions, inserting the krashole into the skull and sliding it. It went smoothly, and he pushed toward the back of her skull, feeling no resistance.

"What am I looking for?" he asked.

"If you notice bleeding, you've either penetrated the tissue, or you found the source of the bleeding."

"I thought the source was where the incision was made."

"It should be, but you will make another test. Let's say for the sake of argument that her husband reported that she had struck her head on the railing of the barge as she got off."

Alec glanced up, following his train of thought. "Then she'd have hit the back of her head, probably not the side of it."

"Indeed. Had she fallen forward, it would have been more likely for her to strike her temple, but if she truly fell backward, we need to ensure that there is no pressure remaining there that needs to be relieved."

Alec continued to slide the device along the back of her head. He felt a hint of pressure and stopped.

"What have you detected?" Master Eckerd asked.

"There's resistance."

"Then you need to redirect. Withdraw the krashole a slight amount and then push forward again."

"What would happen if I pushed forward without withdrawing?" Alec asked.

"We've done experiments on animals and have concluded the risk of penetrating healthy brain tissue is too great. If part of the brain is injured, there are significant detrimental effects. Has your father treated people who've hit their head or injured themselves in such a way that they never completely recover?"

Alec nodded.

"As I suspected. This would be the same thing you would find were you to push too hard here. You don't want to penetrate healthy tissue. There's a good chance she won't survive this, anyway, but we want to give her every opportunity possible."

Alec withdrew the rod slightly and changed the angle, sliding it forward again. He thought he was angling it toward the lower portion of her skull near the back. There was no pressure, and all of a sudden, he felt warmth racing through the rod, and nearly let go of it.

Master Eckerd grabbed his hand, studying it. "Hold it."

A stream of blood began to flow from the end of the krashole. Alec held it in place while the bleeding continued, and it abated slowly.

"Nice work. Now you've done something that very few masters can claim."

Alec looked over to Master Helen, and she nodded to him. "How long do we leave this in place?" he asked.

"There are varying theories. One suggests that we leave it in place until it stops bleeding, and then remove it, allowing the brain matter to settle back into place. Another argues that leaving it in place could provide ongoing drainage of any additional bleeding."

"Which one is right?" Alec asked.

Master Eckerd looked up at him, a hint of a gleam in his eye. "Which do you think it is?"

"I imagine there is a benefit to leaving it in place only

until the bleeding stops. But if the bleeding returns, it could continue to cause pressure, so leaving the krashole in place would be a good alternative, but I would worry about having a wick for infection."

"Both are reasonable concerns," Eckerd said. "You still have not made a choice."

Alec stared at the open skull, trying to determine which might be the best option. "Even if we remove this rod, there will still be a tract for drainage, and as long as you don't replace the bone, or suture too tightly, there will still be a way to relieve pressure. I would favor removing the krashole."

"Go ahead then."

Alec glanced from Master Helen to Master Eckerd. He hadn't given him an answer and had simply let Alec talked it through. Which was the right solution?

Alec had to trust that his analysis was at least close to accurate, or surely, Master Eckerd would not allow him to proceed. He started pulling the rod free, and once it was, he set it on the table next to him.

"Which was the correct answer?" Alec asked.

"You'll know when—if—she survives."

22

A SUMMONS

The knock at his door drew his attention, and Alec looked up. He had been pacing in the room, his nerves on edge since returning from the surgical suite. The rest of the students had long ago departed, sent back to class, or on to find their evening meal.

Alec hurried over to the door and pulled it open. Unsurprisingly, Beckah stood on the other side, tapping her foot with her hand held up to knock again.

"Well?"

She pushed past him and into his room. She turned back and crossed her arms over her chest. "You didn't even want to come find me?"

Alec closed the door and turned to face her. "That's not it. It's more that my heart has been racing so fast that I don't know what to do."

"It was that traumatic? I thought that you had some experience watching minor surgery."

Alec shook his head. "I've stitched plenty of wounds. It

wasn't the observation that was what had my heart racing, it was when Master Eckerd had me insert a flexible rod inside this woman's head. As I did, all I could think about was penetrating her tissue and leaving her in even worse shape."

"You *what?*"

"One of the physickers got sick when she watched the removal of the section of bone. Master Eckerd had me take her place, and then started asking questions."

"Alec, this doesn't just happen. First-year students are never allowed into a surgery. And students, in general, are never allowed to actually *participate* in surgery. What you went in to observe was something that only masters are allowed to assist with. Now you're telling me that Master Eckerd had you actually perform part of the operation?"

"I don't think it was a crucial part. He didn't let me cut into the bone, or remove the first part of blood."

"Still. What you did… that's amazing. Matthias will be so jealous. Can I be there when you tell him?"

"You're terrible."

She shrugged. "Why is that terrible? He tried to embarrass you in front of Master Eckerd. I still think it's great that Master Eckerd invited you into the surgery. Maybe that will teach Matthias to not be such an ass."

"You know, you might be the first highborn I've ever met who uses such language."

"Have you met many highborns like me?"

Alec chuckled. "I don't think I've met many people like you."

"Good. I don't want you to get too complacent here. I mean, I *am* the best student in our year, and so far, you're running a distant second, but more days like today, you might move up."

"Is that right? Didn't you tell me that no first-year students have ever been invited into a surgery?"

"That doesn't mean anything. I think Eckerd felt bad for you. It's probably something that has to do with your father. I imagine he knew him, and maybe he owed him something, some debt, but there's no way it could have anything to do with your diagnostic acumen."

"No way?"

Beckah shrugged. "Well, maybe there's some way. But I don't want you to think too highly of yourself. That's a sure way to get into trouble."

"It doesn't seem to have gotten you into trouble," he said.

"Maybe more than you realize."

Before he had a chance to ask her to elaborate, there came a knock at his door.

Alec looked to Beckah. She was the only person to visit him at the university.

"Maybe Stefan?" she said.

"Stefan wouldn't come here, would he?" Alec said. "Unless…"

"Unless?"

Alec shrugged. "Well, I think his Grandma Helen was in the surgery."

"You had two masters with you in the surgery? And you still were allowed to perform a part of it?"

"I had the sense that Grandma Helen wasn't terribly thrilled with what I was doing," Alec said.

"No? I bet Grandma Helen just loved the fact that

Master Eckerd invited a first-year student into one of the more interesting surgeries that she would do."

Alec made his way to the door and pulled it open, expecting Stefan to be there, maybe having heard that Alec had been in surgery with his grandmother, or maybe he had come for the very same reason that Beckah had come, thinking to hear more about the surgery. He wasn't surprised that Beckah had come but would be a little bit more surprised by Stefan coming. They got along, but Alec didn't know him all that well, yet. He had the hope that they would get to know each other, especially as Alec had so few people at the university that he could talk to.

Instead, a messenger waited for him.

The university used many messengers, though most of them were meant to run between the masters and the physickers. Occasionally, they were used elsewhere, but he'd never seen them inside the students' quarters.

"Can I help you?" Alec asked.

The messenger frowned. "Are you Alec Stross?"

"That's me."

The messenger shrugged. "Whatever. I was sent to find you and bring you with me."

"Why? Where are you to take me?"

"I'm not the one to tell it."

The messenger departed, and Alec glanced to Beckah before following him. She went along with him, taking his hand as she did, and once again, he didn't resist.

What was he getting himself into here? He liked Beckah well enough, but he shouldn't be involved with anybody at the university. Especially since he and Sam...

But there really wasn't anything with Sam. Even if he wanted there to be, he hadn't seen her in weeks. Now that she was at the palace, studying with another Kaver, it seemed that she was no longer interested in working with him. Then again, they had no easar paper so there couldn't be any practice. Without the easar paper, what was the point of them working together?

The messenger led them to the main entrance of the university. A dangerous-looking man waited there. He had the deeply tanned skin and dark eyes of somebody from the outer sections, but it was the pair of knives that were sheathed at his waist that really gave Alec pause. Something about him was familiar, though he didn't know what it was.

The messenger nodded to Alec. "Here's your man."

"I need you to come with me," the man said.

"Excuse me, sir, I think you need to be clearer to my friend," Beckah said.

"Beckah—" Alec said, raising his hand.

Beckah shot him a silencing glance.

"You're needed," the man said. "Bastan sends me."

"Bastan?" Beckah said. "Who is Bastan? And why would he be sending for Alec?"

The other man ignored her, and Alec stared at him, realizing then why he recognized him. Alec had seen him in Bastan's tavern.

"You're one of his servers," Alec said.

"Among other things. Now. Your friend needs you. Are you willing to come with me?"

Alec glanced at Beckah and knew that he had to answer some questions, but he nodded. "If Sam needs me, I'm willing to come."

"Not Sam. Another. The older one."

"What happened?" Alec asked.

"I'll let her be the one to tell you. They need your… special abilities."

Alec's heart raced for a moment. If they needed those abilities, that meant they needed him and his Scribing abilities.

"I'll come."

Beckah grabbed his hand. "Me, too."

23

PROTECTIONS ON THE CITY

S am stiffened. Why would he bring someone else with him?

She lifted her hand off of Elaine's head and stood, clasping her hands behind her back. "Thank you for coming, Alec."

Alec glanced from Sam to Elaine before bringing his gaze back up to meet hers. "What happened? I received this," he said, holding up the note that Bastan had sent with Kevin. "And it said that I was needed urgently. What happened?"

Sam wondered how openly she could speak. How much did this other physicker know? And, more importantly, why had Alec felt comfortable revealing their secrets to her?

"She was attacked," Sam started. "There was an explosion. Like the one in your shop."

Alec's eyes widened slightly, and he studied Elaine for a moment. At least he seemed to understand what Sam was getting at. She had worried that he might be too caught up in this other physicker, and that he might be so interested in trying to impress her that he wouldn't help Sam or Elaine.

"I'll need—"

"I know. Bastan claims to have supplies."

Alec took a deep breath and nodded. "Good." He turned to the other physicker. "Beckah, I need you go upstairs and see if you can grab a few towels and keep them moistened."

The other physicker—Beckah—looked at Alec with a hint of amusement in her eyes. There was something more there, as well, something that made Sam's blood boil, though it should not. She had no claim on Alec, nothing more than their connection as Kaver and Scribe would allow.

"Only towels?" Beckah asked.

"For now," Alec said.

Beckah shrugged and turned back toward the door. Sam soon heard her footsteps on the stairs.

Alec turned to Sam and sighed. "Why haven't you come to me?" he asked.

"Why haven't I... Alec, I tried."

"You tried? It seems to me that with your connections, if you were to try, you would be granted entry."

Sam looked down. Did she share with him that she had come, that she had seen Alec, but had turned and left when she saw him with this other physicker? How would that make her seem? Probably as stupid as she felt right now.

"I went to the university to find you once or twice. The last time, I saw you, but you were..." Sam closed her eyes; she felt ridiculous admitting the reason that she had turned around. Didn't they have more of a connection than that?

"I was what? In class?"

"With her." Sam looked up and met his gaze. Heat rose in her cheeks, and she breathed out heavily.

"That's the reason you haven't come to the university in the last few weeks? I thought I'd done something to upset you. The last time you disappeared on me, you were intent to try to do things on your own."

"I seem to remember you applying for the university at that time," Sam said.

"Wasn't that about the same time you were trailing Marin—and your brother—through the city? I think that's about the same time you were determined to chase the princess throughout every section of the city."

"And for good reason," Sam said.

"It only seems a good reason now, but that doesn't mean it was a good reason then."

Sam stared at him. "Who is she?" she asked softly.

"She's another student at the university. She's—"

Alec didn't have a chance to finish. Bastan burst into the room, carrying a single sheet of easar paper. The paper was distinct enough that Sam recognized it without even examining it closely. There was something about the parchment that was easily identifiable. She could practically smell it.

"Here," Bastan said. "You can use this sheet, but that's all."

Alec took the page from him with a certain greedy excitement. "Where did you get this?" he asked.

"I'm a collector. I find things like this all over," Bastan said.

Sam grunted. "A collector? That's what you would have us believe?"

Bastan shrugged. "Believe what you want but be thankful I have even this page for you."

"And if it were me lying there? How many pages would you suddenly find then?" Sam asked. She knew she was pressing, and she knew that she was making assumptions, but she thought they were somewhat valid. Bastan would help her, wouldn't he? He wouldn't let her die just to protect his supply of easar paper.

"Be thankful it's not you lying there. I know that I am."

Bastan stepped back to the door and tipped his head toward Alec, nodding slightly.

Sam now knew that Bastan had witnessed Alec mixing their blood before and had seen the way that he'd worked his augmentation, but it still felt uncomfortable for her to have Bastan standing there, watching.

"I think she's been poisoned, as well as having a potential internal injury," Sam said.

"Poisoned?"

She nodded. "It's like what they used on me. The Theln we faced was like Ralun. Powerful."

"All of them were powerful."

"This one was incredibly powerful."

Alec watched her and then nodded. "Are you ready?" he asked.

Sam held her hand out, and Alec pulled a foldable knife from his pocket and made quick work of nicking the palm of her hand. Each time he did, it hurt about the same. Each time, Sam hoped it wouldn't hurt, but it always did. He pulled a small glass vial from beneath his cloak, and Sam dripped her blood into it, at least a dozen or more drops.

Alec took a deep breath and made a shallow slice along his own palm. As he held his hand above the vial, he was more cautious than Sam and seemed to count the drops as they fell into it. She noted that he only put in six drops.

"Why that ratio?" she asked.

"The healing has to come partially from me, but it mostly comes from the Kaver," Alec said. "As much as I would like to be the one to take the brunt of this process, healing seems to be tied more to the Kaver than to the Scribe."

Alec brandished a pen and dipped it into the vial, stirring the blood inside. He put the easar paper on the table and smoothed it out. Then Alec made a few notes, almost as if he were testing the easar paper. Taking a deep breath, he began writing.

Sam stepped back, not wanting to watch what he wrote. There was a particular nature to the words that was important, but she had found that watching over his shoulder always seemed to make Alec uncomfortable. She needed him to be focused. Elaine needed him to be focused.

He scratched his pen along the page for longer than what Sam was used to him doing. She glanced over out of the corner of her eye, biting her lip as she frowned, and finally, he stopped.

"Is it done?" she asked.

Fatigue began to wash through her, working through her in the familiar cool wave she always felt when her blood was used.

"It's as done as it can be," Alec said. "I hope this works,

but I don't know. It's like when I attempted to heal the princess."

A gasp near the door caught Sam's attention. She looked over and saw Beckah standing there clutching the moistened towels.

"You… healed the princess?"

"You didn't tell her?" Sam asked. "I thought with your new friend—"

Alec cut her off with a shake of his head.

"Now I understand why the masters treat you the way they do," Beckah said with a chuckle.

"Not because he knows more than they do?" Sam demanded. Beckah turned toward Sam, her eyes widening.

"Sam—" Alec began.

Sam shook him off. "No. You know as much as most of those damn physickers. Don't let them take that away from you. Your father has been preparing you for more than only the university for a long time."

"Sam—" Alec said again, this time a little more firmly.

She shot him a hard look, wanting to glare at him, but it faded as she saw the expression on his face. He nodded toward Elaine, forcing her attention toward her mother.

She thought Elaine blinked once, and then she opened her eyes and managed to look around the room.

"Where is this?" Elaine asked.

"I've already told you. We're in Caster. I brought you to a place that could let me get you some help."

Elaine's features darkened for a moment. "Caster?"

"It's not as bad as most of you highborns seem to think," Sam said. "It's been good enough for me for the last ten years of my life."

"That's not it, Samara," Elaine started.

"No? Then what is it? If you're not offended by the fact that I brought you into Caster, and managed to get you help, I might add, then tell me, why are you so offended that we're here?"

"Because Caster isn't as secure as the city," Elaine managed to spit out.

"Not as secure? It's a part of the city. It's no different from any other section."

"That's where you're wrong. Caster was never part of the original city. It was added later, and that matters."

"Why does that matter?" That was the first question that came to Sam's mind, rather than trying to understand more about how Caster could have been a later addition to the city, especially when many of the buildings were older.

Elaine sighed. "Caster was here long before the rest of the city came. It was annexed as the city grew, but there's something about the section that prevents the same protections. It's probably why Marin stayed here."

Bastan had stepped forward, moving away from the door. He frowned, watching Elaine with a curious expression.

Elaine managed to sit up, swinging her legs over the edge of the cot. She scanned the room, her gaze settling on Sam for a moment before shifting to Alec and nodding as she mouthed the word "thanks." From there, she turned to look at Beckah and tipped her head, something like recognition passing across her eyes. Sam suspected that Elaine had been to the university often enough that she recognized even the students. Or maybe, Elaine was keeping tabs on Sam and had gone and observed Alec and his classmates. That seemed more likely than anything else.

She shook her head, tearing her attention away from the others, and turned back to Sam.

"It's the city, Samara."

"What's the city?"

"You've asked how we've managed to keep the Thelns away, how we've managed to provide protection for as long as we have. That's what I'm telling you. It's the city."

"How can the city provide protection?"

Elaine looked again at the others in the room, before shaking her head firmly. "That's not an answer for here, not one for anyplace that isn't secure."

"Where would you rather this conversation take place?" Sam asked.

"We need to return to the palace. That's the only place we can have the conversation that you need. It's the only safe place to discuss this."

Sam let out a frustrated sigh and turned her attention to Alec, shrugging. "I guess we're going to the palace. I guess that's the only place where she feels comfortable talking about this," she said, having a hard time keeping the annoyance from her voice.

Alec started to reach toward her, and then caught himself.

Sam swallowed, suppressing the rising frustration she felt, knowing that it would do no good. It wasn't Alec's fault what was taking place. And it wasn't Alec's fault that she felt the way she did.

She pushed past Bastan, not waiting for the others to follow.

24

FIRST VISITS

Alec had never been inside the palace. Since learning about Sam's connection to the princess, Alec hadn't had a chance to come here. The only time he'd been near a member of the royal family, he'd been with Sam, but that was in the university, not in the palace. It was somewhat disconcerting being here.

Everything around him seemed more ornate than it needed to be. Chairs were gilded and heavily carved. Floors were covered with expensive-looking rugs that would be unattainable anywhere else in the city. Tapestries on the walls were clearly well-made, though Alec didn't have the same eye for them as he knew Sam—and Bastan—did. Sculptures were scattered around the room where they now gathered, and Alec imagined the cost of them, and could only imagine how much everything in this single room was worth.

Sam took a seat near the hearth, leaning back in an enormous plush chair and kicking her feet up on the table. Alec shot her a look, which she promptly ignored. He stood stiffly near the back of the room, waiting to be invited in, and fearing that perhaps Sam had gotten ahead of herself.

"You don't have to stand there so stiff," Sam said.

"I'm not stiff, it's just that—"

"It's just that your friend isn't here?" Sam asked.

Alec frowned. "That's not it at all. Beckah only came with me because she was concerned. We've been—"

"Beckah? Her name is Beckah? If that's not a highborn name, and I don't know what is."

"Most of the people in the university are highborn by birth," Alec said.

"I would say that all are."

"I'm probably the farthest from highborn at the university."

"And closer to highborn than I've ever been," Sam said.

Alec looked around the room and saw the comfortable way Sam sat, noting the cut of her dress, even the sheen to her skin, now much less tanned than it once had. Did Sam realize how close she had become to the highborns?

Not that he necessarily wanted her to realize it. There was value in Sam not knowing that she had moved up in the world. She maintained an edge, one that helped her as she struggled to improve.

"Where did Elaine go?" Alec asked. It was better to change the topic than to get Sam even angrier. He hadn't seen her in weeks, and now that they were finally in the same room, he didn't want to get into an argument with her. All he wanted was for them to get along.

Were he honest with himself, all he really wanted was

to continue to work with Sam and the easar paper, though he didn't know how much of a supply Bastan had. Probably more than he let on.

"She was injured, so I suspect she went to make sure that everything you did was meant to help, not to harm her."

"Why would I hurt her? She's your mother."

"Maybe for the same reason I would hurt her. She abandoned me, Alec. She... She didn't care that she had left me, alone in the city, and with my mind somehow twisted by Marin and her augmentations. She didn't care that I might still be out there. In all these years, she didn't try to find me."

"I'm sure she cared," Alec said.

"Are you? She didn't care about my father. She said it was too dangerous for him to remain with her, but it feels like she abandoned him, letting him go when it no longer made sense to have him in her life. I think the same thing happened with me."

Alec doubted that was the case, but he didn't know anything about Elaine other than that she was a Kaver and possessed the same types of skills as Sam. Her Scribe came from the highest of the highborns, which made Sam's and his connection feel somehow... less. He suspected that she wished she had someone more like the princess as a Scribe rather than him.

As he stood there, debating what to say, the door opened, and Elaine strode in, followed by someone Alec had not expected to see.

"Master," he said, tipping his head politely to Master Helen.

"You're the Scribe?" Master Helen asked, looking over to Elaine.

"I see you've met," Elaine said. "That might make this conversation easier."

"I don't think any of these conversations will be easy," Master Helen said.

Alec noted that Sam seemed to have tensed, and he frowned. "What is it?"

She stood, her hands clenched at her sides, and nodded toward the master. "Her. She's the one who has been trying to help me with my memories," Sam said. "At least, that's what she claimed she was doing. Have you been telling her what I've been saying?"

Sam took a few steps forward, and Alec reached for her arm, not wanting her to do anything too rash. Sam could be impulsive and had something of a temper. It wouldn't be a good idea for her to attack one of the masters, certainly not one who had the favor of the princess's Kaver.

"I asked her to help you, nothing more," Elaine said. "Anything that took place between you it was just that— between you."

Alec wondered what Sam might have shared with the master.

"Sit," Master Helen said.

Sam glared another moment. Alec wasn't certain whether she would agree, but she sat back down, this time, on the edge of the oversized chair, and turned her attention to the hearth, essentially ignoring Elaine.

"You said we had to come here for answers," Sam said.

"Please explain it to them," Elaine said to Master Helen.

"They are not of age," Helen said.

"Not of age?" Elaine asked. "That one just saved me from three Thelns. Were it not for her, I would have been either killed or dragged out of the city. Tell me that she's not of age."

"Three Thelns?"

"And she didn't have her Scribe with her," Elaine said. "I think it's reasonable to share with her. I'm not sure about him." She nodded to Alec.

Master Helen gave a slight grin. "I believe he is more trustworthy than she."

"Why? Because he's a student at the university?" Elaine asked.

"No, because Master Eckerd felt that he was worthy enough to bring into a head trauma procedure."

"Eckerd?" Elaine asked.

Master Helen nodded. "That was my reaction, as well."

"Why? What reaction are you talking about?" Sam pressed.

"Interesting," Elaine said.

"Are you going to keep talking about us as if we aren't sitting right here?" Sam asked.

"What are the chances that both Kaver and Scribe are accelerated like this?" Elaine asked.

"The Scribe was trained by Aelus. Of course he would be accelerated."

"All right. I think it's time that you explain why you brought us here and why you're talking around us." Sam stood and looked at Elaine. "You promised that we would be told more when we reached the palace. How is the city able to protect us from the Thelns?"

Master Helen's gaze went from Elaine to Sam, and finally to Alec. Her eyes narrowed as she seemed to consider the question. Then she shook her head. "Just know that it does. Without the city, the Thelns would have even easier access, seeking to destroy those with blood magic."

"And you?" Sam asked. "Do you have the same blood magic?"

Helen shook her head. "I am neither Kaver nor Scribe."

"I just thought…" Sam began.

"Yes. You just thought." She turned her attention to Elaine. "It is a mistake to think that we should share with those who are too young to protect themselves."

"Too young?" Sam asked.

Alec was surprised that it seemed the master physicker was commanding Elaine, the princess's Scribe. How many physickers other than Master Helen would have the same confidence?

Helen studied Sam. "Yes. Too young. From the conversations we've had, I can tell you with certainty that you are too young for what you seek to know. Stay and train, become useful. The city is safe."

"Safe? We've been attacked by Thelns multiple times," Sam said.

"In an unprotected outer section. I can promise you that we are perfectly safe here."

"For how long?" Sam snapped. She would have to be careful, especially around someone like Master Helen.

"I thought Elaine said that I was useful? I think the fact that I helped save her from three Thelns proves that I am useful and that I am progressing in my training."

"It proves nothing other than that you have learned some, but you have much still to learn. I will return to visit with you later this week. Perhaps if you make progress there, you will continue to make progress with your training."

Master Helen turned and left, not even paying any attention to Alec as she did. Elaine remained for a moment before she followed Master Helen from the room. It left Alec and Sam alone.

"What is this?" Alec asked. "Why are they keeping things from us?"

"I believe Elaine has been tracking Marin but hasn't found her. I think she ended up having Thelns follow her into the city."

"But if the city has protections that keep the Thelns from gaining access..."

"It wouldn't be the first time they managed to get into the city," Sam said. "If there *are* protections in place, I'm not entirely sure how they managed to get into the city before, but I know that it troubles Elaine. And whatever Marin is doing has to be related."

"You think Marin is somehow allowing the Thelns to enter?"

Sam stared past him and at the door. "The merchant attacks. The Thelns in the city. Marin missing. It has to be related. I just don't know how."

Alec watched her for a moment before deciding to ask the question that had been bothering him. "What's the real reason you haven't come to the university?"

"I told you. I tried, but you were with... your friend."

"This has nothing to do with Beckah. What is it?"

"Well, it was the first time. But the second time, I couldn't get in."

"If you had truly tried, you would have been able to reach me. The university wouldn't have kept you out, not anymore."

He noted the pained expression on her face.

"What? There's something about that which bothers you."

She shrugged. "It's... difficult for me."

"It's difficult for me, too. That doesn't change that I want to—"

"It's difficult for you? You're highborn. You've always known who you were and what you were. But for me, all of a sudden, I have access, and I'm granted access to places that I never could have gone before."

Alec stepped closer toward her. "That's what's been bothering you? You're upset about being granted this access? That you're treated like a highborn now?"

She shrugged. "Well, yeah."

Alec laughed until she shot him a hard glare. "I thought you'd be happy to be highborn. Weren't you the one who kept telling me how much more access the highborns have than anyone else? Why is it now that you're essentially highborn that you are struggling with it?"

"I have never wanted to be highborn." Alec arched a brow at her. "I haven't. I wanted to know where I belonged. I wanted to know where I fit in. Once I learned that my mother was not only alive but also a Kaver, I thought I might actually begin to feel like I had someplace where I belong." Sam swallowed. "Instead, it makes me wonder if maybe I was better off before. Maybe it would have been better for me just to think my mother had died."

Alec shook his head. "You don't mean that. I know you don't mean that."

Sam looked down at her hands. "I'm not sure what I mean. All I know is that I'm no closer to understanding my abilities than I was before I found her. Well, maybe some. But most of that has come from the training of others. She's been gone. You've been gone. And I... I continue to train, but I'm not getting any better."

Alec leaned over and took her hand. Her hands were soft and smooth and fit his. They were hands that he had cut into more times than he cared for, needing blood for their magic, so they could use the easar paper. In the short time they'd known each other, he'd seen her injured and had done things that had hurt her as he'd attempted augmentations, but she'd always seemed so strong to him.

Here she was, more vulnerable than he had ever seen her.

What could he say that would make her feel better? What could he do that would show her that he saw things in her that he suspected she didn't even see in herself?

"Is it true?" he asked.

"Is what true?"

"You took on three Thelns?"

Sam shook her head. "Elaine took on three Thelns. She was augmented, so she took down two of them before she needed any help."

"That means that you jumped in and tried to fight off one Theln?"

"He was the biggest one," Sam said.

"I wasn't saying that because I thought that you

should have done more. I'm just saying that perhaps you've improved more than you realize. You had always needed augmentations to face the Thelns before. If you were able to fight this one without any augmentations…"

"Fight might be a bit generous. I managed not to die. I might have distracted him a little bit, but I don't think I did much more than that."

"You saved Elaine."

Sam sighed. "I saved Elaine. Marin's home is gone. And now, there's no way to see what she'd been up to and no way to find her."

"If you did find her, what would you even say?"

"I don't know. Maybe nothing. Maybe I would demand that she tell me why she used me. Maybe I'd demand that she tell me why she used Tray."

"Even after everything that's happened, you're still worried about your brother?"

"He's still my brother. It's strange. I know that, just as I know that he isn't really, but in my mind—and my heart—he's still Trayson. My brother."

"I don't think it's strange. I think it makes perfect sense. You've only known him as your brother. Anything else would be wrong."

"I wish I could find him. I don't know what I would tell him, and I don't know that if I did find him, it would matter at all, but I'd at least like the chance to try."

"Then find him."

Sam glanced up, meeting his gaze for a moment before turning her attention back to her hands. "Elaine wants me to focus on my training. After facing those Thelns, I understand why. Once I'm better equipped to fight with the staff and the other techniques they teach, I'll be better able to manage augmentations, as well."

"You'll regret it if you don't look for Tray."

"What of you? If I'm supposed to look for Tray, what are you going to do?"

"Helen seems to know something. She might not want to share, but I'm going to get her to tell me," Alec said.

"It seems she's going to come find me later this week, so if I learn anything from her, I'll let you know."

"Has it been helping?" Alec asked.

"I don't know if it's been helping, but I think she's been trying to get to some hidden memories. They're there, but I don't know how to reach them. Whatever Marin did blocked those memories. All I have are blanks where they should be."

"I hope you find what you need."

"What if I do and I don't like what I discover?"

"Do you think that's a possibility?"

Sam turned toward the door. "I wouldn't have thought so, but the more I learn about Elaine, the more I begin to wonder if maybe Marin did me a favor by taking me away from that."

"Sam…"

"No. You're right. All I wanted was to know who my parents were, to have a chance to get them back, and now that I got them—well, one of them—I don't know that I want her." She sighed. "I'd just like to know what happened. Maybe if I can ever find Marin, I can learn what she did and see if it can be undone."

"I'll keep looking, too," Alec said.

Sam swallowed and looked down.

"I miss seeing you," he said.

"I miss that, too."

"Now that we have some paper…"

She glanced up and smiled. "I don't think Bastan was thrilled that he had to reveal his supply. That made me happy."

Alec chuckled. "I'm sure it did."

"He has more. I'm sure of it. I'll go back to him and see what I can get."

25

A MEETING

Sam made her way across the bridge slowly. She took a moment to flash her papers, identifying herself as from the palace, still feeling awkward about the fact that she did—and could. It was an uncomfortable thing for her to be able to claim that she was from the palace, and even more uncomfortable for her to feel like she could travel as easily as any of the highborns.

As she moved farther from the center of the city, she felt increasing comfort with her surroundings. Not because she was necessarily more familiar with them, but more because she was away from some of the formality, and away from people who seemed to watch her with judging eyes. She needed that about as much as she needed to fall into the damn canal and deal with the eels.

If only she had augmentations.

She felt that way most of the time as she wandered between the sections of the city. She had her canal staff, and she had what she'd been taught by Theron, but she still didn't have anywhere near the same level of skill as she had seen from Elaine. Her mother didn't need augmentations to be dangerous.

Had whatever Marin did to cloud her mind forever eliminate her connection to that part of her abilities? She could augment and access them, but nothing more than that. Without them, she was perhaps better able than most to navigate the city, but she still had limitations.

There had been no more attacks on merchants in the city. In the weeks since the Theln attack at Marin's, there had been no further sign of them, either.

Had they disappeared?

Sam had a hard time believing that they had, but if they weren't gone, where had they disappeared to? And why couldn't she learn anything of Marin?

All this time, she should have been working with Alec, preparing for the Thelns. Even with her augmentations, the Thelns made her nervous. More than that. She feared them. Growing up in Caster, she hadn't really been afraid of anything—she was confident she could protect herself —and Tray. But the Thelns did scare her. They had beaten her more than once—and the last time, they'd nearly beaten Elaine, who was better equipped than any to stop them. If she couldn't, what hope did Sam have?

If the protections of the city failed and the Thelns reached them, what could she do to defend herself? How could she keep them from getting to Tray?

That frightened her most of all.

It was Marin's betrayal to her brother, even more than what she had done with Sam.

He had to know what Marin had done before the Thelns came after him.

What if they attempted to recruit Tray?

Sam had no idea if that was something the Thelns did. Elaine refused to talk about them, and every time she'd attempted to bring it up, the woman had changed the topic. Would they learn that Tray was part Theln? Was there anything they could do that would convince him to join with them?

Tray wanted to prove himself. That was all he'd ever wanted. He wanted to prove to Sam that she didn't need to protect him, that *he* could be the one to keep *her* safe. She'd made the mistake of minimizing his ability to do that and pushing him away all these years. Now she needed him. He might be the one person that could keep her safe from the Thelns if they were to attack.

She reached the edge of a section—the Yalling section —and paused at the canal. Standing on the edge, she looked out over the water, listening to the soft sound of the current as it flowed past, and took a deep breath. There was a barge in the canal, and it moved slowly with the current, the captain poling his way along, pushing the boat forward and toward the outer sections of the city. There weren't that many barges willing to travel all the way to the outer sections, so this one must either be poor, or he smuggled something not meant for the center of the city.

Sam waited until he had passed before she assembled her canal staff and took two steps back before jumping over the canal, plunging her staff in the middle of the canal as she leaped.

There was a simple joy found in flying over the canal. Wind whistled around her. The scent of the canal was prominent, but it was not unpleasant from up here, not as it could be from street level. The perspective allowed her the ability to see everything around her, to see the section she left as easily as she saw the one she soared toward.

Then she landed. Sam shook off her staff and disassembled it.

She could have kept it out, but doing so would only draw attention to her. Traveling to Caster and back to Bastan for the second time in a few weeks left her with a desire for anonymity and the ability to appear without warning. Bastan had enough men stationed along the bridges connecting the various sections of the city that he would know she was coming. Sam didn't mind him knowing, but she would prefer to surprise him.

Noise in the middle of the section caught her attention, and she veered away from the road leading along the water's edge.

She should ignore the noise. There was no reason for her to go chasing after things that would only distract her, but curiosity pulled her along.

The section was mostly merchants, though they were lower-level merchants that would not be found in other areas in the city. Some of the inner sections were much more well-off, and the merchants that served those areas had significant financial resources. Merchants found here tended to serve the outer sections, those that had less money, and less prestige.

As she rounded a corner, she saw a commotion in the street.

It was a fight, the kind of street fight that was likely to lead to an arrest, and jailing of those involved. These were the kinds of fights that the city guard disallowed, making every effort to clean them up and do everything they could to ensure that they were short-lived.

Could this be another merchant attack?

It had been weeks since the last.

Three men attacked a fourth. The three men were of average size and build, but they seemed to have some experience working together, and boxed in the fourth man, trapping him in the center. None of them were armed, but they bashed at the other man, pounding him with their fists. The fourth man was larger than his attackers, and he fought back with some amount of skill, his punches sending one after another staggering back.

As she watched, Sam thought he might actually fight them off, but the other three kept coming, managing to get up time and again, only to throw themselves at the other man once more.

One of the men pulled out a pair of knives. The faint daylight glittered off of them, and Sam's heart skipped. What had been nothing more than a street fight—little more than a brawl—now had a different dynamic to it.

Something prompted Sam to rush forward. As she did, she assembled her canal staff and launched herself up and over the outer men, coming to land in the middle of the fray.

She spun, bringing the staff around with a sharp crack, colliding with the nearest man, sending him flying backward.

She flipped the staff around, connecting with the man holding the knives, and the sharpness of the blow cracked his wrist.

That left only one man.

The man getting attacked lunged at him, knocking him to the ground, and began pummeling his face. He struck with a furious intensity, one that battered the other man and left his face a bloody mess.

Sam reached in and tried to pull him back, but he was larger than she was and clearly stronger. Had she any augmentations, she would have been able to restrain him, but, she didn't.

What she did have was her canal staff.

She swung, using minimal force, but caught him in the stomach, forcing him back.

The man grunted. He spun toward her, and Sam nearly dropped her staff.

"Tray?"

"Sam?" Tray's voice had changed, having grown deeper since she'd last seen him. Had so much changed in that short time? "What are you doing here? You haven't been in Caster in—"

"This isn't Caster. And you shouldn't be fighting."

One of the men groaned, and Sam grabbed Tray's sleeve and pulled him with her.

He might outweigh her, but he didn't resist, letting her drag him as they moved out of the street. She wanted to get him away from the fight, not wanting him to get caught near the three men. She had questions and doubted that he'd answer them, but she would press him.

She pulled him along with her as they made their way along the street. Tray remained silent, though Sam wasn't offended by that. He seemed larger than the last time she'd seen him, though that had been months now. In that time, so much had changed for her—and obviously for him.

When they reached the waterfront, the canals

stretching out in front of her, she rounded on him. "What was that about?" she demanded.

"It doesn't matter."

"It matters, Tray. Those men were going to kill you."

"They weren't trying to kill me. They were—" He shook his head, cutting himself off before he could say anything more.

Sam could tell that he was careful about what he said to her and had to admit that she found it a little disconcerting that Tray would censor himself in such a way. He had always been the one who shared everything with her, and she had always been the one to resist telling him anything more than was necessary.

"Well? Are you going to tell me what happened?" she demanded.

"Are you going to tell me where you've been the last few months?" Tray asked.

Sam leaned on her canal staff, shaking her head. "What's there to tell you?"

"Maybe you start with telling me how you learned to fight like that."

She shot him a hard look. "Fight like what? Like my brother's life was in danger?"

"I've known you my entire life. I've never seen you fight quite like that. That was something I've only seen from men who are soldiers. Have you become a soldier?"

Sam glanced up the street, looking for any sign of movement, but there was none. "Why won't you tell me who those men were?"

"Because it doesn't matter. And now that you beat them the way you did, it certainly doesn't matter."

"You're not going to tell me what that was about?"

Tray stared at her, his face unreadable. "You're not going to tell me what your sudden skill improvement is all about?"

Sam began breaking down her staff, pulling the ends apart. "I've been learning how to defend myself, okay? Living on the streets in Caster, you have to learn how to protect yourself."

"It doesn't have anything to do with that boy who likes you?"

"Boy?"

Tray shrugged. "Fine. Man. He's still not all that old."

"This has nothing to do with Alec."

"The last time I saw him—"

Sam jabbed a finger at his chest. "About that. The last time you saw him, it was at Marin's home, and you were watching it for her. How many other jobs have you done for Marin?"

She wasn't ready to say anything more about Marin, or about the fact that they weren't actually related, but maybe she wouldn't need to. Maybe Tray would tell her what he knew about Marin.

"Marin asked me to do a few tasks for her. You know that she wants only to help keep us safe. She knew Mother."

Sam clenched her jaw to keep from snapping at him. It wasn't Tray's fault that Marin had deceived them.

An idea began to come to her. Marin had deceived both of them, but she had always worked on behalf of Tray, had always made sure that he was protected, even sometimes at the expense of Sam. Could Marin somehow be doing that now?

"When did you last see her?" she asked.

He shook his head. "I can't talk about that, Sam."

"She's doing something, Tray. I need to find her."

Tray stared at her, not saying anything, but she could see the look in his eyes, the one that seemed to struggle with how to answer.

"What has she asked of you, Trayson? Is it something that's going to end up getting you hurt?"

He laughed, and there was a hint of bitterness in it. "She hasn't asked me to do anything more dangerous than you ever asked."

"I only ever asked you to watch."

"Watch. And we saw where that got me, didn't we?"

Sam stared at him for a moment, wishing there was something she could say that would convince him she hadn't been responsible for him ending up in prison, but there wasn't. It had been her fault. Had she not asked him to stand guard, to watch over her as she broke into the highborn house, he would never have been captured, and never would have ended up in prison.

Sam had spent only a short period of time in prison. She didn't know what he'd experienced in the weeks that he'd been held captive. How awful must it have been?

And Tray had not said anything to her. He had kept that experience to himself. It was almost like he'd done so to protect her, but she wasn't the one who needed protecting, that was Tray.

"I'm sorry you were captured," she said.

Tray shrugged. "That's not what I'm getting at," he said.

"What are you getting at?"

"Only that I've been in more dangerous situations before. You have to trust that I can take care of myself,

Sam. I'm thankful you've always been there for me, but now, this is something I need to do."

"What does she have you doing?" Sam asked.

Tray looked around, turning his attention up the street where they'd come from, before looking back to Sam. He crossed his arms over his chest, and she felt a sense of enormity from him. Tray had always been large, and muscular. He'd been that way since they were children, and she'd felt slightly jealous about that fact, feelings that only worsened as they grew older, and she remained the same size. Now when he crossed his arms, his biceps pressed against the fabric of his sleeves, and she was completely aware of how much larger he was.

"I've told you. She has me watching."

"Watching what?"

Tray shrugged. "It doesn't matter."

"I think it does. I need to know what's happened to her. Where she's gone. Others will get harmed if we don't find her."

"Others? Like you? Marin made it clear that you had abandoned her."

"I didn't abandon her. I just…"

She couldn't tell him what she had done. If she shared, then she would have to explain more, and not only was she not ready to do that, she wasn't certain it was the right thing to do in the first place.

"You just what?" Tray asked.

"I just—I just want you to be well."

"Then stop trying to save me."

"You're my brother, Tray. I'm never going to stop trying to save you."

Tray watched her, and opened his mouth once, as if he

were going to say something more to her, maybe object to what she'd said to him, but then he clamped it shut once more. He turned and started off down the street, without saying anything more.

Sam blinked, watching him go before anger bubbled up within her and she stormed after him, stopping in front of him and smacking him on the chest with her canal staff.

"That's it? I haven't seen you in months, and you decide it's okay to just run off without saying even good-bye? Tray—I've been worried about you."

"I've been okay."

"At least let me know how to find you," she said.

"It's not safe for you to find me."

"For who?"

"For you."

She tapped him on the chest with her staff again. "I have proven that I can defend myself a little bit. And I'll do whatever it takes to defend you, as well. Don't… Don't do something stupid."

"Like I said, I'll do whatever is necessary to finish this job. That's what Marin asked of me."

"I need to find her, Tray."

"I don't know if that's possible."

"Why?"

Tray gave a half smile. "You haven't said anything about Marin's home, and I know that you were there."

Sam's heart fluttered for a moment. Had he been there? Had he been watching when Elaine had fought the Thelns? She wanted to keep Tray as far away from them as possible and did not want him to learn about his connection to them, not knowing what he might do, or how he might react. If he'd been there, then he might even have seen Sam intervene, and might have seen her carry Elaine off to Bastan's.

"Have you been watching me?" she asked.

Tray shook his head. "I haven't watched you. I don't think I could keep up with you even if I wanted to. I can't get across the canals the same way you do. I have to find a different way across. Don't you remember that?"

Sam smiled to herself. Tray had never been especially skilled at jumping the canal, which was the reason he'd often stayed behind, watching from the other side as Sam did whatever task she needed to. Something had obviously changed though, since Tray was much farther from Caster than she'd expected him to be.

"I remember you trying to chase me everywhere, Tray. I remember us running through the streets, knowing that we should be more careful, but never caring about anything other than where we went. I remember the first time I jump the canal, and you were there with me, watching, encouraging me."

"I'll never stop encouraging you, but I don't need you watching over me anymore. I need you to let me go."

The request hurt, especially considering what Sam had been through, things that she couldn't share with Tray. But she had come to the determination that she wasn't going to lose him. Regardless of whatever happened, he was still her brother. But she couldn't force him to feel the same. If he was determined to have her stop watching over him, and if he wanted her to let him go, she'd already lost him.

"Can you do me a favor?" she asked Tray. It pained her

to ask like this, but then again, it pained her that he wanted her to leave him alone.

"What's the favor?"

"I need to find Marin. I have a question for her."

"What kind of question?"

Sam sighed. "It's the kind of question I can't talk about with you."

Tray watched her, and she worried that he would refuse, that he'd send her away, but he only nodded. "When I see her next, I'll pass on word that you want to speak with her. Does that work for you?"

If it worked, maybe she could figure out what Marin was doing before anyone else got hurt. Maybe she could find a way to keep the Thelns out of the city, away from her—and Tray.

"Have her find me in Caster," she said.

"Where in Caster?"

"Bastan has been offering me a place to stay. She can find me at his tavern."

Was that too presumptuous of her? If Marin came looking for her at Bastan's tavern, there was a real possibility that Bastan—and people that he cared about—could be caught in the middle. That was the last thing that Sam wanted. She didn't want anyone to get hurt as a result of her looking for Marin and seeking the answers she needed.

"I can't promise when I'll see her next," Tray said.

"That's fine. Just… Just let her know that I have a question for her."

"Don't come after me again, Sam. This is something I need to do."

"I'm not going to stop caring about you," she said.

"That's not what I'm asking."

"You know that I'll always be here for you, Tray," she said.

Tray watched her and seemed as if he wanted to say something but didn't. He only nodded and then started away from her, down the street.

Sam watched him depart, and he sauntered off at a lumbering pace, one that picked up speed the farther he went, before practically turning into a run. When he disappeared around a street corner, nausea gnawed at the pit of Sam's stomach. It took a moment for her to understand why. Watching Tray disappear down the street left her wondering if she would ever see him again.

26

THE DANGEROUS PLAN

"You intend to use my tavern to draw Marin out?" Bastan sat at his desk, his arms resting on the table, his face a rigid mask. He wasn't angry, but she had a hard time determining what emotion he was feeling.

"I need to know what she's doing."

"Considering that Marin has not been seen in the last few months, I think that drawing her out will only lead to a potential altercation, especially if she's involved in bringing these Thelns back to the city. And now you have summoned her to my tavern." He drummed his fingers on the desk.

"What if I stay here?" Sam had been thinking about how to make this work, and it was the only solution that she could come up with. If she remained at Bastan's tavern, and if she remained available to respond, then she might be able to counter Marin if she ever did show up.

Sam wasn't entirely certain she would come. Even if Marin did show, Sam still wasn't certain what she would say to the woman who had so betrayed her. Would she open up about her concerns with what Marin had held back from her? Would she demand to know what Marin had done to her mind? Or, would she confront her about Tray?

Probably none of that, Sam decided. She'd probably say nothing, and only try to restrain Marin, and take her to Elaine.

"I didn't think you wanted to remain in Caster. I thought you enjoyed your new access."

Sam grunted. "My new access is only to help me learn how to use these abilities, Bastan. If you don't want me to remain here…"

Bastan's expression softened. "You have always been welcome in my tavern, Samara. I would not chase you away. That doesn't mean I have to like what you've arranged. You've invited trouble into my tavern. The people who work for me our family."

Sam chuckled. "Family? They're your employees."

Bastan met her eyes. "I may compensate them, but you of all people know that I treat those under my employ well."

"Bastan, I of all people have seen how you create obligations. These people remain with you because they have no other choice."

"And what of you? You have another choice, yet you returned. Have I treated you so poorly that you feel that is a mistake?"

"You've been nothing but decent to me."

Bastan grunted. "Decent. And in spite of that, your greatest desire was to escape from me. I still haven't decided whether I should be hurt or impressed that you managed to fend so well for yourself. Perhaps I should feel pride. I like to think that I had some small part in your development."

Sam shook her head. For so long, all she'd wanted to do was get away from Bastan, and keep her and Tray safe from his influence, and now that she had, she thought she understood a little bit more about Bastan, and what motivated him.

He was right. Because of him, she had become the person she was. A thief. And now a Kaver. Her skills had developed because of Bastan, even if he hadn't known what he was doing at the time... unless he had.

Was it possible that Bastan was family to her?

He sat motionless, watching her, almost as if he understood the emotions working through her as she tried to figure out what she should say, and what she should do.

She'd spent the last ten or more years wanting her family, bemoaning the fact that her parents were both gone, and that she was forced to help Tray, but now that Tray had asked her to leave him alone, she thought that she understood Bastan a little better, and the fact that he perhaps saw her as some part of his family.

"Bastan—"

He raised his hand. "I'm not asking you to say anything here that would be out of character, Samara. Of course I will help. I don't want anything untoward to happen to you, especially if Marin has betrayed Caster."

"There would be something else that I'd need," she began. How would he react to her request for easar paper? If she and Alec had access to easar paper, she might be able to use it to augment her, and certainly could use it to keep them protected if Marin attacked.

"You would like a supply of the paper."

"That would be helpful," she said carefully.

Bastan nodded. "I imagine that it would. But, as we have seen, that paper is quite valuable. What are you prepared to offer me in exchange?"

"I thought you said you weren't interested in creating obligations."

"This has nothing to do with creating obligations. This has everything to do with the value of a property."

Sam took a deep breath. She had known that there would be some price. With Bastan, there was always a price. Regardless of the fact that he considered her some strange part of his family, that didn't change the fact that he asked much of her. But then, he'd never asked more than what she was able to provide. He'd never placed her in any real danger.

"What do you need from me in exchange for the paper?" she asked.

"I can think of several uses for your particular talent, Samara."

"Are you going to force me to do these tasks before you will allow me to have the paper?"

"Do you think you'll need the paper to complete the tasks?"

Sam wished she had her staff, but it was leaning against the wall. "Don't make me hit you, Bastan."

"First you ask favors, then you threaten?"

"Would you rather I threaten first?"

Bastan sat back, a wide grin spreading across his face. "It will be nice to work with you once more, Samara. I've missed our banter."

Sam wished she felt the same. She appreciated all that Bastan had done for her but didn't like the idea of getting deeper in debt to him. It wouldn't surprise her to have him ask something of her that would place her new connections in danger.

"What's your request?" she asked.

He smiled. "It *just* might be related to what you're after. Besides, you have the necessary connections for this."

Connections. It was exactly what Sam feared. Bastan would have her use her connections to reach someplace that she did not want to.

"First only the paper," she said, "and then I'll need to have you call Alec back to Caster."

"Why would I need to do that?"

"If your task requires me to use the paper—"

His smile changed, shifting from what had been nothing more than an amused grin to something a little more sly, and a little more devious. It was an expression that made her somewhat uncomfortable.

"The task might require you to use the paper, but you don't need me to summon your friend Alec."

"You've heard that's how the paper works."

"Yes, but it won't be necessary for me to summon your friend back to Caster. What I need from you requires that you travel to the university. There's someone there I need you to find, someone who might have the answers we have been searching for."

With a sense of trepidation, Sam reached the bridge that crossed over to the university. She had little doubt that the papers she'd been given would grant her access. That had not been a problem for quite some time. What troubled her was the idea of risking Alec and his presence at the university. She didn't want anything that Bastan might ask of her to place his status in jeopardy.

She kept her cloak tied neatly around her, the canal staff tucked securely within it, not wanting to give any sign that she carried it. Revealing that she had the staff was a surefire way to demonstrate that she was not supposed to be at the university. She needed to get in, find Alec, and then complete the task that Bastan had asked of her.

The task was not one that she thought would be easy, and Bastan had seemed practically giddy when he told her what it was.

Somehow, Bastan was convinced that Alec would know the solution. It seemed something of a puzzle, but then again, Alec was incredibly smart, and would likely be able to solve Bastan's stupid puzzle.

It was near evening time as the guards waved her across the bridge, and still light enough that she could see everything easily. The massive building of the university loomed in front of her, and Sam's anxiety increased as she approached. This was where Alec studied. This was a place of learning. And she did not belong.

She was nothing but a lowborn, regardless of what Elaine tried to make her feel. She might have papers that granted her access to other parts of the city, but that was all she had. That didn't make her a highborn, any more than Alec spending time in Caster made him a lowborn.

She hurried toward the main entrance. It was late enough that the usual line of people seeking healing had already gone home for the day. In the morning, the line would re-form, and hundreds of people would approach, all of them carrying money, seeking help with whatever ailment plagued them. It still seemed ironic to Sam that Alec had been willing to come to the university, especially after his comments about their requirements that forced people to sacrifice so much of their coin just to get some help. That had bothered him so much from the moment she first met him, but he seemed more at peace with it now. Maybe it bothered him when he wasn't a part of it.

Sam shook away that thought. That wasn't the Alec she knew. She could be frustrated, but she should be frustrated with herself.

As she approached the entrance, she reached into a pocket in her cloak and felt for the sheet of easar paper she had put there. Bastan had offered her a single sheet, claiming that was all she would need, but she'd held out for more. If she had to face Marin, if she had to somehow confront her, she wanted a greater chance for augmentations. More than that, she wanted a chance to practice with Alec and would need more easar paper.

Would Alec still even want to practice with her?

It had been weeks since they'd had a chance to practice together. The only time they'd had together had been when Elaine had been injured, and Bastan had brought Alec from the university to help heal her.

Maybe he was more intrigued with what he was learning at the university than practicing as her Scribe. He'd been very interested in working as her Scribe before he'd been accepted to the university, but maybe that had changed. Maybe the university held some sway over him that she could not. Maybe he would rather use his intelligence to learn things that could benefit others, and not just work with Sam, augmenting her.

She had to stop thinking like that. Alec was her friend.

There was nobody at the main entrance, and Sam tried the door but found it locked.

She knocked. It was a heavy, thunderous sound. She waited, and moments passed before anyone appeared at the door. When the door opened, she was greeted by a young man wearing a simple brown robe belted with rope. She wasn't sure if he was a junior physicker or a student. He looked at her, a hard frown on his face.

"It's much too late for any healing."

"I'm here to see one of your students."

"The students aren't allowed to heal without a master's approval."

"I'm a friend," Sam said.

"Who is the student?"

"Alec Stross."

The man considered her a moment longer before he nodded. He disappeared, leaving her standing at the door, wondering whether she should follow him, or if she should wait.

"Come along then," he called out from down the hall.

Sam shrugged and stepped into the entrance hall. The door started to close, and she took a few more steps to keep from being hit by it. The man waited in the distance, and Sam hurried to catch up to him, and he continued down the hall. The university was nicely decorated, but not nearly as nice as the palace. The stonework was well done, mostly marble. She winced at the thudding of her heavy footsteps, noting the young man's steps were all but silent. Lanterns lit the hall, keeping it bright, and revealed sculptures placed periodically along the hallway. A few tapestries hung along the walls, as well, and her time with Bastan, and in the palace, had given her something of an idea of the quality of the various tapestries.

He led her to a wide stairway, and up. He kept a steady pace and made no effort to speak to her, so Sam refrained, as well. He seemed more put out that she was there than anything, and she didn't want to annoy him any more than was necessary. On the third landing, he veered off and down the hall. The university was enormous, and they made several turns, Sam quickly getting lost as she went, before he paused in front of a door and knocked.

When the door opened, Sam saw Beckah standing behind it. "Can I help—"

The woman cut off when she saw Sam.

"I'm looking for Alec Stross," the young man said.

"He's here," Beckah said, pulling the door open.

Alec sat at a desk and looked up from the book he'd been reviewing. His eyes showed surprise when he saw Sam in the doorway.

"Sam?"

"I need your help. Bastan asked—"

Sam cut off and looked around the room, realizing that she needed to be more careful. If the message from Bastan was anything close to accurate, it might get Alec into some sort of trouble, which she had no intention of doing. Regardless of whatever relationship was brewing between him and this Beckah, he was still her friend. And he was her Scribe. She needed to keep that in mind. There had never been anything more between Sam and Alec, regardless of what she thought she might have felt growing there.

"She's fine, Matthias."

Sam realized that Alec was talking to the man who had escorted her to his room, and Alec's familiarity in addressing him by his first name told her he was likely a fellow student.

The young man shrugged. "Students aren't allowed visitors this late."

"She serves the princess," Alec said.

Beckah's eyes widened as she looked at Sam with renewed interest.

The fellow student glanced over, his mouth pressed into a disbelieving frown. Had it not been true, Sam wouldn't have believed Alec, either. It was an outrageous claim, one that made no sense to her, even though in some ways, she did serve the princess.

"Why would the princess send a servant here?"

Alec met the man's eyes. "Because I serve the princess, as well." There was a clear disdain between the two of them, and that was likely the reason Alec shared as much as he did. He had never been so open about what she and he did.

"I'll make sure the masters know that you had a visitor," Matthias said.

"You do that. Make sure you inform Master Helen particularly."

Matthias glared at Alec before turning and letting his glare linger on Sam for a moment as he departed.

When he was gone, Alec motioned her in. "Don't mind him," he said. "He's not the nicest student. Smart, but he's not always pleasant."

Sam glanced from Alec to Beckah, pushing away the questions that came to mind.

"Alec, I need your help. Bastan sent me here with a message."

"Why would Bastan send you here with a message for me?" Alec asked.

She met his gaze and silently tried to hint for him to have Beckah leave. Sam didn't want to have this conversation in front of her. Maybe she should pull out her canal staff and smack it over the woman's forehead.

She was irrational, but that was only because she felt more and more like a drifter, as if she had no place of belonging. She no longer really belonged in Caster. Tray no longer wanted her, and Bastan would use her, but that was not her home, regardless of what he might claim. And she wasn't a highborn. She did not belong in the palace, in spite of the fact that Elaine—and the princess—and welcomed her, offering to train her, and setting her up with a person who could help her master her canal staff. She had nowhere, and no one.

For a time, she'd thought the two of them would be something, but Alec looked comfortable in this room, the university fitting him in a way that nothing seemed to fit her.

After everything was done, where would her home be?

Maybe the answers would come from Marin. If she could force her to talk to her, to tell her what happened, and to share why she'd hidden Sam's memories from her, maybe she would finally learn where her true home was supposed to be.

Alec watched her, but so did Beckah.

"I ran into Tray out in the Yalling section."

"What? How did you find him? How is he?"

"It's a long story that I can tell later. I asked him to send a message to Marin to find me at Bastan's tavern."

"Oh, Sam. Are you sure that was the right thing to do?"

"The right thing? I don't know what the right thing is. All I know is that I want answers, and Marin has them. And if we can keep.... *them...* out of the city, then it will be worth it."

She knew she sounded hurt, and hated that she did, especially with Alec. No, especially around this other woman.

Sam could see the way Beckah watched him, the interested expression that she had, the distrust that she showed for Sam. This was a woman clearly enamored with Alec. It was a feeling that Sam understood.

"And you told Bastan of your request to Tray? He's okay that you made his tavern your meeting place?"

"Well, everything has a price with Bastan, right? Hence, I am here with his message."

"What kind of message?"

Sam glanced at Beckah. Alec followed the direction of her gaze.

"You can talk in front of Beckah."

"Alec—"

Alec shook his head. "Beckah is a friend. I trust her."

Sam bit back her retort. She didn't want to make Alec feel any worse. Hadn't Sam forced him into situations that had made him uncomfortable? Hadn't she exposed him to people that were less than reputable, making him interact with people like Bastan, and for that matter, Marin?

"Bastan sent me with a message that said you might be able to answer."

"So, what is it?"

Sam shook her head. "It doesn't make any sense. He said that he needed me to find the man who is dead but not dead." And somehow, Bastan thought that had something to do with the merchants—and Marin. He hadn't explained why. "He seemed to think that you would know what that means and seems to think that you can help."

Alec looked at Beckah. "That can't be a coincidence."

"It does seem a little peculiar," she said.

"We haven't heard anything one way or the other. I don't know if the thistle root made a difference."

"I think we would've heard something if it had."

"Maybe not. If the masters were afraid of it getting out that they had misdiagnosed…"

"But they hadn't misdiagnosed it. It just might have been too late."

"We don't even know if the foxglove poisoning was the right diagnosis. We are trusting that it was, only because Master Carl claimed it was."

"You took the foxglove," Beckah said. "You were in the hospital for over twelve hours because of it."

Sam stepped forward. "I don't have any idea what the two of you are talking about. But clearly, you understand Bastan's message?"

Alec turned to her. "I think I understand what he's getting at but am not sure that it's possible to find the person he wants us to find."

"Why?"

"Because he's either dead and incinerated, or he lived and has left the university."

27

SEARCH FOR ANSWERS

Alec glanced at Sam as they made their way through the university. He shouldn't be uncomfortable around her—he knew that he shouldn't—but that didn't change the fact that he was. There was something about having both Beckah and Sam present in the same place that left him unsettled. Alec had never been in a situation where he had two women where he was competing for their attention.

That wasn't quite right—it was the women who were competing for *his* attention.

He felt conflicted. He loved spending time with Sam, and loved the fact that the two of them had the shared bond of both Kaver and Scribe, something that he had never expected to experience, but was that all that was between them? He liked to think they shared more of a connection than that, but in the last few months, that was really all that had bound them together.

Then there was Beckah. The connection between them was different, built on a shared interest in healing and study. She challenged him in ways that he had never been challenged before, and that was very appealing. But he felt a bit guilty that he wanted to share those experiences with Beckah.

They reached the stairs leading down into the morgue. Would this man even still be there? Alec didn't think it likely. He would have been incinerated.

"Why do you think Bastan wants this man?" Alec asked.

Sam looked over and shrugged. "I don't know. It's Bastan. He could want him simply because the man owes him money."

That didn't seem quite right, not to Alec. There was something more to it—though he didn't know what it could be. Did it have to do with the fact that Master Carl had been involved? There was something about the master that made Alec uncomfortable.

"I'm not even sure where to find him," Alec said.

"How do you know about him?" Sam asked. She seemed to make a point of ignoring Beckah, who walked only a few paces behind Alec.

For his part, Alec tried not to spend too much time looking at either of them. At other times in the university, Beckah might have slipped her hand into his, something that Alec would have otherwise enjoyed, much as he enjoyed the vibrant way that Beckah had about her. With Sam being here, as well, Alec didn't want Beckah to take his hand, mostly because he still wasn't sure how he felt about either of them.

"One of the masters brought a man to us to study. He had been given something called foxglove. It's a treatment that slows the heart and gives a person the appearance of being dead."

"Appearance?" This time, Sam did look from Alec to Beckah.

Alec nodded. "Only the appearance. This man wasn't dead, at least not that we knew."

"Alec was the one who recognized that something wasn't quite right," Beckah said.

Sam again glanced from Alec to Beckah. "Is that right? Well, I'm not surprised. Alec always has had a way with healing. The very first time I met him, he made a point of saving my life."

"Oh?" Beckah said. "How long ago did you meet Alec?"

"I've known Alec now for months. At least I thought I did."

"Stop. You know me," Alec said.

Sam only shrugged. "I thought I knew you. But the Alec I knew was interested in healing as a calling."

"Are you implying that Alec is no longer interested in healing as a calling?" Beckah said. "Because if that's the case, I would argue that you don't know Alec nearly as well as you claim. Alec is not interested in healing for financial gain. In fact, I think he makes some of the masters uncomfortable because he would just as soon offer healing to anyone, regardless of ability to pay."

Sam rounded on Beckah. "You don't think it should be?"

"What I think isn't the issue. That decision isn't up to me."

"If it were, how would you respond?"

"As I said. That decision isn't up to me."

Sam smiled. "That seems to be an easy way out of answering."

Beckah glanced at Alec. He wondered how she would answer. They'd never had a conversation about her thoughts on healing others. Many in the university felt much like the master physickers did, believing that only those with means deserved a chance for healing, which meant only highborns or those with money. Alec didn't think there were many like him, who felt that healing should be offered to anyone in need, regardless of their capacity to pay. Maybe that was why his father had left the university.

"I came to the university with particular beliefs, but those have been challenged in my time here."

Sam watched her for a moment, almost seeming to wait for her to say something else, but Beckah didn't take that bait.

"What if he's not still here?" Alec asked as they reached the door to the morgue.

"Still?" Sam asked.

Sam glanced over at Alec. "You've been down here before?" she asked.

Alec nodded. "When we learned about foxglove. Part of the lesson involved the students taking a sample of it, and when we did, it slowed our hearts, but it affected me more strongly than others."

"That's why you were in the hospital for twelve hours?"

Alec sighed. "Apparently, that happens from time to time. I came around."

"What does that have to do with this man?"

Alec leaned against one of the cots, and it started to

slide across the floor. He swore under his breath and stood up, feeling disrespectful of the dead by swearing in their presence. There was something about this place that called for a more solemn air. He didn't want to be the person to disrupt that.

"There was a patient brought to the classroom. He had apparently been dosed with foxglove, which stopped—or seemingly stopped—his heart."

"And you thought to help him?" Sam asked.

Alec smiled sheepishly. "The university doesn't have the antidote. I figured that my father might."

"Why wouldn't the university have the antidote? You'd think with all of these physickers, and all of this brain-power, that they would have a way to reverse poisons like that, especially if it's common enough that they can administer it in the classroom."

Alec frowned to himself. "I didn't think about it that way."

Sam looked up at him. "You didn't? You mean, I thought of something the great Alec Stross did not?"

He shook his head. "I don't understand why the university wouldn't have the thistle root, but when I was hospitalized, they didn't have a supply there, either."

"I'm assuming that your apothecary shop did?"

"It did. We tested it."

Sam glanced from Beckah to Alec. "We?"

"Well, Beckah tested it. She ingested a chunk of the foxglove, followed by a dose of the thistle root that we were able to find in my father's shop to see if it was enough to counteract the poisonous effects."

Sam chewed on the inside of her lip, her attention focused on Beckah. "Did it work?"

"We're not entirely sure. It worked on Beckah. I mean she showed the symptoms of having taken the poison, lost consciousness, and awoke. So, we managed to prove that giving the thistle root immediately after taking the foxglove is successful, but what we don't know is if there is a time limit after which the antidote would be of no effect."

"So, you came here, and you gave it to this man," Sam said.

"We tried. I used all of the remaining thistle root that my father had. It left us with nothing else. I gave all of it to this man, but…"

"But?"

"There wasn't a response. If it worked, we didn't stay long enough."

"So, we go in. We have nothing to lose," Sam said.

"But if he's not here, I don't know where else we might look. We know nothing about the man."

"There would be one other option, but it would be dangerous," Beckah said.

"What option?" Sam asked.

"It would involve breaking into one of the masters' quarters and searching for evidence."

Alec shot Beckah a hard look. "You can't be serious. You can't actually think to break into Master Carl's room because he might have this man sequestered there."

Beckah's shrugged. "If he's not in the morgue, and we believe he's not incinerated, then where else would he be?"

"We're getting ahead of ourselves, anyway," Alec started. "We don't even know if he's still here or not."

"If he's not, there's a log. We can look for a record of

somebody with foxglove toxicity, and if there's not anyone listed, that means that he wasn't incinerated."

"There's a log? How is it that you know this?"

Beckah looked past him. "Come on. Let's see if your man is still here."

She pushed past Alec and Sam and shoved the door open. The inside of the morgue was much the same as the last time Alec had been here. There were dozens of metal cots, each containing a body. Sam gasped and covered her mouth as she gagged.

"The smell," she said.

"You get used to it," Alec said.

Sam arched a brow at him. "You might get used to it, but do you really want to?"

"Not really."

"This is where they keep the bodies?" Sam asked.

"This is where some bodies are kept. There are others that never reach here," Beckah said. She wandered through the morgue, looking at each face as she passed. Alec had a sinking suspicion that they wouldn't find him. Even if he hadn't died—and he found that unlikely—there didn't seem much of a chance that he would still be here. It had been days since they'd attempted giving him the thistle root, and if it had worked, he would have been gone long ago.

"How often do they take the bodies from here?" Sam asked.

Beckah had reached the table at the back of the morgue and opened a book that lay on top of it. She flipped through the pages. "It depends. Sometimes, they'll go nearly a week before taking a body away from here.

Other times, when there are too many, they take them down to the incinerator and dispose of them."

Alec and Sam stood near the door, not venturing into the sea of cots.

"There is no record of anyone with foxglove toxicity going to the incinerators," Beckah said. "Then again, there's no record of anyone with foxglove toxicity getting out of here, either." She stared at Alec and shrugged. "Chances are he didn't make it, and they just didn't record it correctly."

If that was what happened, then they wouldn't find the man. Bastan wouldn't get him, which left him wondering whether Bastan would still give Sam the easar paper.

If Marin returned, and if she tried to attack Sam, Alec wanted her to have all the help she could get, and that meant augmentations, and that meant easar paper.

"We can try Master Carl's rooms," he started.

Sam shook her head. "I can tell by the tone of your voice that you don't think that's likely to work."

Alec shrugged. "I don't know, but I can at least try. I don't want anything to happen to you, which means we have to find this man."

Sam looked past him, focusing her attention on Beckah, and said, "I think you've got a new study partner."

"That doesn't mean I want anything to happen to you," Alec said.

Sam swallowed, ignoring his searching gaze. "Let's go find this master and see if there's anything we can learn."

BASTAN'S MAN

"How much farther?" Sam asked.

Beckah looked back at her, an odd question in her eyes. Sam still didn't like her, but the woman had been helpful. "Not much."

"How do you know how to find the masters' quarters?" Sam asked.

"Sam. She's helping," Alec chided her.

"She says she's helping. Alec, how much do you know about her?" she asked, lowering her voice hoping Beckah didn't hear.

The slight tension in Beckah's back made it clear that Sam hadn't been nearly as quiet as she had intended. Maybe it didn't matter. If the woman discovered how Sam felt about her, what did that matter?

"I know that she's helped me study. I know that she's helped me when I've been injured."

"How often are you getting injured at the university?" Sam asked.

"More often than you would imagine," he said.

They reached a doorway at the end of the hall, and Beckah slipped something out of her pocket, quickly opening the door with it.

Had she just broken into the room or did she have a key? If she used a key, why would Beckah have key access to the master levels?

Alec didn't seem to notice—or if he did, he didn't care. Maybe he'd become too enthralled with Beckah to pay attention to things like that, but she was not.

"Was it locked?" Sam asked.

Beckah ignored her and hurried up the stairs.

"Sam, you need to be nicer to her. She's trying to help."

"Or is she only appearing to try to help?"

Alec watched her, seeming to debate whether she was being serious. Sam was, at least mostly. She didn't know anything about Beckah, and she didn't like the fact that Beckah seemed so familiar with Alec, but Sam didn't have any tie to him other than him serving as her Scribe—and that had been minimal lately.

A wide stairway led up, and Beckah continued without pausing. "She seems to know her way around," Sam said.

A troubled look finally came to Alec's face. "So it seems."

"Nothing about that bothers you?"

"Sam—"

They reached a landing, and Beckah hurried off down the hallway. She stopped at a door at the end of the hall. "This is Master Carl's room."

"How do you know?" Alec asked.

"Because Master Carl is—"

"Your father?" Sam asked. It would be perfectly fitting

for the man who wanted to poison Alec to have been related to his new girlfriend.

"Not my father," she said, a look of disgust on her face. "I've had to come here before."

"Why would you have to come here?" Alec asked.

Beckah glanced from Alec to Sam, seeming to debate her answer. For a moment, Sam wondered if she would even say anything. Maybe she would avoid the question, which would only lead Alec to question her more. Sam couldn't help but feel a sense of satisfaction at that.

"I used to be a messenger," Beckah said.

"A messenger? Highborns aren't messengers."

"They are if they want to get into the university and can't," Beckah said. She looked at Alec, making a point to ignore Sam. "I barely belong here, but they couldn't keep me out any longer. I've tested four times, and each time, I was certain that I would gain admission. When I got notification this time…"

"I don't understand why you would hide this," he said.

Sam laughed. "You don't? It's because you're too close to the highborns to really understand. When you don't have something, and you really want it, you'd do anything for it," Sam said. She hated that she was speaking on behalf of Beckah, but this was something Alec had to understand.

"When have I ever seemed to care about class?" he asked Beckah.

"You haven't," she replied. "I have. I need to continue to progress through the university to maintain my status. My failures have been a huge disappointment to my parents. They stopped talking to me until I was finally able to get into the university."

"But you barely have to study," Alec said.

"Barely? I study all the time. I only give you a hard time about it because you seem to know so much already. Every moment that I'm not in my room studying, I'm looking for something else that I can study."

"But—"

Sam stepped forward, and between the two of them. "Can the two of you have this conversation another time? I think that whatever else, we need to keep moving, and shouldn't remain here for too long. I mean, you said this is the master's quarters."

Alec glanced from Beckah to Sam before nodding. "What do you propose?"

"I think I should go in," Sam said. She'd been thinking about the options as they'd followed Beckah through the halls, and it was the only one that made any sense. If either Alec or Beckah went into one of the masters' quarters and was caught, it would likely mean expulsion from the university. Sam didn't necessarily mind that for Beckah, but she did not want that for Alec.

Sam, on the other hand, had no such issues. What would it matter if she were caught?

Better yet, if she had some augmentation, it was possible that she wouldn't be caught.

"You don't even know what this man looks like," Alec said.

"I know enough that he's dead but not dead. Don't you think I can find that?"

"How will you get in and then out?" Alec asked.

Sam slipped the sheet of easar paper out of her pocket. "Practice," she said, trying to avoid meeting Beckah's gaze.

Alec glanced from Beckah to Sam before nodding. "It

might be the best chance we have," he said. "I'm not sure that I like the idea of you going in there on your own, but it might be our only choice."

"What are the two of you talking about?" Beckah asked.

Sam wasn't sure what Alec would answer. Would he share with Beckah—a woman that he clearly had a connection to—that he was a Scribe and that Sam was a Kaver? There would be questions if he did, and they would be forced to share more than what Sam wanted, but she would trust Alec in this. It was his decision to make about how much to share.

"Beckah, you should head back down. If you're caught here—"

Beckah shook her head. "I won't get in trouble if I'm caught here. I used to be a messenger."

"But you're not now."

"What of you? What happens if you're caught?"

"I won't be caught. I'll follow you in just a minute."

Beckah let out a sigh, flickering her gaze from Sam to Alec before nodding. "Don't linger for too long." She took Alec's hand and squeezed it.

Sam turned away, her heart fluttering and nausea rising in her stomach. Those were emotions she shouldn't feel, that she didn't deserve to feel. Alec had every right to establish friendships—and more—at the university. She shouldn't—and couldn't—begrudge him those.

Beckah disappeared back down the hall.

"We should hurry," Alec said.

Sam nodded and held her hand out. Alec took a knife out of his pocket and made a small nick in the palm of her hand, doing the same with his. When blood oozed to the surface, he scooped it with the knife and smeared it together with his finger.

"This will be rough," he said. "I don't have a pen or any other way to mix this efficiently."

"It will work. We've tried it this way before."

Alec nodded. "I remember."

"I thought that you might have forgotten."

Alec took her hand in his and squeezed. "I won't forget what we can do."

Sam met his gaze. What they could do. Not what they could be. Not who they could be.

It hurt, but she tried to keep the hurt from her face.

"I hope this works well enough that we can keep you from getting caught," Alec said.

He used the tip of his finger and quickly started writing on the easar paper. "Speed and strength will help," she suggested.

"I know."

She closed her eyes, not looking as he continued to write. She didn't know what he would add but trusted that what he chose to write would be effective.

She felt it building within her.

"It's done," he said.

Sam opened her eyes, noting the easar paper with his handwriting across the page—still neat despite using his finger—detailing the method of augmenting her. She grabbed the paper, re-folded it, and stuffed it back into her pocket.

"You don't want me to hang on to that?" Alec asked.

She shook her head. "I can hang on to it. I think Bastan needs to know that I'll return with it."

Alec tried to hide the hurt in his eyes but failed. "I should…"

Sam nodded. "You should head back down with Beckah. I'll find you in the same place as before?"

Alec glanced at the door. "Not the same place. Let's meet in the courtyard outside the university. That way, if you need to escape quickly, you'll be someplace that you can do it."

Was he trying to get rid of her? Or was he simply thinking through it, wanting her to get to safety?

Sam tried not to get caught up in the possibilities. Doing so would only end up with her confused and hurt.

"Go. I'll be fine."

Alec squeezed her hand and then took off down the hall, moving quickly before disappearing altogether.

Sam stood in front of the door, her body tingling. The augmentation had taken hold, appearing quickly. Everything around her seemed to move more slowly, but she knew that was the augmentation for speed. It was she moving more quickly, not things around her moving more slowly. She was eager to test the augmentation, eager to find out whether it would work, but first, she had to break into the room and see if the man who wasn't dead was inside.

If nothing else good came of her visit to the university, at least she had an opportunity to have an augmentation once more. There was something right about it, something that felt good to her.

She tested the door handle and found it locked.

What she did next would reveal her presence, and she knew that there would be no backing down at that point. She could use her strength augmentation to break the handle, but once she did, there would be no concealing the fact that she had been here.

Instead, Sam jerked on the door handle once sharply, forcing the lock within to release. With a loud snap, the handle twisted. The breach would be discovered soon enough, but it was subtler than a broken handle. She pushed, opening the door and stepped inside.

It was an open room, and empty. She saw no one here, nothing that would indicate that the master both Beckah and Alec were concerned about had been here. There was a bed against each wall, each with a trunk at its foot. Shelves rose in between the two beds, and a long table ran along one wall, books stacked on top of it. In the corner was another shelf, this one filled with what appeared to be various medicines. It was similar to what she had seen at Alec's apothecary.

As she took a closer look at the nearest bed, she realized its sheets were disheveled and lumpy. Sam darted over and pulled back the sheets. There was no one there.

Sam sniffed at the air, wishing for a moment that Alec had augmented her sense of smell, as well. There was a hint of a medicinal odor in the air that also carried the scent of various treatments, which reminded her even more of the apothecary.

Beneath it, was something of a sickly odor. This was nothing like the apothecary and left her with an unsettled stomach.

She should have asked Alec to stay with her. He would have recognized the different medicines on the shelf.

Was there anything there that was useful?

Sam hurried to the shelf and scanned it. She noticed leaves in several of the jars, each of a different shape and color. Another jar had what looked to be berries. And another had something like long, thorny twigs.

Sam paused. What had Alec said about the thistle root? They had made an offhand comment about the texture, and the barbs along it.

But, if this was thistle root, why would the master not have used it on Alec when he'd accidentally taken too much?

Sam grabbed the jar and stuffed it into the pocket of her cloak. If nothing else, Alec could replace what he'd taken from his father's shop.

Nothing else on the shelf was familiar. Alec—or Beckah, she had to admit—might have known what was here, but she did not.

She started to turn when something about the nearby wall caught her attention. It was different—and just different enough that she stared at it a moment before realizing why it looked different.

It was a door.

Sam hurried over to it, running her hand along the edge. Her time with Bastan had taught her to notice things like this. Hidden doors were something he was quite fond of. But how was she to open it?

She ran her hand along the edge, looking for a seam, something that might trigger a hinge. There had to be a room on the other side, but she had to find a way to reach it.

But there was no handle, no hidden latch, nothing.

She pressed on the wall.

Something clicked deep within it, and Sam stepped back. The wall had popped out slightly.

Was the entire section a trigger?

She ran her fingers under the raised edge and pried the door open.

On the other side was a room, as she had expected. In it, Sam noted a single cot, but it was empty. There was another row of small jars on a table, and these looked different from the ones in the other room. Sam took a view of the jars and stuffed them into her pockets. Alec could look at them later and maybe tell her what they were.

A moan came from behind her, and she turned her attention back to the cot.

Was it not as empty as she had thought?

Sam hurried over and found a man lying on the ground, his wrists and ankles bound. He had dark hair and what appeared to be a scruffy beard but appeared unharmed. Was this the man that Bastan sought? Was this the man that Alec and Beckah had tried to help?

If it was, why would he be in Master Carl's hidden chamber? Why did Master Carl even *have* a hidden chamber?

Sam lifted him, the augmentations given to her by Alec making her strong enough to carry a man of this size. He moaned again as she did. Sam debated what to do. If this was the man who'd been in a dead sleep for days, who knew when he might awaken. She didn't know how long she had to wait. So, her only alternative was to carry him from the chamber—and hope that her strength augmentation lasted long enough to get them both to safety.

But she also had speed.

She cradled him in her arms and ran out of the hidden chamber. On the other side, she hurried to the door just as it started to open.

Sam hesitated. What would happen if Master Carl appeared—and if he had been the one tormenting this man?

It would be dangerous for her to be caught. She had been seen within the university before, and could be associated with Alec, which she wasn't certain was safe for him, either.

Hoping for the best, she ducked behind the door as someone stepped in. Sam kicked the door and heard a loud crack, followed by a thud as the person fell to the floor.

She bounded around the door, jumping over the fallen form, and raced down the hall, hurrying back toward the entrance to the masters' quarters. She didn't stop as she passed through the door and didn't stop as she raced through the halls of the university, already feeling the flagging of the augmentations. Much longer, and they would fade completely, and she would be left with nothing. She needed to get to the courtyard, to Alec, so that she could get to safety.

When she reached the front door to the university, she barreled through it, ignoring a shout that came from behind her.

Sam stumbled out into the courtyard, searching for Alec—or for Beckah—but neither was there.

Sam stood there, heart racing even as her augmentations began to fade. Without Alec and his ability to augment her again, she would be caught, and this man would be taken back to endure whatever torture she'd rescued him from.

29

KAVERS FIGHT

S am was ready to collapse. Carrying the man had been difficult, but now, with the augmentation gone, and she could no longer hold herself up. Her body ached, and her palm throbbed where Alec had nicked her skin to draw the blood for the augmentations.

That was new. It was unusual for her to have pain in her hand when the augmentations wore off. Had Alec done something different? Maybe it had been the blunt way that he'd used the blood ink to write them.

Or there could be any number of other possible answers. She still didn't know much about her abilities because Elaine hadn't trained her well enough.

Where was Alec?

If he didn't come help her, she didn't think she'd be able to cross the bridge to get out of this section. Even if he did come, she wasn't sure she'd have the strength to move. The effort she used to carry this man had drained her, and she wondered if attempting other augmentations would be too much for her. They had rarely attempted repeated augmentations.

If only she understood that better.

She saw a figure exit the university, but it was too short to be Alec. Was it one of the other physickers? In her haste to escape, she'd shouldered past several physickers at the door. Could they have come after her?

"You have been hard to find," a voice said.

Sam frowned. She recognized that voice, though it took a moment for her to understand why.

"Marin?"

Marin stepped closer, and in the moonlight, she managed to see the woman more clearly. "Samara. I understand that you sent word for me to find you."

Sam's heart pounded as she realized she would have to face Marin alone. Without benefit of augmentation. "I sent word for you to find me at Bastan's tavern."

Marin stepped closer, and she smiled. "Bastan thought you might be here."

Had Bastan told Marin how to find Sam?

No. Bastan wouldn't have betrayed Sam. He wanted to protect her. He wouldn't have done anything that would have caused her any harm.

"What did Bastan tell you?"

Marin continued to approach, inching closer and closer to her. Sam reached for her canal staff and prepared to assemble it, but Marin smiled as she did.

"Samara. You have no need to do anything quite so foolish."

"Don't I?"

"I've only ever tried to protect you."

Renewed anger at Marin's deception surged through

her. "You can't make that claim, Marin. I've learned what you did to me."

Marin arched a brow. "What I did? I think whoever told you might have been mistaken."

"No. My mother didn't die fighting alongside you. You told me that so you could attempt to control me. I don't know how you did it, but somehow, whatever you've done has been with the intent to prevent me from reaching my Kaver abilities."

"I'm not sure how you could believe that, especially since I was the one who shared with you what your abilities meant."

"You didn't share that with me. You tried to hide them from me. And then you disappeared when I had questions."

"Samara." Marin took a step closer and nodded toward the unconscious man at Sam's feet. "I'm going to need to have words with that man."

"Why? What is he to you?"

Marin shook her head. "It doesn't matter. But I need you to release him."

Sam wished she still had her augmentations so that she could lift the man and carry him away, and prevent Marin from getting too close, but they had faded, leaving her weak, with barely any strength of her own remaining.

"Tell me who he is to you?"

"I think I'm done sharing with you."

"Have you shared the truth with Tray?"

Marin tensed but didn't take another step toward her.

"Because I know the truth."

"And what truth is that?"

"The same truth that you didn't want me to find out, I

suspect. It's the same truth that you've hidden from Tray. It's the truth of our connection, the truth of whatever bond there might actually be between us."

"There are reasons for what I've done."

Marin took another step toward her, and Sam prepared for the confrontation. She didn't like the odds of succeeding if forced to face off with Marin. Marin had already proven herself to be more skilled than Sam.

Where was Alec? If he would show up, she could at least try to get an augmentation, but that would require that he get more of her blood. And that just wasn't possible if she had to fend off Marin.

Sam glanced at the man lying on the ground, still unmoving. No matter why Marin wanted him, Sam had to prevent her from taking him. She'd rescued him from whatever the university masters were trying to do to him and was prepared to continue to keep him safe. Somehow. She wasn't entirely certain how she would do that.

"Samara, don't do anything foolish."

"I should say the same to you," Sam said.

"Just hand him over, and you and I can have a conversation."

"Who is he to you?"

"Just a part of a plan. A key part, since you interfered with my other plan."

"I didn't interfere."

"You have always interfered."

"The merchants?" Sam asked, watching Marin warily. "What did you want with them?"

"Not them. What they bought."

"Which was?"

Marin took another step, and Sam would have backed

up, but doing so would have left the man unprotected. She watched Marin, prepared for any sudden movement, but Marin was approaching slowly, carefully.

Did she think that Sam was augmented? If she did, was there some way that Sam could take advantage of that?

Marin's gaze dipped down to the man. "I will be taking him from you, Samara."

Sam took that opportunity to reach for her canal staff and jerked it free of her belt.

Marin smiled tightly. "That's how you want it to be?"

"What's your plan? I know you intend to bring Thelns into the city." Marin didn't respond. "Were you responsible the last time?"

"That was not on me," Marin said dangerously.

"Why now?"

"You can't understand," she whispered.

"Try me. You're the one forcing this. All I want is you to answer my questions."

"We're beyond answering questions now. And you've made a mistake. One lesson I've made clear to you is that you must learn to live with your mistakes, Samara."

Marin pulled out the two pieces of her canal staff and bolted forward, moving quickly. It was fast—but not augmented fast.

Sam swung her staff's two pieces around, blocking Marin's initial attack. Then quickly jammed the ends of her canal staff together, forming a whole. Marin didn't, leaving hers disconnected, and slung them separately, a flurry of attacks at Sam.

Had she not had her staff lessons with Thoren, she wouldn't have had any way of fending her off, but she had improved in her skills in the time since she had last faced

Marin. Sam managed to block most of the attacks and had learned to prepare herself for those that slipped past.

As Marin neared her, a dark grin spread across her face. "You've gotten some instruction."

"Are you disappointed?"

"On the contrary, I'm thrilled."

Marin danced around her and caught her in the back. Sam staggered forward, but jammed her staff into the ground, managing to right herself. She flipped the end of her staff up and caught Marin on the leg. It was a glancing blow, barely enough to slow the woman, but it disrupted the flow of her movements.

Sam flipped up onto the tip of her staff, holding herself upright as she'd once been taught, and quickly considered her options.

Marin didn't give her long. She kicked at the bottom of Sam's staff, forcing her to flip up once more, and spin around. She landed with her staff swinging out in a sweeping arc. Marin jumped over the end of her staff, dancing backward with a hint of a laugh.

"He hasn't lost his touch, has he?"

Sam spun, bringing her staff around, and barely missing Marin. "Who?"

"Thoren. I can tell that you've spent time working with him. You reveal yourself with the technique you use," Marin said.

"What does that say about you?"

"I use many techniques," Marin said. "It reveals nothing."

She spun the staff again, dancing toward Sam. The free ends of her staff moved too quickly for Sam to follow, and she could only block half of the attacks. It wasn't enough.

Sam stumbled. As she fell, she realized that she'd tripped over the body of the man she'd been trying to save. If she didn't do something—anything—she would lose him, and the opportunity to learn whatever the reason was that the masters at the university thought to keep him hidden in that room as they had.

Sam started to get up, but her body ached from the attacks.

"Consider this another lesson, Samara. Be prepared when facing a superior opponent."

"Prepared for what?" Sam asked, swinging her staff around, trying to catch Marin with at least a lucky blow. So far, she'd managed nothing.

"Prepared for defeat."

Two things happened at once. Marin leaped toward Sam, and Sam felt a strange tingling throughout her.

An augmentation.

Alec.

She pushed off with her staff, moving quickly, and it took a moment for her to realize that it wasn't strength or speed that he augmented this time, but that he made her lighter.

They had practiced this before. She knew what it was like to be lighter, to move more quickly with her own strength. It was an augmentation that did not require as much energy from either the Kaver or the Scribe.

That was good, Sam wasn't sure how much she had to lend to any augmentation.

As Sam swung around, Marin eyed her. "Where is your Scribe? I've tried getting to him, but they've kept him protected here, haven't they?"

"You're not going to get to Alec."

"Get to him? I only want to borrow his skills. He would be useful to me."

Sam could only think of one way that Alec might be useful to Marin. Did she intend to use him for his ability to scribe? Was it even possible for her to do so?

Hearing that made her angrier than she had been. Anger wasn't always valuable in a fight. Thoren had made that clear to her when they'd practiced, but there was some benefit to it. It helped lift her waning strength and allowed her to refocus her energy.

There had to be some way of using her lightness to her advantage. When they had practiced with it before, what had she discovered? There was more to it than simply her being able to react more quickly, using her own strength to carry her farther. There was also the fact that she could jump higher and seemed to hang in the air when she did.

Sam gathered herself and pushed off. As she did, she swung her staff around, bringing it toward the ground, and hopefully toward Marin.

Marin seemed to recognize what Sam had done, and flipped upward, kicking at Sam with her pointed boots.

Sam was barely able to react in time, and swung the staff around, knocking her back.

Even augmented, she wasn't going to be able to easily beat Marin. Whatever it was that was special about Kavers, whatever innate ability they possessed, Sam did not have it. Maybe it was locked within her mind, much like her memories.

Marin smiled again, the two halves of her canal staff spinning. "I don't think that I'll end you. Let's consider this a lesson. Besides, you still have value to me."

Sam landed just as Marin struck her on the shoulder

with one half of her staff. The other she jammed into Sam's shoulder, and she realized it had been sharpened.

She screamed in pain. Where the staff pierced her shoulder, it burned. Her arm went numb and limp.

"Useful? I haven't been useful to you."

"Oh, but you have. You've always been useful to me in protecting Tray."

"Because you haven't wanted to tell him the truth?"

"He wouldn't understand the truth. It was better for him to think that I wasn't his mother than for him to know the truth. Much like it's better for you to believe what you think, rather than know the truth." Marin swung her staff again, and this time, it smacked into the side of Sam's head.

As her vision began to fade, she saw Marin grab the man Sam had rescued from the university, lifting him more easily than she should have been able to.

With her fading thoughts, she wondered—*had* Marin been augmented?

30

HOW TO SAVE A FRIEND

W hen Alec reached the entrance to the masters' quarters, he found Beckah waiting there.

"What is this? What are you trying to keep from me?" Beckah asked.

"I'm trying to keep Sam safe," Alec answered.

"Who is she to you? I know that she's not highborn—her skin is far too dark for that—but you two are close."

Alec nodded.

"Is she the one who's been visiting?" Beckah asked.

"Sam hasn't visited me at all. I know she wanted to, but she said that she couldn't reach me."

"Then it was somebody who must have looked like her. Which would surprise me because your friend is too small to be easily confused with someone else," Beckah said. "Is she the one you've gone over to see?"

"Too small?" Alec frowned. In the time since he'd known Sam, he'd encountered a few women who were about her size.

"Do you know who prevented her from getting access to the university?" Alec asked.

"I thought you said it wasn't she?"

"It might not have been, but that doesn't mean I don't need to know who it was. There's another alternative, one that is possibly worse."

"Worse? I thought you were excited to see this friend of yours."

Alec nodded. "I was, but now I'm concerned that someone who is very dangerous might have been getting into the university."

They hadn't seen Marin for months, and Sam believed that she might have left the city, but the city was enormous, and there were many places where she could hide.

There was another possibility, but it seemed too hard to believe. Could Marin have been hiding in the university all this time? Could she have been skulking around someplace?

If she had, why?

He needed Sam, but she was still inside Master Carl's quarters. If they were lucky, she'd find the man poisoned by the foxglove and get him out of there. He knew they had to return him to Bastan, but he hoped they could possibly heal him with the easar paper before that.

Alec glanced back at the door, looking for a sign that Sam might be coming. There was nothing.

What would happen if her augmentations failed while she was up there?

If they failed, she could get caught.

"Alec," Beckah said.

"What?"

She grabbed his arm and pulled, dragging him down the hall.

"Beckah, Sam is still in there."

She dragged him down the hall until they rounded a corner. When they did, she motioned down the hall, pointing in the direction of the entrance to the masters' quarters. When Alec looked, he saw that someone was coming. They'd been lucky so far and hadn't encountered anyone up to now, but the longer they stayed, the more likely it was that they would come across somebody trying to reach the masters' quarters. Worse would be if they came across Master Carl, but any of the masters would question their presence.

"Who is that?" Alec asked. It wasn't Master Carl. Carl was far too fat to be this man. The person coming down the hall was not slender, but certainly not as robust as Master Carl.

"I don't know," Beckah said.

Alec frowned. There was something familiar about the figure.

What was it?

He crept forward, ignoring Beckah pulling on his arm.

As he approached, there was something about the size —the muscularity—that he recognized. It was Tray. Alec was certain of it. Why would Tray be here? Alec hadn't seen him since Tray had caught him breaking into Marin's home.

Why would he have come to the university? And why would he try to get into the masters' quarters?

"Where are you going?" Beckah asked.

If Marin had been somehow hiding out in the university, maybe she'd asked Tray to meet her here. Tray didn't yet know that she was his mother, but she'd used him many times in the past and seemed to have no qualms about putting him in danger.

"I know who that is," Alec said.

"Who?"

"That's Sam's brother."

"Why would her brother be here?"

"I… I have no idea."

Alec's mind was racing trying to figure out what he needed to do. If it was possible that Marin was here, and with Tray definitely here, Sam needed help. Her augmentations would fail. He hadn't used enough blood to keep them functional. Had she only left him with the easar paper, he could make another quick note.

But… He had a piece.

"We have to get to my quarters," Alec said.

"You're going to leave your friend there?"

He shook his head. "Not leaving her. There's something I can do to help her, but I can't do it here."

"I'll help. Anything I can do, just let me know."

Alec should probably send her away. Sam would be angry that he allowed her to participate, but he needed help. He didn't think he could do this on his own.

"Good. I'm going to need you to keep an eye out for me."

He would have to tell her about his ability. What choice did he have?

"What's this about?" Beckah asked. "There is more to this than just finding the poisoned man, isn't there?"

"I didn't think so, but I'm beginning to realize there is, but I have no idea what or why."

They reached his room, and Alec hurried inside. He

grabbed his notes off the table, left there after Sam had appeared.

"What are you after?" Beckah asked.

Alec reached into the stack of notes and pulled out the slip of easar paper. He held it out, and Beckah took it from him, scanning the page.

"What is this?"

"It's called easar paper. There's something about it that grants specific abilities."

Beckah looked up at him, a frown etched on her face. "Abilities? It sounds a lot like you're trying to suggest to me that the paper is magical." Beckah looked back down to the page, and her eyes darted across it as she scanned what he'd written there when trying to help Elaine. "This is your description of the woman you helped in the outer section of the city, isn't it?"

"It is. There's something about the paper that when a specific combination of ink is used grants power. It has the potential to heal, as well as a few other things."

Beckah looked up with a frown. "What kind of combination of inks?"

"Mostly blood." Alec took the page from her and laid it down on the table, next to a few of the narrow pens he'd used before. He grabbed one and pulled out his knife, which still had a dried coating of their blood. He didn't know if it would work to moisten it again, but he had to try.

Using water from his basin, Alec scraped blood off of the knife and started. He dipped the pen into it and took a deep breath, preparing what he would write.

What did Sam need from him?

She'd had speed, and strength, which worked well with

an equal combination of their blood, but to help her now, he tried to think of what else they'd tried. It had been too long since they'd spent much time experimenting. In that time, his comfort and familiarity with the various ratios of blood needed to perform the specific augmentations had changed.

He didn't know what she might be facing. Maybe there was nothing. But if Tray—and Marin—were here, she might need whatever help he could offer.

If only he knew what help that was.

He grabbed his notebook and flipped to the page with notes detailing the various things they'd tried in the past.

Most had a specific ratio of blood, but in order for it to work well, many of them required a greater concentration. What he had now was weakened, diluted. He didn't know for certain whether it would work as he needed it to. If it didn't, did that mean that Sam would be stuck?

Worse, he didn't know what she actually needed. Help of some sort, but what kind?

He grabbed the page and his notebook, and carefully put what little blood ink he'd salvaged into a small vial, then raced to his door.

"Where are we going?" Beckah asked.

"The courtyard."

Alec ran, hurrying into the hall. When they reached the entrance to the university, he found two physickers lying motionless on the ground. They weren't his concern. Not yet.

He raced out the door and skidded to a stop in the courtyard.

Standing there, he saw Sam and a figure lying at her

feet. Was that the man they sought? But then he noticed someone else, as well.

"Marin," he said under his breath. Sam fought Marin, her staff moving more quickly than he could track, more quickly than he thought possible. How had she gotten so good?

Beckah glanced over at him. "Marin? Who's Marin?"

It was apparent that Marin was much more skilled than Sam. Marin was able to spin with more fluidity and easily countered each of Sam's attempts to stop her.

Was there anything Alec could do?

He dropped, and Beckah crouched next to him.

"What are you doing?"

"The only thing I can that will help her."

He pulled out his vial of ink. What would help her here?

An idea came to him, but he wasn't sure if it would work—or if Sam would be aware of the augmentation.

He started writing.

Beckah looked over his shoulder, peering at what he wrote. The scrawl was simple. It was the technique he'd practiced with her in the months before his coming to the university. It came back to him, though he wasn't certain if it would work.

"I don't understand," Beckah said.

"It's the paper. There is something about it."

Alec looked up, and Sam had been knocked to the ground. She lay there, just as Marin was about to attack, when her eyes widened slightly.

She jumped.

It was amazing to watch her do it, amazing to watch the way she quickly responded to the augmentation and flipped up into the air. She hung there a moment, her staff spinning around, and almost connecting with Marin, but the other woman was equally skilled—if not more so.

Marin was augmented. She had to be.

Sam landed and spun around, but Marin was there, smacking her on the side with one end of her canal staff. The other jammed into Sam's shoulder. She screamed.

Alec darted forward, but he wouldn't be fast enough. He wouldn't be able to reach her before Marin finish her.

With a sickening crack, Marin struck her on the side of the head and grabbed the man lying near them—likely the man they were to find—disappearing into the night.

Alec raced for Sam.

He ran his hand along the side of her head, noting the angry wound, the way that her scalp was split open from the last attack. One of her arms was damp, and he realized it was the blood flowing from where the staff had pierced her shoulder. His mind raced through poisons that might have been used, realizing that if he didn't treat her quickly enough, any poison that might have been on the tip of the staff would have too much time to set in, and might be irreversible.

She still had a pulse, and she still breathed. If nothing else, she lived. He didn't know how much longer she would, but for now, he had that.

"We need to get her into the hospital," Beckah said.

"Not the hospital."

"Alec, I know how much she means to you. We need to take her someplace where we can get her help. We're right here. I can go get one of the masters, and we'll do what we can to save her."

Alec closed his eyes, thinking. He couldn't use her

blood, not without knowing if it was poisoned. If it was, it would take too much strength out of her to enact the healing. That didn't leave him with many good options, but maybe Beckah was right. Maybe taking her into the university would be the only thing that could save Sam.

Why did it make him so uncomfortable?

"I need to take her to my apothecary," he said.

"Your father might be able to help her, but don't you think you'd be better able to help her here?"

It came down to what he believed. What did he believe about the university's ability to heal? He believed that they had knowledge and skill, but he also knew that once he had her stable, he could use his easar paper to complete the healing. Would the university allow that?

"I don't think I can leave her here for healing," Alec said.

"Alec—"

Alec shook his head. "They have prejudices that place her in more danger."

"Even if you could help her at the apothecary, you can't get her there. Your section of the city is too far from here. Are you willing to risk her safety for that?"

He wasn't, but he also wasn't sure that he could leave her here, not without knowing exactly what had been done to her. She was injured, but if it was more than just an injury, if it was a poisoning, as well, that was something he didn't think the university was completely prepared to manage.

At the same time, Beckah was right. He couldn't carry her—not quickly enough. If he tried, he'd end up either dropping her or she'd end up dying long before he could reach the apothecary.

He wanted to scream, to yell out to the gods and demand their help, but that wouldn't do anything. That wouldn't get him any of the assistance he needed.

Alec looked up, feeling helpless.

As he did, he realized there was another figure in the courtyard.

He hadn't seen him standing there, hidden in shadows, wrapped in a strange cloak that seemed to shift light around it, forcing his gaze away. But now that he knew the man was there, he couldn't help but see him.

"Tray." Alec stood and started toward him. He wasn't certain whether Tray would flee. "How long have you been here?" Alec asked.

"Long enough," he said.

"Long enough for what?"

Would Tray be upset that Sam had fought with Marin? Would he blame his sister for fighting with her? There was much that Tray didn't know, but Sam hadn't wanted him to know. She preferred to keep him in the dark, mostly so that he didn't have to deal with the stress of what had happened, but also because she wasn't completely sure what to say to him.

"Long enough to have heard."

Alec glanced back to Sam before turning and looking at Tray. "What did you hear?"

"It doesn't matter."

"Can you help? Sam is—"

Tray rounded on him, fury rising in his eyes. "Why should I help?"

"She's your sister."

"Is she? From what I heard, that's not even clear."

Alec licked his lips. Marin and Sam must've argued

about the nature of Tray's relationship to Sam. It didn't surprise Alec. It weighed on her, and she struggled with trying to understand what it meant for them.

"And what do you think this means for you? Do you think it means that Sam cares for you any less? The one identity she never lost, the one truth she held to was that she is your sister."

A trace of the anger faded from Tray's face. "Is it true?"

"I don't know," Alec answered. "Sam thought it was, but..."

"Why didn't she tell me?"

"She hadn't found you."

"She did. She had an opportunity to tell me, but she didn't."

"She found you?"

"She wanted me to get word to Marin. Now I think I understand why."

"No. That's not the entire reason why. Marin... did something to Sam... long ago, something that prevented her from remembering her life before Marin entered it."

"What do you mean that Marin did something to Sam?"

"I don't know what it was, but she somehow wiped Sam's memories from before. She took away what Sam knew of her family."

"Our mother died."

"I thought you didn't believe that?"

"I don't know what to believe."

"Then help me. I need to get Sam to—"

"Bastan. That's where she needs to go."

Would it help to take her to Bastan? He wouldn't have any of the necessary medicines that Alec might need, but then, he might have access to other things that Alec needed. He was well connected.

"Bastan is the one who sent her here," Alec said.

"I know," Tray said.

"Do you know who that man is to Marin?"

"I don't know anything about Marin," Tray said.

He lifted Sam, scooping her with no more effort than Marin had seemed to display when lifting the other man. He started toward the bridge and moved quickly.

"How did you get access to the university in the first place?" Alec asked.

"I don't need to use the bridges, if that's what you're asking," Tray said.

"That's not—"

Tray smiled. "And I don't use a canal staff, not like Sam."

He made it to the edge of the canal and, holding Sam close to him, simply jumped.

His jump carried him across the canal, soaring easily over the water.

Alec had seen Sam jump canals before and had seen her use her staff to carry her up and over, and that had been impressive. When she used her augmentations to jump over the canals, he felt that the fluid strength that she displayed was impressive. With this, it was simply brute strength.

That had to be the Theln side of Tray.

Beckah stood beside him, staring over the canal. "How is that possible?"

Alec shook his head. "I have no idea."

He raced toward the bridge with Beckah next to him. Thankfully, he had the necessary papers to give him access to the other side, and he raced through the streets. Tray was nowhere in sight. With his speed, even carrying Sam, he would arrive at Bastan's long before they would.

"Where are we going?"

"Caster section."

"Caster? Why would you bring your injured friend away from the university and into a lowborn section like that?"

"Because that's where Sam is from."

Alec hurried through the streets, and as he ran over the next bridge, an idea came to him.

He didn't know what Sam might have been dosed with, but the slowing of her heart made him wonder if perhaps there might have been foxglove on the staff. It was possible there was another explanation, but he wouldn't have any way to help her without access to medicines. Even had they taken her to the university, there was no guarantee that they'd have had the medicines he believed she'd need.

That left him with one option, but it would mean a slight delay in getting back to her.

Alec changed course, a brief detour on his way to Caster. He would go to his apothecary and borrow once more from his father, only this time, the supplies he needed were for someone he truly cared about. The last time had been for thistle root and had been for understanding, as much as it had been to help the other man. This time, he went so that he could help Sam—if only it wasn't too late.

As they entered his section, he breathed out, feeling a mixture of relief, as well as trepidation. What would happen if his father didn't have necessary supplies? If it was foxglove, they needed thistle root to help her, but he'd taken the last of his father's supply.

"You're going to raid your father's supplies?"

"The man that Tray intends to take her to has access to resources, and I don't doubt that he will do all he can to help her, but he doesn't know what to use. I know what I might need."

"How do you know what you'll need?"

"Well, I don't entirely. I have an idea—and that might be enough."

He reached his father's shop and checked the door. It was unlocked. That was a surprise, but more surprising was when he pushed open the door, he saw a lantern glowing near the back.

"Father?" Alec called.

His father stepped out from the back of the shop and glanced from Alec to Beckah. "It's awfully late for you to be visiting, Alec."

"I need your help. Sam was possibly poisoned."

"Possibly?"

"I don't know if she was poisoned, only that it's likely."

"Alec, I've taught you well enough to know that you need to know what the potential toxin is in order to adequately counter it."

"It might be foxglove. Then again, it could be something else. It was Marin."

"Marin?"

Alec still hadn't figured out how his father and Marin knew each other, but there was no doubting that they did.

"Why would Marin poison Sam? You told me she's always tried to help her."

"It's a long story, but Marin did something to Sam long ago that wiped her memories from her mind."

His father's eyes widened. "That's a dark use. There's only one thing that would make that possible."

"Whatever augmentation Marin used on her took away memories of her family, memories of who she was before."

"It's not an augmentation," his father said.

"It would have to be. Marin is the one who did it."

"The same Marin who has helped protect a half Theln?"

"You've known?"

"I know many things about the goings on within the city."

Alec would have to find those answers later. Right now, he needed a way to help Sam. "What is it? What would Marin have done that could take away memories?"

"You've seen it before. When you helped the princess, you saw how the Thelns have a way of damaging others."

"The Book of Maladies?" he asked. If it was the book, the only way to counter its effect would be to destroy the page involved. That was how they had managed to save the princess, though he still wasn't certain how Marin—and it had to be Marin—had managed to take that page from the book.

"That's the only thing I know of that could do what you're describing."

Alec squeezed his eyes shut, feeling a bit daunted, before opening them again. "We'll have to deal with that later. First, I need to help her."

"You can't simply use your easar paper?" his father asked.

"She's too weak to use her blood. Doing that would put her in danger, and I'm not willing to risk it."

"If she's dying, you may have to take that risk."

"If she's poisoned, I need to counter the poison before I do anything else."

His father considered him a moment before nodding. "There are a few things that might be able to help," he said, starting down the row of shelves. "If you think it's foxglove, there is only one possible counter for that."

"Thistle root," Alec said. "Did you get my note?"

"A note? Alec, I've been gone for some time. I haven't received any note from you."

Alec looked over to Beckah. If he hadn't received his note, that meant that he hadn't restocked the thistle root. "How hard is thistle root to find?"

"It's difficult. Collecting it requires a careful approach that's not easy to do. I have a reasonable supply that would be enough to help all but the most heavily poisoned."

"You did have enough," Alec said.

His father turned to them, looking at Alec with a curious expression.

"There was a man, seemingly dead, that Master Carl brought into class to demonstrate foxglove toxicity. I was told the university didn't have a supply of thistle root to heal him."

"And you thought to help him."

Alec nodded.

"Oh, Alec. What have you done?"

"What have I done? I was trying to help."

"I am sure you were. The problem is that there are

many uses for foxglove. The university often uses it to sedate dangerous people."

Alec's breath caught. What had he done? If they used it to sedate dangerous individuals, had he somehow inadvertently helped someone who might be dangerous to the university—and the city?

And then he'd helped Sam break into Master Carl's room, and had helped her break this person out—the same person Marin now had.

"Why would they sedate dangerous individuals?" Beckah asked.

His father looked over to her, almost as if seeing her for the first time. His gaze drifted over her, scanning her for a moment. "There are many individuals who seek power and would use that to work against the city. There are many who have no qualms about using what they know and targeting others who might seek to protect the city."

"How is it that you know this?" Beckah asked.

His father met her gaze. "Because I also work to protect the city."

Beckah started to smile. "You're an apothecary."

His father nodded. "I am. One who trained at the university. One who understands the use of medicines for healing... As well as for other purposes."

Alec turned sharply and looked at his father. "What are you saying?"

"I'm saying that I have worked for a long time to facilitate safety within the city."

"Did you know about Marin?"

"I didn't. Not before..." He shook his head. "It doesn't

matter. What matters is that you must try to save your friend. She is important."

"Because she can help the city?" Alec asked.

"Because she is important to you," his father said.

He grabbed a few jars from the shelves, each either a stimulant, or some sort of healing medicine, and placed them in Alec's hands. "Try these. If you give her a boost, if you can help by stimulating her heart a little bit, you might be able to counter the effects of the toxin enough that you can use your abilities to save her."

"Father—"

His father shook his head. "Go. We'll talk later."

Alec turned, grabbing Beckah by the hand and pulling her from the shop, and hurried out into the street.

31

THE TAVERN DESTROYED

The streets of Caster were dark by the time Alec and Beckah arrived. He felt uncomfortable here this late at night, though he knew he shouldn't. No real harm would come to them, not so long as they remained on the main streets.

Beckah looked around, her head constantly swiveling as they made their way along the street. She kept close to him, holding tightly to his hand. "I'm not sure this is safe."

"I had the same feeling the first time I was here. The people here aren't any different from those elsewhere in the city."

A cry echoed through the night, coming from deeper within Caster.

"Not so different? The guard patrols the other sections. They don't even bother in these outer sections at all. It was bad enough the first time, but…"

"You were fine the first time. And the guard doesn't bother because most of the sections like this have a different kind of policing," Alec said.

"What kind is that?"

"The kind they do themselves. These people don't want the guard patrolling here. I can't blame them, either, as the guard has never served them."

"You sound like you're making excuses for them."

"It's not excuses. It's simply the truth of this part of the city."

When they reached Bastan's tavern, none of the usual music filtered out the door. When Alec pulled the door open, he wasn't entirely sure what he would find.

The tavern was empty.

"Alec? I don't like this."

He didn't, either, but didn't want to scare her by admitting that. The tavern should be busy, if only with Bastan's men.

Alec hurriedly guided Beckah toward the kitchen. That had been the way he'd gotten down to Bastan's hidden area before. If he were anywhere, it would be there. They'd taken long enough at the apothecary for Tray to have made it to the tavern with Sam.

There was no one to stop them, and Alec didn't know whether to be thankful for that or worried. Like the main part of the tavern, the kitchen was empty, not the usual bustle of activity. Alec hurried through it and found the door to the lower level open. He took the stairs two at a time, his pounding heart racing in time with his mind. He hoped Tray had gotten Sam to the tavern without any interference.

Where were Bastan's men?

"Something doesn't feel right," Beckah said.

"Because it's not," he whispered.

He checked the first door and found the room empty.

That was where he had been summoned to help Elaine, but there was no sign of Bastan or Sam.

The next door opened onto another storeroom, and it was as empty as the last. There was one door remaining, and though Alec didn't know what was inside, he suspected he would find much the same. There had to be a reason that Bastan—and his men—weren't here.

When he opened the door, the room was as empty as he expected.

"Where are they?" Beckah asked.

Alec shook his head. What had happened? Tray should have easily gotten here—unless something happened along the way and he had stopped somewhere else. But even if that happened, where was Bastan? Why was the tavern empty?

"I don't know."

He returned to the kitchen, and back into the tavern, where he paused. There was one other place to check, but normally, he wouldn't be allowed access. Then again, normally, he wouldn't be allowed unaccompanied access anywhere beyond the main tavern area.

Alec reached the door to Bastan's private office and found it unlocked. That alone was unusual, but everything about this visit felt unusual.

The office was in complete disarray.

Sculptures were tipped, and paintings that Alec suspected were important to Bastan were tossed on the ground in a heap. He motioned for Beckah to wait outside the door, then stepped in slowly, carefully, and looked around, before spotting a small figure lying near a corner of the room.

Alec raced over to it.

"Sam?"

She was still warm, and as he pressed his head to her chest to listen for her heartbeat, he found that it still thudded, and she still had regular breaths. There was that much at least.

How much longer would she have?

Would he be able to heal her?

Alec reached into his pocket and took out one of the vials that contained a stimulant. It would speed the heart but did little else other than give a boost of energy.

Alec took one of the leaves out and rolled it between his fingers. Then he gently opened Sam's mouth and stuck the leaf inside her cheek.

"What are you giving her?" Beckah asked, stepping closer.

Alec held up the jar. "Anfar leaves. They're a mild stimulant and will give a small boost of energy. Maybe it'll be enough to wake her up."

"And if it's not?"

If it's not, he would have to try what his father had suggested, though he didn't like the idea. She was weakened, and if he drew blood from her while she was in such a state, he ran the risk of taking too much. They hadn't practiced that before, but Alec had heard what could happen if too much energy was drawn. It left both the Scribe and the Kaver severely disabled.

But wouldn't he attempt that if it meant saving Sam's life?

After a moment or two, her heart sped up a little, but other than that, there was no change. He took the other vials his father had given him from his pocket, and made a quick mixture using his palm as a bowl, and stuffed the concoction of healing herbs into her mouth. It would likely do nothing, but it was worth trying.

"And that?" Beckah asked.

"These are all different types of healing herbs. I don't even know if any of them will work, but…" He shrugged. "I have to try."

He sat back on his heels and waited. He didn't expect that anything he was trying would make a difference. If it was foxglove toxicity, the only thing that would help her would be thistle root—or to use easar paper.

Alec searched through Sam's pockets for her easar paper but couldn't find it. All he had left to try was his slip of paper.

"I thought you said it was dangerous to do weakened," Beckah said.

Alec took one of the vials that his father had given him and removed the various leaves within it. "I thought you didn't believe in magic," he said.

He pulled his knife out of its sheath and made a small puncture in the palm of his hand, just enough to create a small droplet of blood. He did the same with Sam, debating for a moment, but taking a slightly greater amount from her. He hated that it was necessary, but for healing, the Kaver's blood was more important than that of the Scribe. At least, in their experience, that was the case.

"Can you help me remove her cloak?" Alec asked. He wanted to see the nature of the injury to know whether it was healing as they used their blood.

As he and Beckah shifted Sam, slipping her arms out of the sleeves and settling her back on the ground, he took stock of the injury. The puncture in her shoulder was not only deep but wide, and it continued to ooze.

What was Marin's intent? If it was only to injure Sam, she wouldn't have needed to stab her shoulder like that. As he checked out the wound, Beckah sucked in a sharp breath.

"Alec?"

He glanced over to see Beckah with her hands in Sam's cloak. "What is it?"

She held up a few vials. Two of them were clearly toxins. There was the jagged and sickly-looking leaf of the orson plant. Then there was the equally deadly-looking chatterflax, its leaf a shade of gray that when powdered would stop both heart and breathing.

"Why would she have these?" Beckah asked.

From the way she questioned, it seemed that Beckah recognized them, just as Alec had.

"I don't know. I've never known Sam to have anything like that with her."

Beckah continued to check her cloak and took another sharp breath as she pulled another jar from within it. "And this?"

She handed it to Alec. It was his turn to gasp.

"Thistle root. How did she have a supply of it?"

He quickly opened the jar and removed a piece. He hoped it wasn't already too late. If it worked, if he somehow managed to reverse the effects of whatever poison Marin had used, he'd be more comfortable using the easar paper to heal the rest of her injuries.

Alec cut up the thistle root and crushed it, creating something of a paste. He shoved it into Sam's mouth and tried to force it down her throat. He hated how rough he was with her, but at the same time, prayed that it worked.

"What now?" Beckah asked.

"Now?" Alec glanced down at the paper. He had to try it, didn't he? Even if the thistle root helped, he still needed the easar paper to heal her wounds.

Dipping his pen into their blood ink, he began to write.

He chose the words he used to describe her illness carefully. That was an important part of the healing process. It was much the same way that choosing the right words was important in creating an augmentation.

Alec described the nature of her injuries, at least as much as he knew of them. He described how he would heal them, though he would do nothing of the sort. The easar paper would heal them.

Then he was done.

Alec sat back, glancing from the paper to Sam.

"How will you know if it's going to work?" Beckah asked.

"I thought... I thought it would have started by now. When we've attempted augmentations in the past, it worked right away."

"Why wouldn't it work now?"

He breathed out a shaky breath. "There are many possibilities." He started thinking through what those might be. "It could simply be that the ratio is wrong. The ratio of her blood to mine makes a difference, especially with the intent of how we use it. With healing, it tends to require a higher percentage of Kaver blood."

"I presume that she is the Kaver," Beckah said.

Alec nodded. "I'm what's called a Scribe. The ink

requires blood from both of us to work, but sometimes, the intent needs more of one person's or the others. In the case of healing, it's the Kaver's blood."

He continued watching Sam, but nothing changed. There was no knitting of the wound on her shoulder, nothing that would indicate that his attempt with the easar paper was having any effect. And there was no wave of weakness through him that would indicate it worked.

"It's also possible that she is too far along for her blood to facilitate the magic," Alec said. It was hard for him to admit, but that was what he feared. Maybe the magic didn't burn within her veins when she was as sick as she was.

"What if there's something wrong with the paper?" Beckah asked.

"It worked before, in the courtyard." He'd seen that the augmentation had been effective. She had launched herself, the augmentation making her light, much as he intended. It had to have worked, didn't it?

Unless something had happened to the paper between then and now.

But what could have happened?

"It's possible," Alec said. He remembered the sheet of easar paper that Sam had held on to and reached into her cloak. He found it folded up and buried near the bottom of a deep pocket. Alec reopened the wound in his palm, adding a few more drops of blood to the blood ink.

"I thought you said the ratio was important," Beckah said.

"It *is*, but I don't think I can draw much more from her. It's going to require more of me, though I don't know if it will work."

He unfolded the sheet of paper and smoothed it out on the floor. Dipping his pen into the blood ink, he started writing. The pen scraped along the page, the coppery scent of blood filling his nose. Beckah was silent next to him, holding her breath much like Alec held his.

He made the same notation as before, though this time, he referenced himself more, adding in things that he could do to help her, including willingness to sacrifice to help Sam. It felt almost like he was trying to convince the paper to help him. It was a strange sensation, but it was the only thing that made sense to him.

Then it was done. He felt weakened, and that gave him hope. If the healing was going to work, it needed to draw power and magic from him.

"Did it work?" Beckah asked.

"I don't know." His eyes were heavy, and he felt like drifting, letting himself fall into a slumber, but that couldn't happen. He needed to remain awake, to help Sam if she came around.

He felt hands slip behind him, supporting him. "I'm here," Beckah said. "I'll hold you."

"No. Sam." His mind cleared a moment. "Anfer."

Beckah reached for something, and he felt a leaf pressed into his mouth. Alec sucked on the leaf, drawing from the anfer, hoping that it could grant him strength. All he needed was to remain awake, nothing else. If he could stay awake, he could help Sam.

He felt the juice begin to run down into his stomach, and his heart began to race along with it. He welcomed the sensation of it and welcomed the warmth flowing through him, the steady hammering of his heart, and the quickening of his pulse.

Alec sat up, taking a deep breath. "Thank you."

"I didn't do anything. You did."

He reached toward Sam and saw that her shoulder wound appeared to have knitted closed, the healing taking place following the last notes he made on the paper. Was it the choice of paper that had made the difference, or was it more about the different ratio of blood that he'd used?

Color began to return to Sam's cheeks, enough that he hadn't realized how pale she had been before it did. Alec brushed back Sam's hair and felt a slight sheen of sweat on her forehead. "Just wake up, Sam," he whispered.

The tiredness had faded from him, but he hadn't given Sam another stimulant. Maybe that was what she needed.

"I need more anfer leaves."

Beckah handed him another leaf, and he rolled this up, pinching it between his fingers, and stuck it into Sam's cheek.

Waiting was the hardest part. As he did, he looked around Bastan's office, wondering what had happened. Why was the tavern empty? Where had everyone gone?

Where was Tray?

He had a hard time imagining Tray abandoning his sister, regardless of how angry he might be about what he'd overheard in the courtyard. That made it more likely that something had happened to him.

Clearly, Tray got Sam here, so then what? And if Bastan had been here, would he not have sought out Alec to help her? Or sent some of his men to find him? That he'd seen no sign of any of them on his way to the tavern concerned him even more.

As he continued to gaze around the office, he thought

he saw something along one of the far walls, but a soft moan from Sam caught his attention.

Alec turned back to her just as she opened her eyes.

"Alec?" Her voice came out in a hoarse croak.

"I'm here," Alec said.

Sam tried to sit up, but he kept his hand on her good shoulder, keeping her from attempting to do too much. "Where are we?" Sam asked.

"Bastan's office."

"How... How did I get here? I remember fighting with Marin, and I remember her stabbing me, but not much more than that."

"When you passed out, I knew you needed more healing than what the university could offer. I was going to take you to my father's shop, but..."

"But what?"

"But Tray convinced me to bring you to Bastan. He carried you here, while I stopped at my father's apothecary shop for supplies."

"You saw Tray?"

Alec nodded slowly. "Sam, there's something you should know."

"He knows, doesn't he?"

"He knows. He overheard you and Marin and whatever conversation the two of you had."

"Kyza!"

Beckah sucked in a breath at Sam's swear. "You shouldn't use the god's name in such a way," Beckah said.

Sam rolled her head toward Beckah and blinked slowly. "What have the gods ever done for me?"

"Sam. I don't know where Tray or Bastan have gone."

Sam started to sit, and Alec tried to restrain her, but

her strength had returned enough that she was able to shrug him off. "Then something happened to them." She looked around, frowning. "How did you get into Bastan's office?"

"The tavern is empty," he said.

"Then something is *definitely* wrong. Bastan never leaves the tavern empty, and if he does, there are at least some men faithful to him still nearby, keeping watch. If Bastan is gone, and if the men who keep an eye on the tavern are gone… What happened to Marin?" Sam asked, looking back at him.

"After she attacked you, she picked up the man who had been on the ground—I'm presuming it was the man we sought—and escaped."

Sam sighed. "I don't understand. There has to be some connection, but what is it?"

"What kind of connection are you afraid of?" Alec asked.

"Don't you find it odd that Bastan asked me to rescue a man from the university that only you would be able to help me find and then Marin just happened to appear? And then, Tray shows up following the attack and runs off with me, bringing me here, and now, everyone is missing, including Bastan." Sam stood and seemed to wobble for a moment.

Alec leaped to his feet and slipped his arm around her for support. She gave him an appreciative smile.

"Can you grab her staff?" he asked Beckah, nodding toward the wall.

Beckah went around Bastan's desk and grabbed the staff leaning along the wall. As she did, she sucked in a sharp breath of air. "Alec?"

"What is it?"

"There's… There's someone else here."

Alec glanced at Sam. He helped her toward the desk, and when they reached it, she gripped the edge before looking on the other side. After what Beckah had said, Alec had half expected it to be Bastan, but the figure was too large and too muscular.

"Tray?" Sam whispered.

ANOTHER SCRIBE

S am still felt the effects of whatever poison Marin had used on her. She couldn't believe that the woman had poisoned her in the first place, but she had. She hadn't killed her, but she might as well have.

And now Tray lay motionless in the back of Bastan's office.

She ran to him and fell forward, her legs too weak to support her. She grabbed his face, afraid that he'd already passed, but it was still warm, though blood trickled down the side of his head. He didn't move, and she checked the artery in his neck much like Alec had taught her to do and found that he still had a pulse. That much was good.

"Can you help him?" she asked, looking up to Alec.

Alec knelt down next to Sam and did a quick examination of Tray. His hands ran over Tray's head, then moved down to his sides, working in a practiced fashion. He leaned in and listened, pausing for a moment as he did, and then sat up, a pained look on his face.

"You can't help him?" Sam said.

"It's not that I can't help them, but we've used too much of our strength trying to bring you back. I... I don't have any left," he said.

Sam shook her head. "You have to do something. You have to try. We can't just let Tray die."

"Sam—if we try to heal him, we'll use too much of our own strength. And if we are too weak, I don't think it will work."

There had to be something they could do, some way they could get Tray help. "Alec, he would do anything to help me, so there has to be something I can do."

"We almost didn't survive the last healing," Alec said. "You can barely walk, and I needed a stimulant to bring me back around, otherwise I wouldn't be awake."

It seemed impossible that there wasn't anything that could be done for Tray. After everything they'd been through, after everything they'd learned of their abilities, how could they be at this point, unable to help her brother? That seemed too cruel. Impossible, and... she refused to believe it.

She worked her way around the desk and saw her cloak lying on the ground. She started toward it, but staggered and fell, sprawling forward onto it. All she needed was to reach into her hidden pocket, find the sheet of easar paper, and... What? What did she think she could do alone?

Alec was right. She was too weak. He was too weak. To be effective, both Kaver and Scribe had to have the necessary strength to make the augmentation work. With healing, it required a specific touch, from both of them.

Would she lose Tray before she even had a chance to explain what had happened? Would she lose her brother and never have the opportunity to tell him what he meant to her? What did it matter that Marin had lied to her? What did it matter that he was not her brother by blood? He was still her brother.

"What are you doing?"

She looked up to see Alec watching Beckah. She was kneeling over something—easar paper, Sam realized.

"I thought it was worth a try," Beckah said.

"It requires a specific ability," Alec explained. "You need both Scribe and Kaver."

Sam had a hard time focusing. She really was tired. "Tray is at least half Kaver," she said.

"You're not helping," Alec chided.

"Let her try," Sam said.

"What are the odds that she might be a Scribe?"

"Probably the same odds that you were a Scribe when I stumbled into your apothecary," Sam said. They hadn't discovered what made a pairing of Scribe and Kaver, but she suspected it was little more than chance. It certainly had only been chance that she had stumbled into Alec's apothecary shop. Had she ended up anywhere else, she wouldn't have gotten the help she needed. She wouldn't have survived the poison from the Theln's arrow.

"Are you going to help, or are you going to continue to give me a hard time," Beckah said to Alec. "Or are you worried that I'll be better at this than you?"

Sam smiled in spite of herself. "Does she always give you a hard time like that?" Sam asked.

Alec groaned. "Sometimes worse," he said.

"Good."

Alec sighed. "Fine. Let's prove that this doesn't work.

What you need to do is write down the symptoms and how you intend to treat it."

"How I intend to treat it? That doesn't make sense."

"Pretend that you have access to all of the university resources. Pretend that you have access to everything that my father has in his apothecary shop. Use that and write it down."

Beckah glanced up at him, almost a look of disbelief on her face. "Maybe this was a mistake," Beckah said.

"No. I think it's worth trying."

Sam could tell from the way he said it that Alec didn't expect it to work, but he was willing to attempt it. That meant something to her.

Beckah turned her attention back to the page and started writing.

Sam couldn't see what she was doing, and maybe that was for the best. If she could see her documentation, she might compare it too much to what Alec did, and there was no benefit in that.

"Good. That's good," Alec said.

"Do you think this might work?" Beckah began, and Sam noted the scratching of her pen across the page.

Curiosity got the best of her, and she looked up, turning to watch Beckah as she wrote. From her angle, crouched as she was on the ground, she couldn't read the words on the easar paper.

"That could work," Alec said. "You might try adding a comment about how to heal his wounds."

"I didn't see any wounds, other than the one on his head."

"There are likely internal wounds," Alec said.

Beckah nodded and turned her attention back to the page, the pen scratching along the surface.

And then she stopped.

Sam looked over and saw Beckah leaning back on her heels. "Oh."

She started to wobble and then leaned backward.

Alec was there and caught her before she could fall. He watched Beckah for a moment, his face twisted in an expression of confusion. "Beckah?"

"I… I feel… exhausted."

Alec watched her for a moment before looking over to Sam. "How? How could this work?"

Sam flicked her gaze crawled around to the back of the desk, where Tray lay unmoving. He was part Kaver, which would explain that, but it wouldn't explain why Beckah would be able to serve as Scribe to him. "Do you think it could have anything to do with the fact that you're at the university?"

"I was your Scribe long before I went to the university," Alec said.

"But you'd resisted going." Sam wasn't sure what she was getting at, only that there seemed to be a connection between the university and Scribes. There had to be, didn't there?

The princess had access to the university, as well, and the kind of access she had indicated that she had more than a passing familiarity with it.

"What if there's something about those who succeed at the university?" Sam asked.

"Why would that matter?"

She shrugged. "I can't say that I understand, only that

it would be the only other connection. I mean, even the princess had some connection to the university."

"What of Marin's Scribe?" Alec asked.

Sam thought for a moment before catching her breath. Marin hadn't said anything about a Scribe, but if she had been at the university, there had to be a reason. Was she searching for a Scribe—or was she searching for *her* Scribe?

"We need to meet with one of your masters."

"What will that do?" Alec asked.

"We have questions. I think it's time that we have answers."

33

THE NEXT STEP

After waiting for nearly an hour, Sam's strength began to return. Once it started, it built quickly. She breathed out a sigh, wanting nothing more than to run to the university with Alec, but she had to wait. Tray still hadn't fully recovered.

It still amazed her that Alec's friend was able to connect to Tray, Scribe to Kaver. There had to be some answer, some connection, that made it so the two of them could work together, but if so, wouldn't Marin have known?

Maybe it only required the right potential. Sam and Alec meeting had certainly been chance, no different than this. Could that be all there was? Chance?

She sat in Bastan's tavern, quietly nursing a mug of hot tea. She didn't want anything stronger, not wanting the ale to cloud her mind, not when there was so much still to do.

"He's awake," Alec said. He stood in the doorway of Bastan's office, his face drawn, and his eyes looking tired.

"How is he?"

"Recovering. He doesn't know what happened, other than that when he brought you here, he was attacked. He didn't get to see who attacked him."

"Bastan?" Is that why he'd not returned? What was his connection to the man they'd tried to save?

"You'll have to ask him."

"You haven't told him about how he was healed, have you?" Sam asked. That had been their agreement. They didn't want to reveal the truth until they knew how Tray would react.

"I haven't told him. He deserves to know. If he has this potential, he deserves a chance to work with it and discover what it means. Think about what would have happened had you never learned what it meant for you to be a Kaver."

She didn't like the idea of keeping it from Tray, but until she knew, until she could be certain that he hadn't completely abandoned their connection, she wasn't comfortable with telling him. "When it's the right time, I will share it with him."

Alec took her hands and squeezed. "I'll wait out here." He held her gaze a moment before looking past her, toward Beckah sitting in the back of the tavern alone.

Sam had preferred that she remain that way, but she suspected Alec would go over to her. And she couldn't be jealous—she shouldn't—but she was. She couldn't answer why, though.

Sam sighed and stood, heading for Bastan's office. Sam had picked up the statues and put them back where they belonged, to the best of her recollection, but she left the paintings leaning against the walls of the office. She could only imagine Bastan's reaction when he returned. If he returned, she reminded herself.

"Tray?" She paused at the door, looking at her brother as he sat propped against the wall behind Bastan's desk. He had changed so much in the last few months; his eyes wiser, his body thicker, more muscular, but those weren't the most noticeable changes. There was something else that she couldn't quite put a finger on, but it was just as important.

"Sam. What happened here?" he asked.

"I don't know. There was an attack. I was hoping you would be able to tell me about that."

Tray surveyed the office. "When I got here, Bastan was gone. There were three of them, but they moved too quickly. They knocked me out, and apparently, left me for dead."

"Why did they leave you?" Sam asked, taking a few steps into the room.

Tray shrugged. "I don't know. Probably because I was useless to them."

"Why did they leave me?"

He met her gaze and then shrugged. "I didn't let them see you."

"How?" When he didn't answer, she sighed. "Please, Tray. How?"

"I covered you." He met her eyes for a long moment. "You've protected me my entire life. It was time I returned the favor. What are you going to do?" Tray asked.

Sam walked over to Bastan's desk and leaned against it. "I have to find out what Marin's up to."

"I was only to watch shipments in and out of the university. Nothing more than that." He hesitated. "So...

she's my mother?" There was a bit of defiance in his tone, but she could also hear his confusion. He looked a bit lost.

Sam clasped her hands together and looked into her brother's eyes, wishing she didn't have to answer this. "If what I've been told is true, she is."

"What does that make us?" The question was laced with more than it seemed. It was the question she'd been asking for the last few months, ever since learning about Tray and what Marin had done.

"It makes us brother and sister. It doesn't change anything, Tray. Every memory I have is of you as my brother. Everything I've ever done has been to keep you safe."

"I've told you that you don't need to do that anymore."

"And yet it doesn't change me feeling that way," Sam said. "In my mind, and my heart, you're still my little brother. You're still the little boy who chased me through the city, mad that he couldn't use the canal staff like I could, or couldn't climb up the sides of buildings the way I could."

"I don't need a canal staff anymore. And I have no difficulty climbing up buildings."

Sam stared at him and didn't know quite how to respond. What was the right answer for Tray? What would help him? "That still doesn't change anything for me. I hope it doesn't for you, either."

Tray watched her, unblinking, then let out a frustrated sigh. "Why would she do this to us?"

Sam shook her head. "I really don't know."

"If it was about hurting you, she could have done that anytime over the last ten years."

It was the same thought Sam had. It had to be about

something more than simply hurting her. There had to be some reason Marin wanted Sam close to Tray, and some reason she neededs Tray to be important to her. She didn't quite know what it was—not yet—but she was determined to find out.

"Why were you at the university?" Sam asked.

"I wasn't there," he said, then looked away. "Not until later."

"You were there, Tray. Alec saw you. You came into the master's room. You were there the same time I was." Sam's heart started to pound. "She sent you, didn't she? She wanted you to go in and get him, and she was surprised when I came out with him."

"Sam—"

"No. I've known you well enough—and long enough—to know when you're not telling me the truth."

Tray leaned his head forward, resting it on his hands. "She sent me. She said it was important so that she could help you."

"Help me?"

Tray shrugged. "I didn't know. I didn't know anything. I'm still not sure what to believe."

"You can believe me," Sam said. "You can believe that I have no hidden agenda. My goal is an obvious one. I want to find out why Marin did this to us, and I want to connect the dots with what's been happening. In the end, all of that is to ensure that you and I can be what we've always been, brother and sister."

"Even if we're not actually related?"

"We *are* related. Everything we've done over the years has made us that way. It doesn't matter what Marin—or Elaine—or anyone says."

Tray breathed out heavily, looking up to meet her eyes. "I don't know what she wanted the man for. All I know is that he was important. She thought he was some sort of expert, and she needed his help."

"Why his help?"

"I don't know. She's been studying the canals."

"The canals?" Sam repeated. "Why would Marin care about the canals?"

"Like I said. I don't know anything more than what I've told you."

Sam pushed off the desk and crouched down in front of Tray. She had the sudden awareness of how much larger he was than she, and how much more he was like the Thelns than he ever had been before. But he was something else. He was equally as much like her, having that part of him that was Kaver. That was the side that she needed to appeal to.

He smelled different than he had before. There was something almost sharp about it. It was a strange odor that she never would have associated with Tray in the past. It was almost medicinal and reminded her of the smells in Alec's apothecary shop.

She sniffed him again. "What has she had you doing?"

Tray shook his head. "Don't make me tell you."

"What if she intends to hurt me? Is that what you want?" Sam asked. She jabbed him in the chest as she did. Would he react dangerously? She never would have questioned it before, but she began to wonder how much she really knew about Tray. So much had changed between them over the last few months, and she'd spent so little time with him, certainly not enough to know how he might respond.

"She doesn't intend to hurt you," Tray said.

"You still think that even after you saw her attack me?"

"I…"

"She's letting dangerous people into the city, Tray. Possibly the same people who attacked you." And maybe that was why Bastan had disappeared. "I need to find her before others get hurt."

"I think I might be able to find her," Tray said. He started hesitantly and wrung his hands together as he continued. "I'm not sure if she'll even be there, but I overheard her earlier when she was talking about the canal around the palace."

"Why the palace? With the guards there, it's too well protected. She wouldn't even be able to get close enough to do anything."

"I don't know. Ever since you saved the princess, Marin has been angry about something. She blames the royal family."

"But you don't know why she's angry? What does she blame the royal family for?"

"If I knew, I would've told you. The fact is, I have no idea. There are quite a few people in the city who don't care for the royal family, Sam. You know that as well as I do. When you grow up in Caster, you see plenty of people whose lives would've been better had they not been lowborn."

Sam rocked back on her heels, wishing she could deny what Tray said, but she couldn't. He spoke the truth, and before she had known what she was, she had no real affinity for the royal family. The only reason she'd agreed to help the princess was because she'd hoped it would somehow help her get Tray out of prison, otherwise she would have left her to waste away.

"Come with me. We're going to see what Marin is up to."

"I'm not going to do anything that harms her," Tray said.

"I haven't asked you to."

"I want you to be prepared. If it comes to it, I'm not going to hurt her. She's been kind to me."

"Even after what might have happened?" Sam said.

"I have only your word for it. It might not even be true."

"It *is* true. I learned it from"—Tray watched her, a strange expression on his face. How could she tell him what needed to be said?—"my mother. She's still alive. And she's like me—a Kaver."

Tray stared, dumbfounded. "Your mother? A Kaver?"

They had no time for this right now. Sam needed answers. "Yes. I can tell you more later, but right now, I need you to take me to Marin."

"But what if she's not telling you the truth? How can you trust her after she abandoned you?"

She shook her head. She wouldn't argue with Tray about this. It wouldn't do any good if she did. Besides, she didn't need him to harm Marin, she only needed to convince him to go with her so that she could find Marin and figure out what exactly the woman was after.

"I won't ask you to do anything you're uncomfortable with."

Tray watched her, the darkness behind his eyes difficult to read, before he finally nodded. "When are we going?"

"As soon as you've recovered enough."

34

APPEAL TO THE MASTERS

Alec reached the university with Beckah hurrying behind him. He barely paused at the bridge leading to that section of the city and hurried over. Neither of them had spoken in the race toward the university, but there would be time for that later. Alec needed to help Beckah understand what it meant that she had Scribe ability, but first, he had to get some answers, and neither of them knew where those answers would come from.

They needed to reach the masters. After that, they needed to get to Sam and Tray before they risked themselves by facing Marin near the palace.

Why had he agreed to come without Sam?

He shouldn't have. With each step, he felt a growing certainty that she needed him now more than ever before, but he needed to come here, and they both needed answers, otherwise they would continue to flounder in the dark.

"What if they won't see us?" he asked Beckah.

She shook her head. "They'll see us."

"How can you be so certain?"

"You don't see yourself the same way they see you. They might not be interested in me, but you present a different appeal to them."

"There's no appeal. I think the fact that my father is an apothecary angers them more than anything."

"I don't think it so much that he is an apothecary that upsets them, but the fact that he chose a different path for himself than what they chose."

His father still had secrets, and there was more that he needed to learn from him, but much like understanding what had happened with Tray and Beckah, it had to wait. Right now, there were more important things, though his curiosity was getting the best of him. Alec wasn't good at waiting. He wanted answers when he had questions.

They entered the university building and raced up the stairs toward the masters' quarters. He'd already decided that he was going to try to find Master Eckerd, or even Master Helen, since both of them seemed willing to acknowledge him. As they rounded a corner, they encountered the master he least wanted to see.

Master Carl frowned at him, his deep jowls seeming to draw shadows into them. He stood with a slight lean to him, tipping forward, almost as if his enormous belly was threatening to drag him down.

"You shouldn't be in the masters' section."

"We're looking for Master Eckerd." Beckah stepped around him, speaking in a more confident tone than what Alec would have managed. She never seemed quite as impressed by the masters as Alec did.

"Wait until his next class. Students don't get to come and summon the masters."

"It's important," she said.

Carl grunted. "I have no doubt you perceive it as important, but whether it is important is a very different thing." Master Carl started down the hall, using his bulk to drive them along. He had a tendency to use his size to bully others, and it worked on Alec.

Alec tapped Beckah on the arm. "We should go."

Beckah glanced over at him. "No. We're not letting him get away with this again."

Master Carl paused. "Just what do you believe I've been getting away with?"

"You've had it out for Alec ever since you saw him in class," she said. "You didn't like him for some reason."

Master Carl's lips peeled back into a grin. "Is that so? Do you think that I care what happens with one of the students? I care only that the university continues to meet its mission."

"You care only that the university makes money."

Master Carl wrapped his arms above his belly and laughed. "You say that as if it's such a bad thing. Without the university acquiring appropriate funds, we would not have the same level of scholarship. You should be thankful that we do and that we allow you to study here." He arched a brow at her. "Perhaps you most of all."

"You think insulting me because the masters chose not to include me will work?"

"Beckah—" Alec said.

"No. If you've taught me nothing else, it's that we have something we can offer to others in the city, and we do nothing other than restrict access to it."

"Restrict access? Is that what you truly believe?" Master Carl looked from Beckah to Alec. A sneer spread across his face. "How many do you think we could help if we offered our services to everyone? How many do you think would come, seeking healing, unmindful of the fact that others might need it more? If we use the ability to pay as a filter, it allows us to serve that much more."

"Master Carl, we mean no disrespect," Alec began.

"You absolutely mean disrespect. Much like your father meant disrespect. You think we don't know what he does? Do you think we don't know that he sells services in such a way that he bastardizes what he was taught?"

"My father has done nothing other than offer healing services. He's never charged anything for those services, other than what people were able to pay."

Master Carl laughed a dark laugh. "Never charged? Your father never charged because he didn't need the money. He had another source of income."

"My father doesn't have any money."

"If he has no money, how do you think he has so many supplies? I seem to recall hearing about a fire in that section of the city. How can a man with no funds manage to rebuild so quickly?"

"What are you saying about him?" Beckah asked.

"You better be careful who you associate with, Ms. Reynolds. If you have any political aspirations, you might see them extinguished before they even have a chance to come to fruition." Master Carl started toward them again and push them down the hall, pressing them with his size.

They were forced backward. Beckah took his hand, and together they tried to resist. Alec looked over to her, desperate to find Master Eckerd—or even Master Helen—

but they would have to get past Carl, and there just didn't seem to be a way to do that.

"Please, Master Carl. This really is important. I need to find Master Eckerd—"

They had reached the top of the stairs that led down, and Master Carl did not relent in his effort to remove them. Alec took a step down but kept hoping the master would change his mind and be willing to at least listen, but he didn't seem to care. And he clearly had something against Alec's father. What did he mean about his father having money? Master Carl seemed more familiar with his father's business than he should be. More questions for later.

"Master Carl. What are these students doing in our quarters?"

Alec breathed out a sigh of relief. It was Master Eckerd.

Carl turned away from them, shielding them from Master Eckerd as he approached. "The students decided to violate the masters' quarters."

"And after your room had already been broken into," Master Eckerd said.

Master Carl hesitated. "Indeed."

"Which students are you trying to force down the stairs using your considerable girth?"

"It does not matter. You should return to your studies. I believe that you were quite concerned about the nature of the shortage of various healing compounds."

Alec had to say something now, or he risked not getting a chance. "Master Eckerd," he began. "I came looking for your help."

Carl glanced over his shoulder, giving Alec a hard glare, but Alec ignored it.

"Mr. Stross. It is awfully late for a visit." Eckerd stood near Carl and looked over his shoulder. "And you brought Ms. Reynolds with you. The only person you're missing is Mr. Jaffar."

Alec was glad they hadn't involved Stefan and didn't know whether he would even have been willing to come along with them. Maybe having him with them would have been helpful, especially if they were able to reach his grandma Helen. But with Master Eckerd's fortuitous arrival, they now simply had to get past Master Carl.

"I have a question that needs an answer," Alec said.

Carl shot him a look. "I could have answered any question for you, Mr. Stross."

Alec ignored him. "This one has to do with a particular paper, and the skills required to use it."

Master Eckerd watched him for a moment and then nodded slowly. "Why don't we discuss this in class tomorrow."

"That isn't soon enough," Alec said.

"Mr. Stross, you are a talented student, otherwise I wouldn't have brought you into the surgical suite. But you get ahead of yourself." Eckerd looked at Carl. "I think you're right to send them away. Some of the students really do think more of themselves than they should."

Carl grunted. "You only now see that? What have I been telling you about his father for the last two months?"

"And what have I been telling you about judging the son by the father's mistakes? I think if anyone would understand the importance of avoiding that, it would be you."

Carl frowned at him before shrugging. He turned back to Alec and motioned for them to head down the stairs.

Alec looked over to Beckah, a helpless feeling coming over him. What choice did they have but to comply? He had thought that coming to the university and finding one of the masters would give them answers, but it seemed the masters had no interest in helping.

Could Eckerd be no different than Master Carl? Could he be only interested in how much money the masters could make?

Alec followed Beckah down the stairs, having no choice but to do so. They reached the bottom and the entryway leading out of the university, and Beckah glanced back at him, shaking her head. "We can still try to help them," she said.

"I don't know if we will be enough," Alec said.

"You're going to try, though, aren't you?"

"I have to. Sam needs me."

As the door closed behind them, Beckah pulled him away from the building. She breathed out in a sigh. "I used to think that you had an unusual connection to her. After experiencing the power that I did, I'm beginning to understand."

They reached the courtyard and hurried toward the palace section. "I was hopeful that Master Eckerd might be able to answer—"

"Answer what?"

Alec spun. Master Eckerd was walking toward them, having come out of the building from a doorway that Alec didn't even realize was there.

"I thought you said we thought more of ourselves than we should?"

Master Eckerd waved his hand. "That was for Carl's benefit. He's always wanted more political capital but has never managed to get it. Instead, he's been forced to remain a physicker, and I think he resents that. Now. You have discovered that you're a Scribe?"

Alec blinked. It was much blunter than he had expected. "I've known for a short time that I'm a Scribe. Beckah just discovered that she is one as well. I thought there was some connection required between the Kaver and the Scribe."

Eckerd waved his hand again. "The connection is basically the first Scribe who mingles with the Kaver. That first union is what is important. Occasionally, a strong connection is made, though that's not always the case."

"How… How do you know this?" Beckah asked.

"Why do you think the testing at the university is so rigorous?" Eckerd asked. "Rarely is a Scribe's talent revealed so early. Usually, it takes years of study to understand the appropriate techniques to document and make scribing effective, but I'm not surprised that Mr. Stross managed it. I am, however, surprised that Ms. Reynolds has discovered her affinity for scribing."

"I… may have had something to do with it."

Master Eckerd glanced from Alec to Beckah. "Perhaps that is for the best. Now. Why have you come looking for me?"

Alec considered how much to tell Master Eckerd but decided telling him everything was best. It might be the only way they would get his help.

35

AT THE CANALS

The canal stretched out wide in front of them. Sam stood at its edge, her canal staff fully assembled, and a sense of anxiety rolling through her. What would she do when she encountered Marin? What would she say?

Maybe she didn't have to say anything. Marin hadn't earned a response from her. All she had earned was her capture. Then Sam would force her to explain what she'd done to her so that it could be reversed.

"Where do you think she'll be?" Sam asked Tray.

The canal through this section of the city was incredibly wide. It was patrolled more diligently, and few barges were allowed through here, certainly none without the royal family's blessing. In the distance, Sam could see the palace rising, the gleaming stone reflecting the moonlight. Did Elaine even know what was taking place? She'd fought the Thelns, and presumably worked to keep the city safe, but she hadn't managed to find Marin.

Somehow, only Sam had managed that.

"I didn't hear all the details," Tray said. "All I know is that she was going to be near the palace, and the man you grabbed was important to her, though I don't know why."

Sam had thought that maybe he was a Scribe, but if so, for him to be "useful" as Marin had said, they would need easar paper. That might be why Bastan was missing, too. If nothing else, Bastan had shown a talent for acquiring the paper.

Sam walked along the canal, every so often glancing over at Tray. He had surprised her as they'd crossed from Caster to this section. She'd used her canal staff to make the jump, but he hadn't needed it. Always before, Tray had needed to use the bridges to cross, but now, he was able to jump them. Was it a Theln ability or was it something else?

It was late, so they were cautious in their movements. Sam didn't want to reveal their presence to Marin before she had a chance to understand what was taking place. She had little doubt that Marin had planned something. The challenge was determining what it was and what it meant for her.

"There," Tray said, pointing along the canal. It was rocky here, with a sharp drop from the street's edge down to the water. The closer they got to the center of the city —and to the palace—the steeper the drop off to the canals. It was one way of regulating access.

Sam followed the direction where he pointed and saw a cloaked figure standing at the canal's edge. "That's not Marin." The figure was much too tall to be Marin.

"Maybe not Marin, but..."

Tray raced toward the figure without finishing, moving faster than Sam could without augmentation. She hurried after him, clutching her staff tightly, uncertain what she might encounter. As they neared, she could tell it was a man. Tray reached him and struck the man in the back of the neck, crumpling him to the ground.

"Tray!"

"He works with Marin. If you're trying to reach her, you'll need to know what she's after," Tray said.

Sam looked down at the man, who lay unmoving. As Alec had taught, her she took note that he still breathed, his chest rising and falling steadily, and checked his neck to see that his heart still beat. Tray hadn't killed him.

She noticed a bag lying next to the man. She reached into it and found several empty clay containers. What would have been in them? And why would the man have these here along the canal?

When she sniffed inside one of the containers, she noted a familiar, almost bitter odor. "What was in this?" she asked Tray.

He glanced at the container and shrugged. "How would I know? I told you, I was only assigned to try to find information."

Sam had a feeling he had been asked to do more than that. "How would you know? Because you smell just like this jar smells."

Tray stared at her blankly. Sam set the container back down, stood, and started toward him, preparing to jab him in the chest and demand answers, when she noticed something floating in the water near the side of the canal.

What was it?

It was too far down for her to see easily, and much too dark for her to make out. She glanced back at the clay containers, and the man lying on the ground. There had to be a connection, didn't there?

"What was in those containers?" she asked Tray again.

"I don't know. I wasn't given details about what she wanted. All I knew was that she needed particular experts, and I was told how to find them."

"What kind of experts?"

He held her gaze. "The same kind of experts as your friend's father."

"Alec? His father is an apothecary."

"Is that all he is? Marin believes he has a greater role than that."

What more could Marin think Aelus had done? "Why are you making this so difficult?"

Tray sighed. "Because... I don't know what she was doing."

"And you don't know why you smell like whatever was in that jar?" She tapped the container with her staff.

Tray shook his head. "I didn't realize I smelled like anything."

Sam watched him for a moment before deciding she needed to know what was in the water.

Retrieving the jar from the others, Sam carefully placed her canal staff just at the water's edge. She shot Tray a look and then flipped up, suspending herself above the water. Balancing like this was difficult, and she hadn't completely mastered it, but each time she'd tried it, she'd gotten better than the time before. It was easier now. She shimmied down the staff, until she was just above the water, and realized the object in the water was some sort of leaf. Actually, many leaves. Dozens of them—possibly hundreds.

As her staff began to slip, she scooped the jar into the water, collecting a few of the leaves, and flipped herself back to shore.

"What is this?" she asked, pressing her nose into the jar and taking a long sniff. It wasn't clear what it was, but the odor was the same as what she'd first smelled in the jar. And the same thing that Tray must have been around often enough to make him stink of it.

"I don't know."

Sam glanced at the man still lying motionless. "Bind him. If Marin is up to something, I don't want any of her men to come after us."

"I'm one of her men," Tray said.

"I'm hoping that you're one of my men, too."

Tray watched her for a moment, saying nothing. Sam turned away from him and started down along the edge of the canal, looking for signs of anything else. Every dozen feet or so, she saw more leaves in the water. Every time she did, she glanced back at Tray, but he didn't seem to notice, or if he did, he gave no indication that he cared.

They found no one else depositing leaves into the canal, no more than what they had already discovered. Why had Marin wanted this man to put these leaves in the canals?

They followed the canal as it circled around this part of the city until it came to another bridge that led over to the palace side. Sam had papers that would grant her access, but Tray did not. She wasn't certain she even wanted him crossing to the other side, gaining access to the palace. He had changed enough that he made her uncomfortable, especially not knowing his allegiances.

"It's okay, Samara."

Tray never called her by her full name. "What's okay, Trayson?"

He grinned at her. "You don't have to stay here. If something's happening near the palace, and you have access, you should go."

"I can't bring you to the other side."

"I know. I'll see what else I can find here, and you go and make sure Marin isn't doing anything dangerous near the palace."

Sam gave Tray a hug. He stiffened as she did, then relaxed slightly. "Thank you."

"All I've ever wanted was to help you," Tray said.

"And all I've ever wanted was to keep you out of trouble. Kyza! I went to jail to try to get you free."

Tray grinned. "That wasn't necessary, you know."

"I know that now. At the time…" She hugged him again.

When she released him, she ran toward the bridge, reaching for her documentation. She glanced back, noting that Tray simply stood there watching her. She wasn't sure what he would do, or where he would go. Whatever Marin was after involved the canals, but what?

She was granted quick access to the other side, and ran across the bridge, scanning the palace grounds, but found nothing. What did she expect? Marin had skill and cunning. Would Sam even be able to detect her presence?

Had she made a mistake?

Sam ran back toward the canal, this time to the east. As she approached it, she saw fighting on the bridge.

She'd come across a different bridge—three bridges connected the palace to the other sections of the city—but if there was fighting on this one, what might be taking place on the others?

There were two massive men on the bridge facing the soldiers.

Thelns.

The commotion drew other soldiers out from the palace, and they raced toward the bridge. Sam got out of the way, not needing to get involved in a battle. The men were trained for that. She was able to use her staff, but this was a more open conflict.

Too late, she felt a buildup of heat.

"No!"

The bridge exploded. Chunks of stone went flying, and she ducked to avoid one striking her on the head.

Dust and debris scattered, and the bridge collapsed into the canal with a rumble and an enormous splash of water.

Another explosion struck, this time from the north side of the section. Sam didn't need to see it to know that another bridge had collapsed.

That left one bridge.

She ran, sprinting toward it.

She would be too late—she knew she would—but if she could stop the explosion... How? What could *she* do that would stop the explosion?

She reached the bridge and wasn't surprised that it was the same one she had just crossed. Guards ran along the bridge, filling it. She spotted a single man on the opposite shore. He was enormous, looming against the night, and fought against three Thelns of the same size.

Tray.

What was her brother doing?

As Sam watched, she saw someone flipping toward him, a canal staff spinning.

It was Marin.

If Marin got to Tray, he might give up the fight, he might allow those men to cross the bridge and blow it up as the others had been destroyed.

There were too many people on the bridge for her to pass.

That meant having to jump to cross the canal, but she'd never jumped that far. Even when she'd trained, even when she had been practicing, she had never managed such a distance.

It wasn't possible. Not without an augmentation, and Alec was at the university, trying to get help from the masters.

She watched helplessly as Marin got closer. Within moments, she would be there, reach Tray, and Sam didn't have to imagine how that would go. Marin would convince him of what she was doing, and Tray would stop fighting.

One of the Thelns fell, leaving Tray facing two.

Sam had to reach the other side. She had to help.

Could she jump?

Elaine had proven that it was possible and had shown that without an augmentation, a Kaver could leap even the widest canal, but Sam didn't have that ability. Or if she did, it was locked in her mind, trapped there when Marin erased who she was and who she could have been.

Sam had to try. She didn't like her chances, but she was willing to do her best. If she failed, what was the worst thing that could happen? She'd splash into the water, and not for the first time. She thought of the eels, but was there something worse? She didn't know what Marin had placed in the water, but if Tray had been working with it, it couldn't be fatal.

Marin neared Tray.

Sam took a few steps back, then sprinted, jumping into the air and plunging her staff to the bottom of the canal.

The jump wasn't far enough.

She pressed off, the staff flexing, forcing her up, and she flipped, swinging her staff back around, hoping to complete enough of a rotation that she could reach the other side.

She started to come around and felt herself going too far, so she quickly plunged the staff down, using the energy of her rotation to send her up, and all the way across.

It was a double jump, one that she'd never attempted before, and when she landed in a roll, she felt her heart pounding wildly as she looked back across the canal, amazed at the distant she'd just cleared.

She didn't gaze for too long.

Not hesitating, Sam threw herself forward.

Her staff smacked into one of the Thelns, knocking him down. The distraction was enough to give Tray an opening, and he dropped the other.

Sam didn't have the time to marvel at what she'd done.

Marin reached her.

As she did, Sam knew that she wouldn't be fast enough —she couldn't be fast enough—without augmentations. Marin moved quickly—too quickly.

She was augmented.

"You shouldn't have come back here," Marin said.

"What choice did I have?" Sam asked.

"There's always a choice. And you made the wrong one."

Marin lunged at her, and Sam knew she wasn't going to be able to stop her.

36

THE PLAN

They reached the canal, and Alec was breathing hard. He clutched his satchel against his side, afraid of losing it. Beckah had tolerated the run more easily, as did Master Eckerd. Neither seemed to be panting quite as much as Alec was.

As they turned to head down toward one of the bridges, thunder rumbled. "A storm?" Alec said.

"Not a storm," Master Eckerd said, pointing down the canal. Alec looked and saw the bridge collapsing into the canal. Dust from the explosion filled the air, and there was a strange energy there, as well, one that he'd felt before, and recognized.

Was it Thelns?

He had thought they wouldn't be able to reach this far into the city, but the explosion, and the power he detected, had traits of the Thelns.

"Where are they?" He asked the question mostly to himself, but Beckah answered anyway.

"I don't see anyone here," she said.

Another explosion thundered, and Alec's breath caught as it did.

That left one bridge leading to the palace side. All of them seemed to wait, the air within the city—in this section of it—still, as if the city itself seemed to wait for what happened next.

Nothing came.

"By the gods!" Master Eckerd said.

"What about the third bridge?" Beckah asked.

"It's not the bridge," Eckerd said. "Look."

Rather than pointing toward the bridges connecting the palace section to the others, he pointed toward the water. Alec stared, trying to make sense of what would have drawn the master's attention, and realized that it was something in the water.

Alec crept closer, not wanting to get too close to the edge, and saw leaves floating there. "Are those—"

Eckerd sniffed. "Foxglove."

"Why would they want to put foxglove in the canals? Diluted like that, it wouldn't have much of an effect on anyone in the city, even if they were to drink it." Alec looked to Eckerd, whose face had gone ashen. "It's not about the supply of drinking water, is it?"

Eckerd shook his head. "It's harvest time, and we've had our suppliers collecting all of it."

"Suppliers?"

"Foxglove is incredibly difficult to grow in this climate. And we pay a hefty premium to all who collect it."

"That's what money from the university goes toward?" Alec asked.

"There are many purposes for the money the university collects."

"Why foxglove?"

"You aren't far enough along in your studies to hear the answer to that," Master Eckerd said.

"I think we've shown that we are a part of this," he said.

Eckerd sighed. "The city was originally designed as a haven for those with Scribe and Kaver abilities. It was designed that way to ensure certain protections from those who would cause harm."

"How could it be designed..." Alec looked to the canals. "The water?"

Master Eckerd nodded. "The greatest canvas ever attempted. Those ancient Scribes used the canals to create an augmentation for the city itself, one that provides protection to all of those within it and excludes the Thelns."

"But it hasn't excluded the Thelns," Alec said.

"It has, until recently. Something has changed. There has been activity, an intentional attempt to bypass the protections placed upon the city."

"How would foxglove poison affect them?" Beckah asked.

"The canals have particular qualities that make it work."

Alec nearly asked what qualities, when he realized what they had to be. It was the reason that even the strongest person he knew was afraid of them. "The eels? They're real?"

Master Eckerd studied Alec for a long moment. "You really do have an astute mind, Mr. Stross. Very few have ever come to that understanding."

"So, the foxglove is designed to poison the eels,"

Alec said.

"And, I suspect, it will work," Master Eckerd said. "The eels share something in common with Scribes, and it makes them quite sensitive to the effects of foxglove."

"Is that why it affected me as strongly as it did?" Alec asked.

Eckerd nodded. "Master Carl has never administered the foxglove test before. It is typically administered by those within the university who understand its purpose. It served as something of a screening process, and those who pass are typically those with the potential to become Scribes."

"But Beckah didn't have the same reaction," Alec said.

"Ms. Reynolds had not had any training as a Scribe. I suspect that if she were to take foxglove now, the effect would be even more potent."

"We have to stop this, don't we?" Beckah asked.

"I think you need to help your Kavers," Master Eckerd said, nodding down toward the only remaining bridge.

In the distance, Alec saw Sam leap across to the other side, somehow managing to stick a second jump before landing safely. What would have prompted her to make such an attempt?

Then he saw the reason. Tray was there, fighting several others, and… Marin approached.

"What will you do?" Alec asked.

"Others have already been notified," Master Eckerd said. "Now that I know what she intends, I think I might be able to counter it, but… It will be painful."

"There's not enough thistle root to counteract the foxglove."

Master Eckerd smiled tightly. "Thistle root is the antidote that we have allowed known. There is one other. Unfortunately, as I said, it will be painful." He motioned toward the fight. "Go. Help your Kavers."

Alec nodded, and they started off. As they approached the fight, he slowed.

"What is it?" Beckah asked.

"We need a sample of blood for this to work," he said. "That's the unfortunate side of this magic. It requires blood ink in order for it to be effective."

He watched Sam, as she was tossed back, jumping toward him.

But... Tray remained ignored. It was almost as if Marin had chosen to fight Sam first, thinking—probably rightly—that Tray wouldn't attack her.

"You're going to have to draw Tray away, and get a sample of blood from him," Alec said.

"How do you suggest I draw him way?"

"I don't know. Harass him the same way that you harassed me?"

"What about you? What are you going to do?"

Alec looked over at Sam, watching her fight. She was getting thrown back, and Marin moved much more quickly than what Sam could do. It was not a fair fight, especially since Marin was augmented, and Sam was not.

"I need to find a way to reach Sam."

"Alec—be safe."

He tore the easar paper in half and handed her a piece. "Go and help your Kaver."

She sighed. "Why do I feel that I might have been better off never learning about this magic?"

There were times he felt the same way.

37

A KAVER ATTACKS

S am was thrown back again, the end of Marin's half-staff striking her shoulder. She managed to block, but only deflected it slightly. Marin fought with each half separately, moving faster than what Sam could keep up with. She'd been struck a few times, and each one stung, but so far, Marin hadn't poisoned her as she had before.

It was almost as if Marin toyed with her.

"Tray knows the truth," Sam said.

Marin glared at her. "Neither of you knows the truth."

"Why are you poisoning the canal? What do you think you can accomplish here?"

"Accomplish? I think to right an injustice. Unfortunately, you are in the way."

Sam managed to block two blows. She continued to dance back, and when she glanced over her shoulder, wanting to ensure that she didn't trip over anything, she saw Alec and Beckah.

If she could get to him, she might be able to even the fight.

"Where's your Scribe?"

Marin grinned widely. "What makes you believe that I need a Scribe?"

"Because you're a Kaver. Kavers need their Scribes."

"Ah, Samara, how much you have to learn."

She attacked with a renewed fury and sent Sam staggering backward.

"It's time for me to end this, so I can complete my task."

"Why are you doing this? Why won't you help me understand? Why let Thelns into the city?"

"Ask your mother."

"What does that mean?"

"It means that not everything is what you believe."

"Like my mother being dead? Like how Tray's mother was dead?"

Marin's eyes narrowed, and she flicked her staff at Sam.

It sent her dropping to the ground, rolling so that she could get away from the attack. She crashed into Alec, thrusting out her hand, hoping that she timed it well.

She felt a sharp pain and rolled toward Marin, swinging her staff as she did.

Sam hoped she'd given Alec enough time.

Marin grinned and jumped into the air, flipping before coming back down, driving the ends of her two staff pieces toward Sam.

If she rolled either way, she'd be hit. Sam flipped back, dangerously close to the edge of the water, and jabbed with her staff before flipping backward.

As she did, her body began to tingle.

Had she given Alec enough time? It seemed too much to believe, but she felt power flow through her.

Sam jumped.

She surged higher into the air than what Marin had managed and swept her staff around in a rapid arc.

With the augmentation, she caught Marin off guard, the staff crashing into her shoulder, knocking her to the side.

Sam landed in a roll and swung again, this time connecting with Marin's leg.

Marin had recovered, and reacted, twisting her staff as she did so that it forced Sam's up, leaving her body exposed.

Marin thrust forward, and Sam twisted, barely managing to evade the attack.

"Clever. Now we can see what you've learned." Marin lunged forward, and Sam jumped again, tapping her staff as she did so that she flipped higher into the air.

She rotated, spinning her feet as she swung the staff around, and connected with Marin's back.

Sam kicked again, but this time she missed, and Marin grabbed her leg and swung her. It sent Sam sailing nearly to the water. She twisted, throwing her staff down to push off, and managed to flip back to shore.

As she landed, Marin kicked, catching her in the chest. Something struck her arm, and then her leg. Each blow was harder than before.

Marin had been holding back.

Sam spun around, trying to get her staff into position, but she was too slow.

Three more blows rained down on her, catching her

legs and her arms. One of them left her arm hanging limp, her shoulder likely broken.

It left her with only her right arm.

She couldn't fight with only one arm. She could barely manipulate the staff.

Marin toyed with her, swinging one of her staff ends at her, and danced away as Sam flicked her own staff in her direction.

She could barely stand, pain shooting down her legs, and she staggered with the movement, nearly falling over.

"It's a shame that you are so unprepared. You have potential. I thought you could be useful, but it seems I will need to make other arrangements."

"Why?" Sam asked. She hoped to draw Marin in, wanting the opportunity to strike her one more time, hoping to use the last of her augmentation to maybe keep Marin from doing any more damage.

"Why what?"

"Why do what you did to Tray?" she asked, nodding to where he had been. Where had he gone during the fight?

"All that I did was to keep him safe. Ask your mother about that."

"By poisoning the canals?"

"That's for a different purpose."

"What are you going to tell him?" Sam asked.

"Nothing. He needs to know nothing. And soon, you will know nothing."

Marin approached, near enough that Sam had one shot.

Tingling washed over her again.

Another augmentation?

Pain shot through her injured arm, and she felt it knitting back together.

With a scream of pain, and frustration, and all of the emotions she'd held bottled in over the last few months, she swung her staff.

Marin didn't react in time.

Sam connected with Marin's head, sending it rocking backward, and she fell, striking her head on the cobbles.

Sam fell backward, landing on her injured arm, breaking it once more. She screamed out and couldn't move.

A shadow appeared, and she recognized the bitter scent from when she'd been with Tray. He lifted Marin and carried her away.

"Tray—" Sam called out.

Tray paused.

"Don't. She needs to face punishment for what she did. She needs to give me answers."

Tray looked over his shoulder. There was a haunted expression in his eyes that Sam had never seen from him before. There was something else there, as well, something that looked to be a mixture of pain and frustration.

"She'll face punishment, but I need answers first."

"Why?" Sam asked.

"If she's my mother, I need to understand. You know what that means, don't you?"

Sam could only nod. Her body began tingling again as another augmentation coursed through it, and she felt healing, her arm repairing once more. Even healed, she wouldn't go after Tray.

She'd been so focused on having him help her find Marin for her own reasons that she'd overlooked reasons that Tray had to find her. And he deserved answers, the same as Sam did.

"If you find out what she did to my memories…"

Tray nodded. He looked as if he was going to say something but simply clenched his jaw and disappeared down the street.

Sam watched, wondering if it might be the last time she would see Tray.

Alec waited in the decorative room inside the palace, an uncomfortable feeling making his heart race. Were it not for Sam, he wouldn't be here. Everything around him was ornate, and he found his gaze jumping from statue to candleholder to painting, never resting. Everything here was incredibly valuable. Everything here would be more than enough to purchase his father's shop once more.

The door opened, and Sam entered. She moved slowly, still recovering from her injuries. The easar paper had helped, but he'd needed to use so much of their strength to keep her safe during the fight with Marin that not much was left to heal her fully.

Despite his efforts, they hadn't managed to catch Marin.

Alec jumped from his chair and went to help her. She scanned the room before settling her gaze back on him. "Just you?"

"What do you mean?"

"You've had Beckah with you lately. I thought maybe you'd bring her with you."

"Sam—"

Sam shook her head. "It's okay. I understand you have a connection with her."

"I do. But I have one with you, too."

Sam sank into one of the plush chairs and leaned back, closing her eyes. "I can't challenge you the same way that she does."

Alec chuckled. "You always sell yourself short."

"I don't sell myself at all. I know my limitations."

"You don't have the limitations that you believe."

Sam sat silently for a moment. "What of the canals?" she asked.

Alec had shared with her what Master Eckerd had told him about the eels. At least others believed they were real. She was tired of trying to convince everyone about what she'd experienced with them. It was still hard to believe the eels were helpful. The stupid creatures had tried to bite her!

"The canals are cleansed."

"How?"

Alec shook his head. "I'm not entirely certain. The masters who were involved in cleansing them are all still lying in the hospital." That had been a surprise. Master Eckerd and Master Helen, along with three others, masters that Alec had very little experience with, had all been involved. If nothing else, they had revealed to him which of the masters were Scribes. "They are all still quite weak, but they'll all pull through."

Sam rested her head, letting her eyes drift closed again. "Good. I still can't believe they used the canals to protect the city and prevent Thelns from gaining access." She sighed, and it seemed that she was simply exhausted. "Marin claimed that disrupting the canals was part of her task."

"When the masters recover, I'll make sure they know."

"We have to find out what it was."

"The man you pulled from the university was the one responsible for helping Marin gain access to the university supplies of foxglove. The masters had kept him sedated until they figured out what he intended." He fell silent, watching Sam's reaction for a moment. "How is Bastan?"

"He'll be fine. He's angry the tavern was attacked again, but he'll get over it."

Alec nodded. He leaned forward, twisting his hands together. What he needed to tell Sam would be difficult, but she deserved—and needed—to know.

"My father thinks he knows what happened to your memories." Sam's eyes opened, and she bit her lip. A hopeful expression came to her face. "He doesn't think it's the result of any augmentation."

"Your father isn't a Scribe so how would he know?"

Alec had begun to realize that his father had more connections than he had ever known. He had questions for him, and he would find out the answers, but that would have to come in time. "He tells me that the only way to disrupt memories the way that yours were is by using the Book of Maladies."

Sam stared at him, saying nothing. Both of them knew what that meant. If the Book of Maladies were involved, there would be no easy way—or possibly no way at all—of reversing the effect.

"How certain is he that's what happened?"

"It was the first thing that came to mind for him. He said the power required to disrupt memories that way called for more magic than an augmentation could provide."

Sam stared at her hands and breathed out a long sigh. "Then I'm going to have to find it."

"Find it? Sam, there's no way to reverse it short of—"

Sam leaned forward. "Short of destroying the page. I know. Marin said that not everything is what it seems. I can't trust her, but there *is* more going on than what we have learned. Which is why I need to find the Book of Maladies. And you're going to help me."

Pick up the next book in The Book of Maladies: Tormina

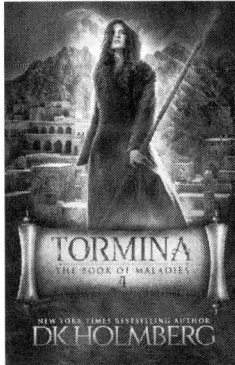

Finding the truth means risking everything.

While trying to track down her brother, Sam discovers she isn't through with Marin quite yet. An attack proves that a traitor sympathetic to Marin remains active in the city, but training prevents Sam from finding answers. With the Thelns once more in the city, Elaine doesn't believe Sam should be involved in the search, which means she has to go off on her own. Doing so risks her position at the palace, but any other choice puts her brother in danger.

Alec continues his studies and realizes how much he still has to learn at the university. Now that he knows some of the master physickers are also Scribes, he wants answers, but his search places him at odds with someone far more powerful than him. When Sam asks for his help with her quest to find the traitor, Alec has to make a dangerous decision and the fallout will change their lives in the city.

Failure means more than another Theln attack upon the city—it means they might lose everything they have discovered about themselves.

NAMES AND TERMS

People:

- Aelus Stross: An apothecary and skilled healer. Alec's father
- Alec Stross: an apprentice apothecary
- Bastan: a thief who essentially runs Caster
- Hyp: a moneylender in the Arrend section who frequents Aelus's shop
- Mags: a painter with a unique talent
- Marcella Rubbles: owner of a stationary store in Arrend
- Marin: a thief who knew Sam's mother
- Samara (Sam) Elseth: a thief
- Trayson (Tray) Elseth: Sam's brother

Places and Terms:

- Arrend section: a merchant section

- Balan Day: a day to celebrate the festival god
- canal eels: possibly mythical creatures living in the canals
- Callesh section: a merchant section
- Caster section: a lowborn outer section of the city
- Central Canal: the canal that separates the lowborn sections from the merchants and highborns
- Drash section: a merchant section
- easar paper: magical paper
- Farnum section: a merchant section
- Highborn: a term for the wealthier living in the center of the city
- Jaku section: a highborn section where easar paper was found.
- Kyza: one of the many gods worshipped in Verdholm
- Lostin section: a merchant section
- Lowborn: a term for people living in the outer sections of the city
- Lycithan: a southern nation. Known for their skilled artisans.
- Narvin Plains: east of the city, thin stretch of land
- Physicker: healers with specialized training at the university
- Piare River: connects to Ralan Bay and the canals
- Ralan Bay: a trading hub along the coast of Verdholm
- Sacred Alms: the healing religion Alec follows

- Sornum: Bastan's tavern
- Thelns: dangerous brutes
- Valun: a country known for various artifacts, including the stout rope Sam uses
- Verdholm: an isolated city situated near the coast with canals running through it separating it into different sections
- Yisl: one of the many gods worshipped in Verdholm

Printed in Great Britain
by Amazon